Run to You

CHARLOTTE STEIN

T0337288

mischief

Mischief
An imprint of HarperCollins*Publishers*
77–85 Fulham Palace Road,
Hammersmith, London W6 8JB

www.mischiefbooks.com

A Paperback Original 2013

First published in Great Britain in ebook format by
HarperCollins*Publishers* 2012

Copyright © Charlotte Stein 2013

Charlotte Stein asserts the moral right to
be identified as the author of this work

A catalogue record for this book is
available from the British Library

ISBN-13: 9780007553426

Find out more about HarperCollins and the environment at
www.harpercollins.co.uk/green

CONTENTS

CONTENTS

Chapter One

Sometimes I'm sure Lucy hasn't really gone on holiday. Something else has happened to her, something terrible, like the little scene at the start of a gritty crime drama. The police are going to find her tomorrow, floating in the Thames. In fact, I can almost see it when I close my eyes: that pretty under-slip of hers drifting around her pale, still body, like transparent water weeds. Her red hair so bright against those murky depths.

She isn't somewhere exotic, living the life of Riley. She wouldn't leave with only a note for a goodbye. And yet, when I search for some other answer, there's nothing to be found. Her apartment is as clean and featureless as ever: an open book. There's no clue stuck on her refrigerator, in the form of a shopping list she suspiciously never went out for. I can't find clothes she didn't take, or arrangements she didn't make.

'I'm moving to my Mediterranean heaven – rent's paid for the next three months,' she said, which should be explanation enough, really. It's only because I'm left with an absence, and a sense that I meant far less to her than I thought I did. I was just a blip to her, in a life filled with jagged edges and full Technicolor. I am a speck, a stripe of grey.

But that's Oean+K, because I like it that way. It's not nearly as bad as it sounds. I have a sensible job at a sensible company, and every night I eat sensible meals in my sensible flat, before retiring at a sensible hour. My pleasures are few and simple, but they *are* pleasures.

And even better: they can never hurt me. I don't have to flee to some far-off place because I did something very wicked – though I don't know if this wickedness of Lucy's is just my imagination. It certainly seems like it might be when I flick through the little date diary she's left in the upper right-hand drawer of her desk.

'Dentist at three,' it says, in that looping, dangerous-looking scrawl of hers. 'Floor waxing at nine.' Dull appointments like that almost look disingenuous, dressed in those slashing black 'T's and her big, all-consuming 'S's. The latter letter seems to devour entire pages, and puts my own handwriting to shame. My words creep across the bottom of pages, narrow and cramped and completely unobtrusive. I can't bring myself to turn my 'C's into great, gaping mouths. And I certainly don't know how to write in red.

But she does. She has. Every third Friday, there it is – the one appointment that doesn't seem quite as dull as the rest. 'Assignation', it says, in bold, bloody crimson. And then as though to emphasise how incongruous that one word looks and sounds, she's circled it three times. She's circled all of them three times – these sibilant, secretive marks of the thing she must have been doing.

She was meeting someone. Someone she didn't tell me about, someone dark and deadly. Or maybe it's worse than that: an affair, an embroilment in the underworld … anything. It could be anything, which probably explains why I then pick up the telephone, and call the place she's listed under every instance of that word.

'The Harrington', her diary says, and I immediately picture a great, grand dinosaur of a place. It will be one of those hotels that's been caught between the wealth it once commanded and the seediness it's disappearing into, and when a woman answers the phone she does nothing to dispel this impression.

'How can we be of service?' she says, in a tone designed to put the casual patron off. It's both haughty and bored, like a person who's just stepped out of the nineteenth century. She could kill with a voice like that, but my answer spills out of me anyway. I stretch my neck out, and put it on the chopping block.

'My name is Lucy Talbert,' I say. 'I believe I have a reservation with you for Friday.'

And the woman says, 'Yes. Yes, Lucy, you do.'

* * *

The place is even more intimidating than I had initially imagined – mainly because that seediness simply isn't present. There are no holes in the velvet curtains, or cracks in the yellowing plaster. Everything gleams like the inside of a wine glass, and for a moment I stand transfixed in the doorway. I'm afraid to walk on the glossy marble floor, in case my cheap heels crack it.

Or maybe I'll slip. Yes, slipping seems likely. It's practically an ice rink in front of me, and I've never been known for my poise. Whereas the woman descending the elegantly curved stairs in front of me … well. She has poise in abundance. She's wearing a skirt so slim and tight I'm surprised she can walk, and her heels are daggers.

But she doesn't falter on that smooth floor. She doesn't even seem aware of it. She glides to reception with all the grace of a swan, murmurs something to the equally elegant lady behind the mahogany desk an wigany ded waltzes on.

It doesn't surprise me that I hold my breath when she swings past me. If I inhale her perfume I might die of wealth. Her sheer classiness is on the verge of swamping me – or at the very least it's about to mark me out as the impostor I am.

Suddenly, the difference between me and Lucy is immense. It's a chasm. She came here, and she came here *often*. There are a lot of assignations in her little book, and if she attended them all she must have known how to operate in this environment. You couldn't come here as a misfit, in ill-fitting clothes.

Though somehow that's what I have done. I shamble up to the reception desk like an old washerwoman, skirt riding up my thighs, jacket gaping open. These heels are crippling me, and they aren't half the height of that other woman's. It's really no wonder the receptionist looks at me with clear disdain, though I suspect that's her default expression. Her eyes are the cool, clear blue of an arctic ocean, each framed with the kind of artistic sweep of eyeliner that I can never hope to achieve. And her hair ...

I've never seen such neat, complicated coils. She's wearing a snake on her head, only the snake is beautiful and blonde and so much better than me. I'm embarrassed to be in my own body, right at this moment.

'Yes?' she asks, and for a long second I can't think what to say. I've forgotten how to speak, in a presence as imperious as hers. She isn't even trying to be imperious, either. It just comes naturally to her, in the middle of casual conversation.

'I'm Lucy Talbert,' I say, but this time the lie stings. She's quite clearly going to know that I'm not telling the truth, because she's not just some receptionist. A person like her won't mistake one guest for another, or fail to pay any attention at all.

I bet she knows everyone who's ever walked through those doors. I bet she knows the random visitor who only stayed once last June, all the way up to the pretty red-headed girl who used to come once a month. And she knows … she absolutely knows that I am not that girl. My hair isn't red, for a start.

It's a dull, dense black.

And I'm biting my lip, where I imagine Lucy didn't. In this, she was definitely different from me. She must have used that flicker of iron I saw in her sometimes – that confidence that I lacked. She was the one who said to some guy in a bar, 'Buy us a drink.' I was simply the one who reaped the benefits.

I can't pass for her.

And the pressure of trying to is too much for me. Before the woman has said another word I turn to leave, defeat like ashes in my mouth. My head is down; my eyes are on the floor. That flame of sudden jolting curiosity will never be extinguished.

Instead, I make an even greater fool of myself.

There's a man behind me, and of course I stumble into him as I go to leave. Of course I do. He's a suited wall, grey and heavy and ominous, and the moment I glance at him I rush to back away. It's bad enough that I'm surrounded by all of this opulence. I don't want to smear my poverty and inelegance all over it.

But that's what I do. I skid on the ice rink, and rather than avoiding him I blunder in closer. My heels shove forward; my body arches back. It's only his quick reflexes that stop me landing on my ass. He shoots out a hand, so quick I hardly see it coming – and I certainly don't have time to graciously pass it up.

'No, I'm fine,' I imagine myself saying, in this imaginary world where I didn't actually need his h bay need elp. In the real one, he grabs my elbow and jerks me back up – but that isn't the humiliating part. No, no. The humiliating part is how indifferently he does it, as though saving girls from embarrassment is on a level with swatting away a fly. There's no concern to the gesture, or acknowledgement of me as a person.

He sets me right and then simply keeps on moving towards the desk, oblivious.

Whereas I'm left with the opposite feeling. I'm on the other end of the spectrum from oblivious, whatever that's called. Extreme noticing, perhaps? Severe and chronic attention-paying? At the very least, my eyes are refusing to move away from this man – this guy who's barely registering my existence.

I can't blame my eyes, however. He looks as though he's just stepped out of a Hugo Boss advert, if Hugo Boss adverts usually featured much burlier, intense-looking men. Instead of the flat, moody look of a model trying too hard, he has an aura of focus, of effortless masculinity. His suit has settled on his body like a second skin, and beneath it you can clearly see all the things you usually wouldn't.

How broad his chest is, how immense his shoulders are. I'm sure I can make out the heavy slab of one shoulder blade, in a way that should mark him out as a wrestler, or a boxer. It should make his suit seem ill-fitting.

But of course it doesn't. He's so at ease he could probably wear a coat of armour and seem comfortable and proper. He just looks at the receptionist, and she goes to retrieve whatever it is he came here for – while I remain, gawping.

I can't help it. His face, oh, Lord, his *face*. I haven't even gotten to that part yet. I'm still stuck on his grey woollen suit and his massive hands – the ones he's currently easing into leather gloves. I'm almost afraid to analyse anything else, in case it proves too much for me.

And I was right on that score. His face is far, far too much.

Of course he's handsome, in that Hugo Boss way, but he's also handsome in a way that's not. As though he maybe models for some obscure Eastern European equivalent of that scent – Hurgo Bsosch, maybe. It's there in the heavy-lidded look in his eyes, and the softness of his mouth. He doesn't have a grim slash, of the kind that seems so popular these days.

He has a sensuous mouth, a decadent mouth, a mouth you want to plunge into and swim around in. If his mouth was sculpted out of chocolate, I'd cram it down my throat like a starving person – hell, it's possible I'd do that anyway, chocolate or not. He's just so rich-seeming, and not just in the monetary way.

In the solid, fleshy, *real*-seeming way. In the big, masculine way.

And yet when he speaks, his voice is so gentle. So unassuming. He has a slight accent, just as I suspected, but I'm not close enough to make out what it is. He doesn't speak loudly enough for me to make out what it is. He just murmurs a few words as the receptionist hands him his long overcoat, and all I'm left with is a hint of musicality.

It seems quite incongruous to hear such an imposing man speaking in such an unimposing manner. Shouldn't he be more commanding? How on earth does he pay for suits like that, and go to work at the Hungarian branch of Hugo Boss, if he barely speaks above a whisper?

And then I realise what I'm doing, in a rush of humiliation. I'm actually leaning forward, to hear him better. In fact, I'm practically on tiptoe. And I've held my breath again, as though breathing is just some irritating habit, getting in the way of my ability to listen.

He doesn't have to speak in a commanding way, I realise.

He's already got your complete and undivided attention, just by being.

I watch the way he writes on a little notecard she gives to him – with a jewel-like fountain pen, naturally. I don't think he needs it to make his script so neat and fluid, however. I think that's just the way he is: both precise and effortless.

He has precisely and effortlessly brought me to a standstill. I can't even move when he turns, abruptly, though I know he's going to see me. He'll take in my wide eyes and my gaping mouth, and then he'll sneer, I know it. He'll be disgusted.

But somehow it's worse when he doesn't seem that way at all. The look he gives me is a punch to the gut, mainly because I can finally see those twelve-past-midnight eyes of his but also because of the weight behind his gaze. He considers me gravely, as though I'm somehow as important as the glossy girls he usually sees. I'm as important as his latest business meeting; I rival the world for his attention, in that one moment.

And then something like a smile hovers around his lips, a second before he moves past me and glides back out of the main doors. Strange, really, that so slight a thing leaves a burn mark in my brain. I can't shake that barely-there smile, long after he's gone – and I know this because the woman behind the desk has to get my attention.

'I assume you wanted your room key, Ms Talbert,' she says.

It isn't a question. She brooks no refusal. I'm in this for real, now.

The trouble, I suppose, is that I don't know what *this* is. 'Assignation' implies a meeting of some type, but it has other connotations too. Nerve-wracking, impossible, problematic sorts of connotations that I don't quite know how to deal with.

So I don't. I put them out of my mind as I climb the winding staircase, still marvelling at the air of utter luxury. I'm almost afraid to trail my hand over the banister, in case I get my sticky, plebeian fingerprints all over it. And at the top is a hall lined with doors, each one glossier than the next. The wood is so dense and dark I'm certain it must have a smell, but when I lean in close there's nothing.

There's just the odour of sheer, intense class – more class than Lucy could have possibly afforded. She earned the same as me, which puts this place out of reach. But then I think over that confidence she had, again, and my mind goes back and forth on the matter.

True, she didn't have the money for a place like this. But she had the chutzpah.

And that thought pushes a sudden pang of loss through me. She'll probably never tell me some shocking story again. She'll never persuade me to do daring things. If

I want anything above a simple life of simple pleasures again, I'll have to persuade myself.

Which seems unlikely, until I get to the door on my room key: One-One-One. And then despite my pounding heart, and that impulse in me to always turn back at the point of no return, I'm somehow putting the key in the lock. I'm compelled to, by the look of the thing. It isn't one of those modern card-type affairs with a light that turns green when you're allowed in. It's a proper brass key with an ornate and shadowy hole to slide it into, and, when I turn it, it creates such a solid sound.

Just to make everything that little bit more final. I've come to a hotel with a name that isn't mine for an assignation I didn't arrange, and now I'm in a room I didn't pay for. A ear pay foroom that *hasn't* been paid for, if I know Lucy. She was probably going to meet someone here and then finagle them into footing the bill, but of course I don't know how to do that.

I'm not even sure how to stand in a room like this. The luxury downstairs was bad enough, but in such a closed space it's almost oppressive. I feel as though I'm being mugged by expensive furniture and artwork, and there's nothing I can do to get away. The three-foot-deep carpet has me mired, like quicksand.

And then I see what awaits me on the bed, and the effect gets worse. I'm smothered in shock and anxiety, to the point where I can't breathe, for a long moment

– though I do understand how silly that is. I'm sure this is all perfectly normal and ordinary to someone who isn't as dull as me.

People are probably using handcuffs on each other all the time, in all the places I'm not. It's not even a big deal to have kinky sex any more. It's old news, it's beyond boring, it's passé. Those glittering gunmetal loops on the bed are simply a sign of how out of date I am.

As is the leather strap next to it, and the puddle of red silk like spilt blood, and the thin silver cane that makes me think of the kind of school I never went to. This is the dusty place of my Enid Blyton imagination, filled with answers you can't give to questions that don't make sense and professors in tweed with icy eyes.

Professors who might be very angry to find me trespassing where I don't belong. I've somehow slipped into Bluebeard's cupboard without knowing it, and now I'm dancing amidst the dead girls. I'm seeing things I shouldn't and feeling things I'm not prepared for, and it's at this moment of supreme confusion that the door handle starts to turn.

I hear it before I see it. I hear old metal grind against old metal, and then I move without thinking. I don't even stop to consider how insane this is. I simply step backwards into the double-door closet behind me, and pull the doors closed with every bit of grace I didn't think I possessed. I'm almost proud of myself for the sound they make: soft as a sigh. And for the stillness I sink into, the second I'm cocooned in sultry darkness. Usually I trip, I stumble, I knock something over. I've never been known for my stealth.

But I feel stealthy here. I've erased myself from the room, as though this is actually the reverse of that Bluebeard tale. I took myself out of the equation, before he could do it for me. I guessed and found my sanctuary behind some secret door, somewhere to hide while he does whatever he's going to do outside it.

Oh, God, I know he's going to do *something*. All the hairs on my arms have stood up, before I'm even aware it's a *him*. And then once I've heard his heavy footsteps – somehow thudding, despite the plush carpet – and understood that it definitely *is* a man, the sensation gets worse. The prickling, bristling, squirming sensation, as though I've done something to be ashamed of, despite knowing I haven't.

I've only pretended to be Lucy, I think at the heavy presence outside the doors. Please don't be a Russian mobster, hell-bent on killing me.

Because that idea, though ridiculous, has a ring of truth about it. This is the moment in the movie when the heroine hopes she's safe. She holds her breath, waiting and waiting for the drift of shadows through the gap between the doors. Hearing the creak of leather shoes, the thud of heavy footfalls …

And then just when she's sure she's safe …

Just when she breathes a sigh of relief ...

That's when he drags her, screaming, from her hiding place. That's when he does whatever Russian mobsters do – teeth-pulling and eye-puncturing and lots of shouting about treasure that I have no knowledge of. Any second, I think. Any second.

Only the second never comes. It just goes on and on until it's practically a whole minute, torturing me endlessly with its refusal to end. If this moment goes on much longer I swear I'm going to burst out and make a run for it, and the only thing that stops me is my need to check first. I just have to look.

And then I lean forward, trembling, and peer through the gap between the doors. I see who he really is, in a rush of breathless bravery.

It's the man from downstairs.

The man in the suit, with the inescapable face.

Apparently he had such an impact on me I can recognise him in parts and in pieces. I see a sliver of black and know that it's his big, burly right arm. And that flash of gunmetal grey ... that's the hint of stubble on his great granite face.

Though I think I try to pretend otherwise, at first. I turn him into a jigsaw, and rearrange each tiny bit I can see into something else – that's a leg, not an arm, and it's far too small to be his. That flash of dark hair I can see? It's not dark enough to equal the black pelt I saw

15

a little while ago. It's not him, I think, it's not him, and even if it was I wouldn't care.

Only he chooses that moment to speak, and after he has I have to face the fact that I do care, after all. I care *a lot*. I want to slump against something, but of course I can't. If I do, he'll hear me. He'll know I'm here, and worse – he'll see the effect his silken voice is having on my usually reasonable behaviour.

My breath actually catches in my throat, when he speaks words into his phone. And I can't blame what he might be saying, either, because I don't know what it is. It could be 'I'm going to kill her,' thus justifying my bizarre shivering reaction to the sound of him. But it could just as easily be dry-cleaning instructions for his assistant.

Because he says it in another language.

He speaks in a different language with a voice that's already like sand shifting over metal, and my insides just flip out. He's inadvertently flicked some weird switch inside me, and there's no turning it back once it's there. Apparently, I really like hearing someone speak in Hungarian or Polish or Russian or whatever it is he's speaking, while trapped in a closet. I'm a secret subscriber to *Trapped In A Polish Closet* magazine.

I'm practically the President of the TIAPC.

Though I don't exactly know how that happened. I've never noticed a predilection for accents before, in my back catalogue of sexual encounters. The only thing I can come up with is that time Steven Tate pretended to be a caveman, but ended up sounding like a Brummie taxi driver.

Needless to say, it wasn't sexy.

But this ... *this* is sexy. Suddenly I know exactly what sexy is, which is in itself a revelation. I wasn't previously aware that the word really existed, or could be applied to things that happen in life. It had seemed like some abstract concept that other people probably only pretend to understand, the way women pretend about orgasms.

No one is actually sexy. Nobody really has an orgasm.

Only now I can see I was very wrong about the first one, and am getting scared about the second. Because the longer I watch him – like some furtive per th furtiv-vert, unable to help themselves – the more I understand what sexy is. And the more I understand what sexy is, the stranger I feel. A heavy pulse starts to beat between my legs.

And when he passes too close to the closet and I catch a whisper of his cologne ...

Suddenly I can feel that pulse beating all over my body. It's running down my arms to the very ends of my fingertips, before doubling back to blast me in the face. My teeth are rattling because of it – this drumming inside me that has never previously existed. This drumming that shouldn't exist now.

It's embarrassing, really. What sort of person gets

so excited over something so trifling? A silly person. A weak-minded person, who's so unused to the finer things she falls to pieces when she sees them.

I don't like being her. So I close my eyes and count to ten. I think of all the ways I can make myself reasonable again. He isn't here for me, I tell myself, and he could never be. The kind of woman he's here for will be like the one downstairs at reception, beautiful and elegant. And she'll have called to organise this meeting by doing something effortless and classy, like ringing a special number on an antique phone.

She wouldn't hide in a closet, wrestling with her suddenly emerging libido. Her heart wouldn't beat hard to see someone like that, and hear him say a string of alien words. *Tar-zu*, he says, and something else that sounds like 'camera', and then another thing that reminds me of that castle I thought I was in again.

Only this time it's real, and on top of a mountain in Transylvania. If I look again he'll be wearing a cape, and have a pronounced widow's peak.

Though when I really peer through the gap he doesn't. Of course he doesn't. He's still this perfect picture of a businessman, all smooth clean lines and big angles, inside his second-skin suit. He's still so handsome I want to open the door, just so I can see more of him.

But I stop myself in time. I hold back just as he picks

up that red silk and lets it trail through his fingers. He's still on the phone, talking in this uninterested way, probably about stocks that need transferring into bonds, but he's playing with something so sensuously as he does it. And he *is* playing with it too.

I can't pretend he's doing something more manly, like mining the material for coal. He lets it slide over the back of his hand, and just when it's about to drift back down onto the bed, he catches it. He's so deft, I think, before I can kick myself for mooning over him again.

God, *mooning*. Like a teenager.

Seriously, I don't know what's wrong with me. I don't know why I'm still watching with bated breath for his every little move. He finally finishes his call and snaps his tiny phone shut, and I jerk like he fired a bullet into the ceiling. And then he strides across the room, quite abruptly, and I almost do the thing I prided myself on avoiding.

I almost stumble into the shoe rack behind me and give myself away. In fact, I'm certain I *have* given myself away, just by jerking back. I fully expect the doors to swing wide at any moment. I'm sure that's what he was intending to do anyway.

But when I dare to look again, the room is empty. He wasn't going for the closet, I realise. He was going for the exit. He came to meet his lovely Lucy, and, once he realised she wasn't here, he made a call to the complaints department of the Assignations Bureau, before taking his leave.

Or at least that's how it goes in my head. In reality,
Iysen reali have no idea if there's such a thing as the
Assignations Bureau. For all I know, this could be some
kind of sex-trafficking drugs ring. Lucy could have been
moonlighting as a high-class call girl. I was almost in an
episode of that TV show with Billie Piper.

If I hadn't hidden in a closet.

But I did, and that's how it is, and so now I have to
fumble out into an empty room. And though I know,
rationally, that this should be a relief, it somehow isn't.
I'm not pleased that I avoided him. I'm boiling hot and
absolutely furious with myself for being the same person
I always am: frightened, foolish, clumsy.

I didn't even speak to him. I couldn't even ask him
about Lucy. I let myself be intimidated by his brilliance
and lamped by my own weird arousal, and now I'll never
know. I've missed my chance, because God knows I'm
never coming back here. Never, never, never. Wild horses
couldn't drag me.

However, I suspect his business card might.

He's left it on the desk by the window, propped up
against a bottle of champagne he didn't drink. It's probably worth more than every drop of lemonade I've ever
consumed, but he's just abandoned it here. He's used it
as a backdrop for that little innocuous rectangle – the
one that probably doesn't mean anything at all.

He's left it for the girl that didn't come. That red

writing coiled across its surface will say, 'Lucy, lovely Lucy, why didn't you meet me?' Or at least that's what I tell myself, as I try to leave without reading it.

And then somehow I find myself crossing the carpet, to get a closer look. I see the word 'girl' and the word 'wardrobe', and I know what's coming, though I try to deny it for another moment. I was so sure he didn't know I was there. I was so sure I got away with it. He gave no sign, you see. There was no indication he'd guessed – I thought I was safe.

Now I know I'm not.

'To the girl in the wardrobe', the card says, on its blank white back. Then on the front: his name, and his number, and one simple instruction:

'Call me.'

Chapter Two

When I get to my desk I do everything the same as always. I put my coffee on my little Garfield coaster and turn on my computer. I check my emails and send out various messages, then call down to Finance to make sure they've got my updated details. It's just another ordinary day, I think to myself, though I can already tell it's sliding into something else. I'm concentrating too hard on work tasks for it to qualify as normal. Usually I hardly care; now I can tell I'm caring too much.

Once I'm done with the typical morning tasks I straighten my desk, as though it really needs straightening. Everything needs to be at right angles, and there are far too many paperclips lurking behind sheets of paper. The sheets of paper themselves shouldn't be here, so I file them away in a filing system I don't yet have.

But I soon will.

I spend a good hour creating one – with tiny tabs and little plastic inserts and everything. Michaela snorts at me over the divide of our two cubicles, wanting to know why I'm suddenly so busy ... but of course I can't tell her. I can't tell anyone about this, because my usual go-to confessor has flown the coop and I'm still no closer to finding out why.

I don't want to be any closer to finding out why. I've already dialled his number twice and hung up, and I really can't risk a pany more. The night before last was frightening enough, and maybe explanation enough, and I'd far rather be normal and busy and a customer services operative again. The phone rings and I answer it like I always do: 'Alissa Layton speaking, how may I help you?'

And I expect the person on the other end to be boring and possibly stupid, the way they always are. 'My payment went out at the wrong time, I don't understand these forms, I don't like what I've signed up to, do you sell milk?' I even have my sigh pre-planned, soft and low and aimed at something other than the phone receiver. Just beyond our dividing wall Michaela rolls her eyes and makes a winding finger around the edges of her own phone conversation, like every other day in this mundane place.

So I suppose it's more of a jolt to hear that voice, in the middle of all of this. Back there at The Harrington he belonged, but even then it was a shock. Now it's almost impossible ... like hearing a lion roar in a library. You turn around expecting dusty books and there it is, sleek and predatory and ready to devour you whole.

'Hello, Alissa,' he says, and I think he might devour me whole. In fact, I know he will. He's barely said a word and I'm already speechless and frozen, unable to process his presence in my silly basic office. How did he know where I was? Why does he care where I am? He wrote those words – 'Call me' – *but I didn't think they were serious.*

'I'm very disappointed in you.'

Or that I was capable of provoking an emotion like disappointment. I've never been important enough for anyone to be disappointed in me. No one has ever expected me to make something big of myself; I've never done anything so awful that it let anybody down.

This is entirely new territory, and so disturbing because of that fact. It's like I've stepped into another dimension, while drunk. The world slants sideways and my stomach goes with it ... if this carries on for much longer I'm going to lose my lunch. I'm sweating already, and my skin is prickling, and worst of all: I don't know how to answer him.

I don't know.

I don't belong in your world, I think at him, but phones don't pick up thoughts. He has to make do with my stupid silence, and my shaky breathing.

'Calling then hanging up? That's hardly polite. Why would you do such a thing?'

'I don't know,' I tell him, while the image of my own

fear and panic rises inside me. It's like seeing a bird caught inside a bottle.

'Perhaps you were busy, and couldn't complete the call,' *he says, in this purring persuasive tone – almost as though he's daring me to say yes. Make it easy on yourself, he seems to be suggesting, but weirdly I can't quite do it.*

I can't say, 'Yes, go away, I'm busy' *now.*

'Perhaps.'

'Or maybe you had an appointment you had to attend.'

'That could be the case.'

'You have such an important life,' *he says, and I know for sure then. He's teasing me, in the most subtle and strange way I've ever been teased in my life. I can almost hear a lick of laughter in the back of his voice, but it's not unpleasant. It's not even infuriating.*

It's something else, instead.

'I really do.'

'So many matters to attend to.'

'Absolutely.'

He makes a little hmm-ing noise ins, ing noi the back of his throat, like some friendly psychiatrist. I can almost see him nodding with understanding, though of course it's obvious the understanding is fake. It's obvious even before he knifes me with his next words, hard and fast and right under my ribs.

'Nothing at all to do with being afraid and intimidated.'

I fall silent again then – mainly because I have to. It's impossible to talk when your throat has sealed itself up, and your body is frozen in one weird position. I'm almost bent double over my desk and my hand has made a fist in my best suit jacket, as though my body just had to prove him right. Naturally I'm afraid and intimidated.

I'm a completely ridiculous person talking to this scion of business. He probably eats people like me for breakfast. I'm probably not even good enough for his breakfast. I'm the water he swills around his mouth after brushing his teeth with his gold toothbrush, before spitting me into the sink.

'*Are you still there, Alissa?*'

I wish I wasn't. I wish I could tell him where to go, but there are so many reasons why I won't. There's Lucy and what happened with her, and that place and its mysterious allure. And then of course there's the real reason:

Him.

'*Possibly.*'

'*This makes me think of you as something ephemeral, that I might blow away with a whisper. Is that so?*'

'*I'd probably phrase it a different way, but generally yes.*'

'*Really? How would you phrase it? Tell me, enlighten me, let me hear your voice.*'

That's too much pressure. He has to know that's too much, right? Just the idea of enlightening him is making my armpits prickle.

'*I wouldn't use the word ephemeral.*'

'*I see. And there is a reason for this?*'

'*Yes. It's too ... pretty. It needs to be more basic.*'

'*Ah, then perhaps insubstantial would do.*'

'*That's better.*'

'*Or invisible.*'

'*I could deal with invisible.*'

'*Of course you can. Of course. Because that is how you feel, is it not? You feel so perfectly invisible, like no one could ever notice a single thing about you. And, in fact, you've grown so used to this state of affairs that you've started to fall in love with it. You like being in the background, hidden from view ... lingering around the edges at parties ... keeping out of conversations in case someone finds you as insufferably dull as you've always suspected you are. You can't even talk to me because what if I don't care either? Surely my life must be so expensive and jaded that anything you say will sound like the simperings of a child.*'

He pauses just long enough for me to say something here – a denial, perhaps, or an accusation. But truthfully, I think he knows I'll only answer with this hollow, horrified silence. I think he was hoping for it, so he can just go ahead and fill it up with this:

'*And yet I feel I have to ask: if this is all the case, and you are so little and so weak ... why is it that I could feel your presence through five inches of wood? Can you tell me, invisible Alissa? Why are you – in silence – stronger and stranger than any woman I've actually met?'*

* * *

I don't know why I hung up on him so abruptly. When I look back saI look on it now it seems like something a person would do if the phone suddenly bit them, and they really needed to get away. I can even picture it in my head: the receiver clattering back down onto the cradle, my hand jerking back.

He probably thought I was insane.

But that's OK, because I think he's insane. I think he's so insane I can't stop thinking about him. What did he mean by invisible, exactly? And more importantly: how did he know that I was? Surely the point of being invisible is that no one can see you. He must have X-ray vision, I think, but doing so doesn't help me.

It only makes things worse, because who wouldn't be intrigued by a man with superhero eyes? If I call again I might find out he has other skills, like the ability to fly in through a window and save me from this stultifying existence.

And for a while I come close to calling him. I get as far as the last digit, but before I can hear the purring ring in my ear I slam the phone back down again. I'm not a weak person, tricked by strange mind games and just waiting for some Superman to come rescue me. I know that he never will, for a start.

But oh, my foolish heart.

How my foolish heart fails me when my phone suddenly goes, ten seconds later. It actually seems to jerk in my chest, before slowly dissolving through my insides. I flick my gaze to that previously innocuous piece of machinery, angry at it for changing. Angry at the ring that now seems as sharp as a knife and dark as midnight.

It makes me think of horror movies, when you know the killer's calling. The startled heroine, that lonely drilling tinkle, the wide-eyed stare in the phone's direction … it's all there. I actually catch myself with my mouth open. I have to compose myself and close it, before I pick up the receiver. And it's a close call, even then.

I almost go get myself a drink of water.

But I'm glad I decide otherwise.

'Hello, Alissa,' he says, and for one mad second I know how Lois Lane feels. I threw up the signal and he came calling, right on cue. 'Are you ready to finish our conversation now?'

I'm amazed he even remembers our conversation, in-between million-pound meetings and making himself so slick and flawless. The suit alone must take a thousand years to put on, with all of its buttons and extra bits and the always imminent threat of ruining something so expensive. I bet he has to lever it on with tweezers. I bet geishas roll it onto his body using their breasts.

And yet here he is, just waiting to finish something so pale and slight.

It makes me think it wasn't pale and slight at all. Somehow I've stumbled into a Very Serious Discussion about important things, and now I have to finish it. How do I finish it? What were we even saying?

'Describe your face to me.'

I definitely don't think we were discussing that.

'Why? Don't you know what it looks like?' I ask, confused. He saw me in the lobby, didn't he? Though when I think back ... how would he have known I was the same person, hiding in the wardrobe? He couldn't have, not for sure.

And I don't feel like explaining. Everything might end, if I do.

'How would I?' he says, and I can almost hear his shrug through the phone. Just one big shoulder, as lazy and casual as a basking lion.

'Well, you know where I work. You must have found things out about me.'

'So you ven">'Sothink I'm some obsessive stalker. From invisible to so sure of yourself in under a day. Very impressive.'

'No, I don't think ... that's not what I meant,' I say, but I flounder over what I did actually mean. In the

end I have to settle for the truth, even though doing so makes me picture that lion, suddenly baring all of its teeth. 'It's just that … well … you seem like a stalker. And also a mind-reader.'

'You think I found out where you work because of mind-reading?'

He sounds so amused I almost take the words back. But in the end I think it's better that I stand my ground. If he is a maniac, he'll know I have him pegged now. He'll picture me with my thumb on speed dial to the police, and never put me in a box beneath his stairs.

I'm not fooled by you, I think at him – though my actual words sound weak.

'Possibly.'

'Ah, possibly again. Not sure, can't decide, don't want to commit.'

'Why would I want to commit something to someone I barely know? You haven't even told me your name,' I say. He doesn't have to know that I've invented hundreds for him, in my head. Stanislav, Arvikov, Amritza, my mind murmurs, even though I'm sure none of those are actually words. 'And I have no idea how you know mine.'

He laughs, low and dark. I swear the sound rattles my bones.

'You keep calling me, remember?' he says, and I want to smack my hand over my face to see my own silliness spelled out like that. Of course, of course, I keep calling

31

*him and hanging up. I really am sending out a signal.
'If you hadn't, I would have surely bothered you no
longer. But seeing your work number in neon was too
tempting, so I simply called you back and listened to
your delightful answering machine message. How does
it go again? "You have reached Alissa Layton, please
leave a message after the beep."'*

I'll admit it. I love the way he says the word 'beep'.
It's almost a click, instead. It snaps out of him, oddly
abrupt and oh, so interesting.

'That does sound like me.'

'Why do you think so?'

'It's straightforward.' I hesitate, wanting to hold off
on the final verdict. It's just too damning. I want to claw
my way out of the outfit it puts me into, and run newly
bared down the nearest street. 'And dull.'

'So now we have dull to add to your collection. What were
your other terms for yourself? Invisible, and insubstantial?'

'I might have said something along those lines.'

'So you don't think there is anything beneath all of
this? Nothing of interest?'

'Certainly nothing as interesting as the life you lead.'

'And what makes you think my life is so interesting?'

I see the entrance hall of The Harrington behind my
eyes, glossy and glorious. The coil of the receptionist's
hair, the three neat items laid out on the bed like bowls
of porridge in the Three Bears' house.

Which one is just right?

'You do those things at that hotel.'

It doesn't come out the way I want it to. It comes out fumbled and childish, with a hint of judgement I didn't realise I felt. I mean, just because I don't understand sex doesn't mean other people can't, and in a second I'm sure he'll tell me as much. 'Shouldn't people explore if they wish?' he'll say, though when this doesn't happen I'm not grateful. His amusement is back, and it's just as prickling as it was before.

'Is that what you think happens there? "Doing things"?'

'You know what I mean.'

How can he? I don't even know what I mean.

'I really don't. Speak plainly.'

'I thought I was,' I say, because I'm a fucking liar. That laughing lilt to his voice just makes me want to lie and lie and lie – but that's all right.

He tells the truth for me.

'No, you were speaking in a vague way because you're afraid to say the actual words.'

How does he do it? Years of reading people over the boardroom table, I suspect, though there are other options. Perhaps he operates in some shady, cut-throat world I can't even fathom, where everything dances on a knife edge.

Or maybe I'm just really easy to read. I'm a neglected

book that's been left somewhere damp, swollen to twice its size and suddenly filled with enormous words. Most of them probably ask for help. Some might mention loneliness.

All of them must be hidden, immediately.

'Maybe that's just because you're a stranger.'

'My name is Janos Kovacs,' he says, casually. He doesn't know that I cradle those two names to my chest like rare and ready-to-fly birds. 'There, now we are no longer strangers.'

Indeed we are not. He is Janos, pronounced with a curdled call for silence at the end. He is Hungarian, as I had guessed, and suddenly so large in my head I fear I'll never get him out. I have to tear away the rest of him with claws I don't have.

I'm not this fierce, I think.

I'm not this able to resist.

And yet I am.

'I don't think that's enough.'

'How about if I tell you I work in finance?'

'Lots of people work in finance.'

'I have a penthouse that overlooks the city.'

'Doesn't everyone, these days?'

I marvel at the boredom in my own voice. My palms are sweating so much I have to keep switching the receiver from one hand to the other, but somehow I keep up this charade. When it's just our voices, I can do it.

'My favourite opera is Madame Butterfly.'

'You could be any anonymous millionaire suit.'

'So if I was poor you might say what you mean?'

'I might.'

'Then I am penniless.'

The words themselves are not unusual. But, I confess, the sudden conviction in his voice gives me pause. There's something steely about it, as though he's carving each word into a tree with a knife.

It makes me shiver, but I pretend it doesn't.

'You can't change the dynamics just by saying.'

'Of course I can. That's how the game is played.'

'And is that what The Harrington is about? Playing games?'

'If you say the real words I might tell you yes or no.'

Whatever this game is, he's extremely good at it. I didn't agree to dancing, and yet somehow I'm doing it anyway. Idoinanyway.m doing it right here in the middle of the work day, with Michaela to one side of me yakking away into her own phone and my boss over there by the water cooler.

He gives me a slight nod, like he thinks I'm fielding an important call – and I suppose that is how I must look. I'm hunched over, near-whispering, one fist clenched over my keyboard. The other clinging to the phone for dear life.

'All right. All right,' I hiss at him. 'People meet there to have illicit liaisons.'

'*I'm not sure that's quite real enough. It sounds like something from a tabloid newspaper, about the swinging the neighbours have been doing.*'

'*People meet there to have sex, then.*'

'*Sex is better, but I think you can do more.*'

I glance across at my boss. He's no longer looking, but that doesn't matter. This conversation is definitely giving off a vibe, now, that people should be able to feel across long distances and without glancing at me. I can feel it pulsing at my core like some nuclear reactor, so it must be spreading outwards.

Soon everyone will be irradiated.

At the very least, they'll know. Alissa is having an oddly sexual conversation with a complete stranger, and doesn't want to stop. Look at her there, shamelessly not stopping.

'*They meet to touch, and kiss, and lick,*' *I say, and though my voice shakes I'm proud of myself. It feels like he shot a tennis ball at me with a cannon, and somehow I miraculously managed to smack it back.*

'*And is that all?*'

I close my eyes and take a breath, hovering on the brink of not obeying. He's just toying with me, pushing me, daring me to go too far. I shouldn't care. I should put the phone down. But I suppose the trouble is:

I want to go too far. I'm tired of living in the land of not far enough.

'*They meet to screw in every kind of position, all over each other and upside down and inside out. And when they're done with all the things I can imagine, they start on the things I can't. Threesomes and foursomes and things with toys ... things with handcuffs and canes and red silk sliding all over their bodies ...*'

By the time I'm done my face is flaming, and I'm trembling all over. I barely even remember what I've said – it just came out in such a tumble, one word racing after the other, all of them so eager to emerge. I didn't realise how eager I was to emerge.

But I think he does.

'*What a wonderful way with words you have when you really try.*'

'*It's nothing to do with trying. It's just you and how goddamn persuasive you are.*'

'*If I'm so persuasive then why are we talking about what you want to talk about?*'

I frown at nothing and no one, the inside walls of my cubicles suddenly gone. Instead they're replaced by his indomitable face, and its every infuriating line and curve.

'*No, we're not.*'

'*Of course we are. You wanted to know about The Harrington, and now I have told you – even though it is the most closed of all secrets.*'

'*But this is ... this is what we started out at. We started talking about it and then you wanted me to talk dirty.*'

'Oh, darling. If I wanted you to talk dirty there are a hundred other ways I would have gone about it. No no no, when we began talking I wanted to know what y so know wour face looked like, and you led me down an entirely different path. I must admit I am enjoying the view here, but even so – it's your view, not mine.'

Oh, God, he's right. How is he so right all the time? It would be impossibly frustrating, if he wasn't so calm about it. So inoffensive. He doesn't force his point of view on you. He just leads you down a certain path inside the labyrinth, and suddenly you're lost.

'It wasn't … I didn't do it on purpose, though.'

'Didn't you?'

'Of course not. Why would I?'

'Because you don't want to talk about your face.'

This labyrinth is dark, and deep. I don't know where I am any more.

'Maybe I'm hideous,' I say, so faintly I hardly have to worry if anyone can hear. Only he can, down a million miles of phone wires to his lair that lies beyond the goblin city.

'I think it's more likely that you think you're hideous.'

'No, I really am. I'm sure you think you're talking to some gorgeous babe whose presence pushes through wood, but in reality I'm monstrous. I'm six foot tall and three hundred and fifty pounds, with no ears and one eye,' I say, and I know why I do it. It's so I can be the

minotaur instead of the girl. I'm marching around his maze, hungry for his blood.

But he doesn't care either way.

'Are you just trying to turn me on now?'

'A man like you isn't turned on by no ears and one eye.'

'Perhaps not – but I am turned on by the sound of your voice, and the way you watched me, and by your resistance. I've never known anyone long for something so much and yet be so afraid to take it when it's offered.'

I'm the girl again, just like that. I'm running around the insides of myself, blind and fumbling – only I think I was wrong about him having a lair at the centre. I think I can see him atop one of the walls with a rope, and he just threw it down to me.

I won't take it though. I don't know him well enough to take it. This could be a trap, and once I'm up there he robs me of my self-esteem and makes a run for it.

'You don't know what I long for.'

'How can you imagine so when you make it this clear? You long for something different, and lovely, and exciting,' he says, as my eyes drift closed. 'You long to be outside your own skin, for just a little while.'

I've never ached before over something someone's said. I'm not used to the sensation, so sweet and hollow inside myself. It makes me swallow too thickly and keep my eyes closed in case someone sees I'm having feelings, and most of all it forces me to deny, deny, deny.

'That's all wrong.'

'Is it?'

'Yes.'

'Then why are you still on the phone?'

'I'm putting it down.'

'Of course you are.'

'We'll never speak again.'

'No, never.'

Is it my imagination, or does he sound strangely sad when he says that last lonely 'never'? It must be the former, and yet I can still hear the word echoing in my head a long time after he's said it. I let the silence spin out, just so I can feel it for a little while longer.

nd n="justBefore I have to say: 'I'm really not pretty, you know.'

'Tell me all the ways in which you think you're not.'

'My face is too square.'

'So you have a strong jaw that I should angle up to the light, before I leave a trail of kisses over its perfect slant.'

'And my upper lip is hardly there, while my lower one …'

'Is so full and soft and sulky, as I lean in to steal a kiss.'

'You wouldn't want to. My skin is almost see-through and my hair is as thin as paper. I can never do anything with it.'

'*Except lie back and let me wrap my hand around those soft strands. Is it dark?*'

'*It's almost black.*'

'*And your eyes?*'

'*A muddy brown. A boring, dull, nothing brown,*' I say, though that's not strictly true. It's just that I don't want him to recognise me as the girl from the lobby, not yet. Not while he's so content to imagine me into someone else.

'*But you would look up at me with them, wouldn't you?*'

I know what he means. He means that I would look up at him as I took his cock in my mouth. He means it because I make him, in my head. I push him back on the bed, and lick along the length of him, wetly, greedily, oh, God.

'*I would.*'

'*And what would those eyes of yours say?*'

'*More, now, yes, please.*'

I don't know if I mean more of his words, or of the sex he doesn't know we're having in my head, or just everything, everything would be fine. He's nothing like I thought and everything that I want, and if that means I have to take a leap of faith and grab the rope, I will.

'*Oh, so greedy. Are you greedy, little Alissa?*'

'*You know I am.*'

'*Then tell me what you want,*' he says, and the fantasy

suddenly bleeds into reality. I blurt out words before I'm even sure he's ready for them – words like 'I want you to fuck my face.'

But he doesn't let me down. Of course he doesn't. I'm halfway up that rain-slicked granite-grey wall, and he's still hauling me.

'Yes,' he says, only he stretches that one beautiful word out to twice the size. He packs it full of delicious satisfaction, and ends it on this: 'You want me to fill your hot, sweet mouth, over and over, as deep as you can take it and as rough ... and then just as you're sure you've reached your limit ... just as you think it's too much with my fist in your hair and my cock so swollen and eager ...'

He leaves the last word hanging, like the hand I imagine reaching down to me. I'm almost at the top, now. I'm almost able to look out over the labyrinth if I can just take this one last little step ...

'You come all over my tongue. All over my face. Oh, God, yes, come all over me,' I tell him, sure for a second that I've gone too far.

And then I hear that amused lilt in his lovely voice.

'Do you see now how lovely you are?'

Chapter Three

The problem is that I now know what the phone is. It isn't a device through which I can make deals or contact friends I don't have or order a Chinese takeaway. It's a hotline to him. It's a way of revealinen

Even though I'm not the sort who suspects anything, of anyone. I usually get it wrong in some spectacular fashion. I imagine someone's watching me and it turns out they'd just noticed my skirt tucked into my knickers. I believe I'm loved and discover it's just a mild affection. This is the usual way of things, and for a while it makes me pace the living room like a trapped animal.

I put it off and put it off, by turns angry at myself and almost pleased. I don't care who he is or what he does, I think to myself. And then I call quite suddenly, when I least expect it, and thirty seconds later he calls me back.

The moment he does, a half-made circle in my head clicks closed. I guessed, and was proved right. For once,

I was proved right. I wasn't punished for imagining something amazing, only for reality to fall so very short.

He's right there, on the other end of the phone.

'Hello, Alissa,' he says.

It's practically his catchphrase.

'Hello, Janos,' I say.

His name sounds like something sacred and unspoken, in my mouth. My clumsy English accent stumbles over the J that should be a Y and the missing H at the end. It's a travesty, really, but he doesn't seem to notice.

'You remembered,' he says, as though I could ever forget now.

It's burned onto my brain. I say it in my sleep.

'Of course I did.'

'I get an "of course"? Well. I do feel privileged.'

'You shouldn't.'

'No?'

'I'm hardly anyone important.'

'And you believe that is how I weigh things? By importance? Perhaps I would like you better for being the undiscovered queen of a small country.'

'It would make more sense.'

'Then I shall make you one. You can be queen of my island.'

'What island?'

'The island that all men are, naturally.'

He sounds like he's laughing, again, but I'm starting to

think that's his default state. Or at least it's his default state with me. I make his voice go all rich and rolling like that, with a faint curl upwards on the end of every sentence.

'That sounds like a lot of responsibility. I'd probably have to wave a gloved hand from inside an expensive car. Accompany you to functions I'm not prepared for. Wear outfits I look terrible in, with hats I can't afford.'

'That isn't the sort of island I had in mind.'

'No?'

'No.'

'Then what? What sort of island are you?' I ask, but I'm picturing it in my head before he's even said. I see tangled jungles lit by a thousand lurking eyes ... great jagged rocks turned black and nightmarish by a storm that's always raging.

And me, swept up on the beach.

'One where it's always night.'

'I can see that.'

'And the ocean rages.'

'My little boat hardly stands a chance.'

'No, probably not. But you needn't worry.'

'Why?'

'Because I am waiting for you on the shore.'

'In your suit?'

'No, I'm never in my suit, on the island inside me.'

For some reason it makes my breath catch in my throat, when he says it like that: *'island inside me'. I have to*

45

sit down on the edge of my bed, because my legs don't want to hold me up any more. I'm almost in the same state I was before, at the office.

Flushed, famished, eager to get lost again.

'Then what?'

'Barely anything. A savage animal stripped to the waist.'

'I think you're just telling me things you think I want to hear, now.'

It's not the first time I've wanted to say it. It's just the first time I've been brave enough to – and not just because of how intimidating he is. I wanted to hold onto the illusion a little longer. I wanted him to be real, to honestly find me interesting, to wonder what lies beneath my cloak of invisibility.

But now it's OK if he doesn't.

Because I'm pretty sure he does.

'I'm disappointed in you, Alissa. Do you really think I'd be so dishonest?'

'I think you'd do a lot of dishonest things to get what you want.'

'It's true. I have. I do. And yet not with you.'

'Why not with me?'

'Because you are already sure everything is a lie. My only defence is the absolute truth. My only power over you is the truth. And if I keep telling it, eventually you'll believe.'

My breath is caught again. Actually I think it's been bound and gagged and sent before the firing squad. And when I finally speak, my voice is shaking slightly.

'How do you know this stuff? Did Lucy tell you?'

'Lucy?' *he asks, and my heart sinks before he's even finished.* 'Who is Lucy?'

'The woman you were supposed to meet that night.'

He laughs, low and startling.

'So that's why you were hiding in the wardrobe. It was not meant to be you.'

'That's right, it wasn't. Which means everything you think about me is wrong.'

'On the contrary. Everything fits a little better, now. I thought you'd merely changed your mind, but this is much more you. Slipping into the skin of someone else, just as I said.'

Damn him. Damn damn damn him.

'It's not like that. I wanted to find out what she'd been doing. That's all.'

'Are you sure?'

I close my eyes briefly.

'Not even a little bit.'

'Ah, that's good. It's good to hear your honesty.'

'Then tell me yours. You said you would. How do you know me?'

He hesitates, then. His silence is almost as overwhelming as his words.

47

Almost.

'Do you think you are so very hard to read? Perhaps no one has ever bothered before, and this has led you to believe you are inscrutable. But no, I think not. I think it is more likely that these other people are lazy. You take a lot of studying and so they let you pass them by, even though everything you do says so much. You hide when you don't wf sou donant to; you hang up when you want to complete the call. You deny the things you feel the most and admit what matters least. My little study in opposites, are you not? Heart on her sleeve, though she would say it was only the pattern of the piece of clothing she was wearing.'

He's right again in many ways, but this time I only swallow thickly and try to change the subject. I try, even though it's difficult. My heart is thudding through my body like an oncoming army, shuddering my foundations as it goes.

'Maybe you should tell me something about yourself now,' I say, despite knowing what path those words are putting me on. It's the path that leads to him, not away. And worse: I think I like that this is the case.

I shiver strangely when he answers.

'And what would you like to know?'

'Anything.'

'Will you tell me anything in return?'

'You mean you don't know it already?'

He laughs that low laugh. It's almost a growl, but not a threatening one. More like the sort you'd hear as an animal sleeps, and dreams of defending his home.

'I don't.'

'All right, I will.'

'Very well, then. Ask me a question,' he says, and in the silence that follows I pick and discard several options. Some seem too personal, others too flippant. And all of them lead me back to the real issue.

My every word apparently tells him a thousand things about me. A single slip and I'm suddenly wretched and shallow, to go with all the other things he's uncovered so easily. My habit of doing the opposite of what I want to, my tendency to hide – he had it all.

So I have to be careful here, and completely innocuous.

'How old are you?'

'Worried that I am older than you'd like?'

Dammit, question, you were supposed to be innocuous.

'I hadn't thought about it.'

'Really?'

'Why would I? What would it matter to me if you were?' I say, and try to laugh lightly somewhere in the middle. I largely fail. And even if I had succeeded I don't suppose it would matter, because he soon blows all of that nonsense away.

'It would matter because my intention is to do all of those things you spoke of to you, and far more than that

besides. I intend to bring you pleasure and sweetness of the sort I'm sure you have not yet known, and so you can see: how old I am is of some importance. Many women don't like to be with someone twice their age.'

'I don't think the idea would even enter most women's heads, when it comes to someone like you,' I say finally, and only because I'm afraid of something else escaping. My body pulsed once, hotly, over several of the things he's just said, and if I give it too much leeway I know what it will make me do.

There are so many words it wants me to say, always hovering beneath the surface of our conversations. 'Yes' is one of them. 'Please' is another. Both broke through last time and embarrassed me, but I won't let them out again.

'Oh, really?'

'Yes, really. Don't pretend you don't know what I'm talking about.'

'Am I pretending?'

'Of course you are.'

'And why would I do such a thing?'

'To get me to admit it.'

'Admit what?'

'How handsome you are! You want me to admit how handsome you are. You want me to say that you're gorgeous, that you're amazing looking, that I was mesmerised by your great granite face and your hooded eyes and your mouth like an imprint of a kiss, and I want to because you said all of those things about me and I can't stop thinking about any of them even though none of them are real and God, God, you're the most frustrating person in the world.' I pause to take a breath. 'Why do you even need to hear this? Everyone on the planet has probably told you how handsome they find you.'

'Yes, of course,' he says, so coolly, so clearly. I could almost believe there was nothing else coming, until it hits me around the head. 'But it only matters to me that you do.'

I can't be held responsible for the one word I croak out. I'm still stunned after the blow, and probably sprawled all over the floor of my own mind.

'Why?'

'Because I want your pulse to quicken when you think of seeing me.'

'You do?'

'I want you to be wet between your legs when you imagine my face.'

'Oh, God.'

'Are you wet now, Alissa?'

'Can I plead the fifth?'

'You can, if you wish. Of course it will mean that I have to be honest while you do not, but if you really must …'

'All right. All right. I am,' I say. 'But it's not just about your face.'

'*I see. How intriguing. Perhaps you could tell me what it is about, then.*'

He knows I won't refuse, now, but oh, it's agonising to get the words out. Words he said so easily to me, so freely, and I'm struggling like I'm in a straitjacket.

'*The way you say things.*'

'*So it's the sound of my voice.*'

'*Not just the sound, though that's nice enough,*' *I say, then immediately want to make it more than that. He was so generous, I think. Why don't I know how to be generous with him? Why do I keep thinking that he's heard it all before, when I can almost hear him waiting on every single thing I say?*

He's waiting now, I can tell, and the longer he does the more the pathways in my mind begin to rearrange themselves. The one marked sex no longer has a beware sign barring the way. And the one marked Janos is a thousand miles wide and as smooth as silk.

I could probably slide down it.

'*It's more than nice enough. It's so beautiful I hear it sometimes in my dreams. The first time I heard it in the hotel room it was like I'd known it all my life, and just hadn't listened before.*'

'*Ah, Alissa.*'

'*And your words …*'

'*Tell me about my words.*'

'*They make me crazy.*'

'Which ones, specifically?'

'All of them. Any of them.'

'So mostly "and", and "when", and "if".'

It's another challenge, ten hurdles high. I can clear it, though. I can.

'No. Mostly "sex" and "pleasure" and the way you just said "wet".'

'Like it excites me.'

'Yes. Exactly, yes.'

'Like I want you to tell me all about that slippery seam between your legs, and how eager you must be to have someone lick their way over it.'

'Oh, God, yes.'

'And how I would, if I were there. I'd kiss your pussy until you forgot every little sliver of that restraint, play with your nipples to make them so pretty and stiff, slide my fingers inside you just as I think you might be doing now. Are you?'

I'm sitting with my legs squeezed so tightly together you couldn't pry them apart with a crowbar, one hand a tight fist just above that place he's talking about. However, my imagination is an entirely different matter. In my imagination I'm sprawled back on the bed, fingers sliding through my absolutely soaking folds, everything so frantic and furtive it's almost real anyway.

I don't suppose it matters if I lie a little.

'Yes.'

Only I think it does matter that I lie a little. I can tell. There's a silence after I've said it, as though he's considering saying one thing. But in the end, he goes with the other.

'Good. And then just when you're at the point of begging … just when you're ready to tell me your every secret without dissimulation …'

'Yes, oh, yes.'

'I'd stop.'

'No, don't,' *I say, and am shocked by the urgency and desperation in my own voice. I sound like I've lost my mind, or at the very least would be willing to trade it for more. And worse, he definitely knows that this is the case.*

'It has to be so.'

'Why?'

'Because this way I can make you take another step, without even really trying. You're ready now, aren't you? You're just waiting for the next part, hovering on the edge. So I will leave you here, sweet Alissa, with a promise.' *He pauses, almost unbearably.* 'I'll carry on, if you come to me.'

I could kill him. I want to kill him. At the very least I want to cry and kick and scream, and have to fight with myself to stop it happening. I'm not a child who's been denied something. I'm a rational adult, who needs to tell him rational things like:

'I won't be what you expect, you know.'

But he defeats me again, as easy as anything.

'Of course you will. You're the girl I saw in the lobby, aren't you?' he says, and when I answer with a shocked silence he laughs. 'Oh, my darling. Did you really think I didn't remember?'

Chapter Four

There are so many reasons why I'm standing in the lobby of The Harrington again. Obvious ones, like the curiosity which now burns through my body unchecked and uncontrolled. Undeniable ones, like the draw of that voice and the deal I made with him.

And then there is the real reason:

He lied.

Or, at the very least, he didn't say. Either way it doesn't matter, because the result is the same: I'm here and waiting for him, angry and stupefied but most of all safe, oh, so safe in the knowledge that he knew all along. I won't be a shock to him. I've never been a shock to him. He saw my face and my clothes and my body, and carried on with all of this even so.

In fact, he carried it o

He's not a magician after all.

Though it seems like he might be one, when his hand suddenly smoothes over my back. I don't hear him cross the skating-rink lobby, or see his shadow out of the corner of my eye. He keeps everything drawn in, so that this one touch will have the strongest possible impact. And oh, it does.

I think my whole world lights up to suddenly feel him. My skin bristles all over, so sharply aware of that one innocuous touch. That one *nothing* touch. He doesn't even cup my waist or linger for a while, and somehow I'm feverish over it. I'm flaming hot and hardly able to stand it – though I suspect the reason why.

The very casualness of the gesture is what makes it so very potent. Only intimate acquaintances would touch each other like that, with some unspoken hint of all the years between them. Somehow, I think, we have years between us, even though we've never actually and properly met.

This is the first time, and despite those years it feels like it. I'm shaking in the semi-shelter of his arm, afraid to meet his gaze but dying to do it anyway. Will he be as magnetic as I remember? It seems impossible, and yet I know the answer before I look. I don't have to see those eyes. I can feel them on the side of my face: a slow caress.

And when I finally turn my head he's even better than I expected.

I do it in increments, starting at his stubble-roughened throat, before moving onto his muscular jaw. There's something so fist-like about his face, so brutal … until you get to the centre. Until you get to that mouth like melted butter and those eyes, oh, those eyes. Had they seemed so alive before? I would have called them hooded and sultry, I think, but I can't quite call them that now.

They still are, but it's different. It's like he's searching for something; I can see the restless pacing behind that gaze. I can feel him wandering through my insides, trying to find something I don't know how to give. I'm sorry, I think at him, but it doesn't seem to matter. Once he's done with this looking, his mouth lifts a little at the corner. Just faintly, hardly anything at all.

But I recognise it for what it is.

This is the same smile I heard in his words – only now it comes with confirmation of its warmth, of its affection. I can see it in his eyes. I can feel it in the hand he raises to brush aside an errant strand of my insane hair.

And most of all, I can hear it in his words.

'Hello, my Alissa,' he says.

* * *

The room is just as I remember it: opulent, and filled with the kind of awed hush people usually find in museums. It makes me want to be very, very quiet, in case I accidentally breathe and disrespect the drapes. I almost fail at following him inside, for fear my shoes will dirty the quicksand carpet.

And for other reasons, too. Now that he's not holding me and caressing me and saying the one word that turns my insides upside down – 'my', I think, mine, my own – *I'm not quite sure how to behave. I feel as though I'm trailing in the wake of an enormous dark ship, and if I draw too much attention to myself I'll be crushed by its jagged edges.*

He could definitely crush me, if he wanted to. He's much taller than I remember. Perhaps sit i. Perhax foot two or three, though his overall size makes it seem like more. He really is built like a boxer or a rugby player, which probably explains why I jump back when he suddenly turns to face me. I just wasn't expecting him to move. I was quite content following a couple of steps behind, and in one abrupt movement he closes that gap too quickly.

It isn't a shock that I slam into the door behind me.

But it is a shock to him. He raises one eyebrow, which I suppose is his version of that feeling. It's measured and a little amused, and it makes the corner of his mouth lift a little.

'You're not afraid, are you?' he asks, though I think he knows I am. He just wants to show me how silly that is, how bemused it makes him. He isn't going to do anything horrid to me, so why did I almost barge my way back out into the corridor?

Because he's big? Because he's a prowling, dangerous

*predator? He certainly walks like one, all from his hips
and with the minimum of excess movement. It's almost
like his upper body remains completely still and ready
to lunge, while his legs do all the work. It's impossible
to describe fully and so insanely masculine.*

But it doesn't explain why I wanted to run.

No, what he says next explains why I wanted to run.

*'You do understand that I'm not going to suddenly
perform strange perverted acts on your innocent young
body, don't you?'*

*'Of course I understand that,' I snort, but I'm still
standing by the door. And he's still raising that one
eyebrow. We both know I'm not fooling anyone. 'All
right, maybe I didn't completely understand that.'*

*He turns to the drinks cabinet by the window, that
great broad back now to me. It doesn't make any difference, however. I could no more read his face than I can
his shoulder blades. They're both a blank slate.*

*'Then let me be very clear: I didn't bring you here to
do anything you don't want.'*

'So what did you bring me here for?'

*He glances over his shoulder at me, smile now as
sharp as a shark's.*

'To find out what you do want, of course.'

'Don't you already know?'

'I told you. I'm not a mind-reader.'

He has a glass of what looks like Scotch in his hand

when he turns, and for a moment I think he's going to give it to me. Instead he simply sits down by the table in front of the window, free hand working the buttons on his jacket until the whole thing hangs loose. One big leg jutting in my direction, the other tucked back.

It's neither a relaxed pose nor an aggressive one.

It just is. He's just himself, utterly contained and totally compelling.

'I suppose the other women are pretty clear.'

'The rules of the assignation are pretty clear. We always know beforehand what particular game we might be playing, though we never see each other more than once. Everything relies on an unspoken understanding between participants. But you and I don't have that understanding.'

'So what do we do now, then?'

He rolls the liquid around inside the glass, but doesn't drink.

He speaks instead.

'We do it the old-fashioned way. I ask, and you tell me.'

'Can't you just guess?widtrea guess?

'I could, but that would make it ever so easy on you.'

'I don't think that's such a bad thing.'

'Perhaps not.' He sets the glass down on the table, and I know something's coming. He's gearing up to it, if he even needs to do anything like that – which I doubt. He seems to have two settings: bristling silence and sudden

action. And I think I'm about to get some sudden action now. 'Perhaps we could play that way for a little while.'

Oh, God, I should never have asked for guessing. I was wrong, I take it back. Guessing is for people who understand everything about themselves. I do not understand everything about myself. I don't even understand why I jerk when he stands up, because he doesn't do it in an aggressive way.

He doesn't do anything in an aggressive way, really. His voice is soft; his movements are measured and precise. And when he starts circling me, he does it in such a slow, casual manner it's almost like he's not doing it at all.

I doubt I'd notice, if I wasn't so completely tuned into him. My body hums the moment he gets close, and even after he's stepped behind me I'm aware he's still there. I'm almost leaning towards him, in fact, as though he's a magnet and I'm made of metal.

And of course he notices.

'I could, for example, intuit from the sway of your body that you like it when I draw close, and don't when I step away. Am I correct?'

He's so correct it's painful. I think he's starting to pull my fillings out.

'Yes.'

'And when I do this …' he begins, but naturally he doesn't have to finish. The back of his hand against my cheek is enough. It's more than enough. It's a sort of bliss

I've never really known before. 'I can tell how much you like it by the way you lean into it.'

He could say more and embarrass me, I think, because really I'm not just leaning. I'm almost sliding off my chair. If he were standing beside me now I'd slump into his side, and I'm not even sure I'd care. All that matters at the moment is how hard and high my heart is beating, how prickly my skin seems to be, how warm I am right at my centre.

I want to be my body and nothing else, for once.

And oh, it's easy to be that way with him. He makes you forget without even really trying. He says one word and every frantic thought I've ever had just flies away.

'Yes, you like that,' he tells me, and I feel no need to say no. Saying no might make him stop, and, dear God, I don't want that. His knuckles are just about to graze my jaw, and if I hold my breath I know he'll do more. He's right on the verge … right on the cusp … just a little bit more and then he gives it to me.

'And this?' he says, as his hand slides under the collar of my shirt.

He doesn't go right for my breasts, however. Of course he doesn't. Schoolboys with sweaty hands do things like that, and he's the absolute opposite. He's from another world where men are calm and cool, and capable of just letting the tips of their fingers trail over a woman's collarbone.

I feel him press lightly, briefly, barely there, but just as I'm starting to enjoy it he backs away a bit. He lets those fingertips brush against the material instead of my skin, touching buttons in a suggestive way. He might undo them. He might not.

All I have to do is say.

So I do.

'Yes, that,' I tell him, fumbling and bumbling over word choice and finally settling on something that makes no sense. Yes, that, I think, and want to roll my eyes. He's like the endless coils of a clever snake, and I'm this humiliatingly literal and oh, so basic creature.

Not that he cares. In fact, my stunted attempts at being a real person only seem to spur him on. I stutter out the only words I can and he responds with a sultry 'and more, I'm sure?'

Before that maddening hand does just that. It gives me more – far more than I expect. Running through my head is the image of him cupping my breast, or maybe unbuttoning my shirt a little bit, before I explode. Instead he touches two fingers to his lips, like he's blowing me a kiss.

And then he licks them. He licks them.

It's probably the dirtiest thing I've ever witnessed. Dirtier than actual sex I've had, dirtier than movies filled with sex. He's still in his suit, and he looks so elegant and refined, and yet he's lewdly easing his tongue all over and around his fingers, right in front of me.

Of course it's then that I realise I'm not going to survive any of this. He hasn't even done anything, and I'm staring like a maniac. I'm thinking like an unprepared teenager. I can't even fathom why he's doing what he's doing, even though I should absolutely know. Why else would he be making his fingers all nice and wet?

He's going to touch me, I think, but the thought doesn't connect with his actions. I watch his hand lower back down to my trembling body, as though everything is suddenly in slow motion. My lips are parted; my eyes are wide. I must look pretty comical, following his fingers as they slide beneath the material of my shirt.

And even more comical, when they slide beneath the material of my bra. I make a little sound and come pretty close to grabbing his wrist, but I swear it's not because I'm a prude. It's because I'm far too excited. My nipples are stiff unbearable points, clearly visible through my shirt. I really need more time to compose myself before he does this.

But he gives me none.

He simply eases those slippery fingers over that one tight little tip, rubbing and rubbing before I'm ready. I'm still choking over the first burst of sensation, and he's making slow, slick circles around one of the most sensitive spots on my body.

Or at least, it's one of the most sensitive spots now. Great aching tingles surge down from that point of connection, turning most of my lower body to liquid. I'm shuddering all over, and so stuffed with heat I could set fire to the carpet with very little effort – and over such a minor thing. It's nothing really, I think. It's nothing.

And yet at the same time it's everything.

He catches the stiff tip between those fingers, and I cry out. I strain towards his touch, without shame. How can I be ashamed when it feels so good? I think I could actually come like this, all mired in the heat and the tension of his presence, stirring restlessly beneath his cool and perfectly assured touch.

And I so desperately want to test that theory. I'm gagging to test that theory. Go on, go on, I think at him, just a little more. Just pinch it a little harder; just lick like that for me, again. Give me everything you've got, go on.

But instead he waits. He waits for the perfect moment, when I'm writhing and reckless and ready for so much more. Then he leans down as though he's going to kiss me, and whispers in my ear:

'ostjustifyNow tell me what you want to happen next.'

'That isn't fair.'

'Of course it's fair. If you want something, you have to ask.' He walks around me again, only this time it's more like pacing. It's more like prowling. 'I did say that you couldn't expect me to do all the work. You have to offer me something at least, and really I'm requiring so little. Am I not?'

The answer is yes, obviously. Yes, you're requiring so little. Words are barely anything when you really boil them down, and I know I could compress them even further. I could mash 'fuck' together with 'me' and he'd understand.

He would.

So why am I floundering? It's simple, really.

'All right,' I say. 'I'd like to touch you.'

There, I think. There.

And just as I do he strikes me down.

'Liar,' he says, like a fist rapping against glass.

A little harder and it will break.

A little gentler and everything will stay the same.

'That's not a lie.'

'Of course it is. You don't want to touch me. You want me to carry on touching you. You want me to peel off your blouse and your bra and get right underneath. And when I'm finished there, you want me to start on other items of clothing.'

He gestures to my skirt, though perhaps gesture is the wrong word. It's much more like a caress, from the curve of my hip over and down my thigh to my knee. And I suppose it would be, if his hand wasn't around two feet away from any of my actual body parts. It just dances through the air over certain places, and I shudder as though he really touched me.

I'm fighting a losing battle.

'You're wrong. I hate being naked.'

'*You hate being naked because you think you're unappealing. But secretly you long to be confident … to have a man's eyes following your every move as you strip out of your clothes, so sure and certain that he wants you. That he craves you. Isn't that so?*'

'*No.*'

This time he stops in front of me, and tick-tocks his finger back and forth.

'*That's another lie, Alissa.*'

'*How can you always tell?*'

'*I make my living from being able to tell.*'

'*Really? True or false, then: I threw my childhood pet in a lake.*'

'*Are you challenging me?*' *he asks, laughter in his words.* '*Very well: true.*'

'*You honestly believe I'd do something like that?*'

'*Whether I believe or not, it's obvious you aren't lying.*'

'*Why?*'

'*Because you wanted to trick me, so told me the most ridiculous thing you could think of in the hopes I'd get it wrong.*' *He sits back down in his seat by the table, while I make every effort to close my gaping mouth.* '*Correct?*'

He's so correct it hurts. My pride is still reeling from the blow.

'*Correct.*'

'*I don't know why you did it, however. Are you going to enlighten me now?*'

'You really want to know?'

'Of course.'

'I killed it by accident. It was justnt. It ust a mouse and I was mostly afraid of it and it jumped out of my hands when I tried to hold it too tight.' He was right about the ridiculous part. This story is so absurd I'm blushing over it, and not just because of the content. There's also the fact that he's making me tell it to someone like him. What does he know about petty concerns like this? I wish I wasn't telling him about petty concerns like this. 'And then I was scared my parents would find out, so I got rid of the evidence.'

'That's a sad little tale.'

'It's a stupid, meaningless little tale.'

'Yes, I'm sure it's meaningless that you were afraid, and that you tried to hold on tight, and then couldn't tell the people closest to you,' he says, and something rises in my throat after he's done so. It kind of feels like a knot of frustration on the way up, but it comes out in the form of a word.

'God,' I snap. 'Do you really have to be like this? You can't work me out so easily, you know. No one can work out another person so easily.'

'I never claimed I could. I only claimed that I can interpret some of the things you say and do, and that I know when you lie. And I believe I've proved that much, at least.'

He's right. He has. But I'm not willing to accept that. I'm not willing to accept any of this. I just want to go back to the touching and the guessing, and that urge is so strong it's making my teeth ache. Before I answer I have to clench them together, and the words come out all grating and ground up.

'Not enough for my liking.'

'No? Then perhaps we should play another little game,' he says, in a way that suggests it isn't going to be little, and it isn't going to be a game. People don't brace themselves over little games – but that's what I'm doing. I've stiffened my shoulders and tightened my hands into fists, and when he finally speaks I close my eyes. It seems better to close my eyes for something like this: 'If you tell me a lie about your desires and I catch you, you then have to do whatever it is you tried to conceal from me.'

'And how would you go about catching me?' I ask, in some vain attempt at injecting some bravado into this. I already know it's the wrong thing to say, however. The second I speak that word aloud, my mind starts picturing him chasing me down hallways. In some of the scenarios he has giant metal hands or a big chainmail net, but in all of them I'm exactly the same way. I'm panicking and stumbling and completely unable to escape.

He'll have no trouble, I think.

And apparently, we're of one mind on this.

'I don't believe it will be so very difficult.'

'*I could lie about lying. I could tell you it isn't true no matter how hard you pressed me, and then what would happen?*'

'*Then the game comes apart.*' *He picks at lint that isn't there, somewhere around his right knee.* '*Though I trust that you won't let that happen. No matter what you say, I think you like it when I guess.*'

He's right and wrong at the same time. Sometimes he speaks and my insides soar, but I always have an urge to punch him afterwards. I have an urge to punch him now, and it's really only being eclipsed by the need to play this game until it reaches some probably nightmarish conclusion.

He'll ask me if I'd like some anal sex, and I'll lie and say no.

And then I'll have to do it.

Oh, God, yes,e oem>yes< I'll have to do it.

'*All right. I haven't the faintest clue how this is going to work, but all right.*'

'*Excellent.*'

He shrugs around inside his jacket, as though to make himself comfortable. And when he finally is – when he's completely at ease and the master of his own domain – he speaks in this casual way.

It's just a shame that the words themselves aren't casual at all.

'*What are you waiting for, then? Take off your clothes.*'

'What? That's not the game.'

'Of course it is. You lied about not wanting to be naked, and I caught you. So now you have to remove every … little … thing.'

For a moment I'm too taken aback to speak. He's like a wizard. He's like the designer of terrible traps for foolish people, and somehow I've stumbled right into one without even realising it. My leg is caught and I've lost my map, and I've really got no one to blame but myself. I actually feel stupid for complaining, though I have to do it.

'But we weren't playing then.'

'I don't remember that being in the rules. You didn't specify a starting point, as far as I can recall, though you can try to tell me otherwise if you like.'

I bet he'd let me, too. I bet he'd let me talk just to see how deeply I can tangle myself in him and all of his craziness. And the answer is, of course: very deeply indeed. Oh, so deeply I'm never going to get back out again.

'I don't want to tell you otherwise.'

'So then,' he says, and holds out a hand – like the conductor of a symphony, I think, awaiting a command performance. I can even hear the strings singing in the background, everything rising and rising to the point where I have to do this.

Doesn't he realise I can't do this? I've never learned;

I don't know how. The instrument is unfamiliar and clumsy and the notes are all wrong. I can't I can't I can't, I think, about a second before he speaks again.

'Begin,' he tells me.

And somehow I can play.

Chapter Five

I start out quite simply, slipping out of my shoes and casually tossing my jacket aside. But after a moment I realise this is meant to be more than that. It's meant to be a striptease, I can see. It was in his words, and that hand gesture he made, and now it's in his expression. That near-smile is dancing around his lips, though it hasn't quite reached his eyes.

Oh, no, his eyes are as dark as midnight and twice as intense. They glitter at me like onyx from all the way across the room, and they never waver. They don't even flick to something else when I reveal the silly thing I've done.

I wore tights, instead of stockings. I wore big, clumsy, grey woollen tights, unthinkingly. All I considered was how good they'd look with the only expensive suit I own, and in truth they do. They look great when I'm fully dressed.

They just don't when I'm not.

Why didn't I think about not? I knew what I was coming here for. There weren't any illusions, though I suppose I might have pretended otherwise. I erased our final phone conversation from my mind, and just focused on other things. His voice, the island, this room.

I'm such a fool, I think, but there is nothing fogn=r it now. I have to reach under my skirt and wriggle out of these ugly elasticated things, and I have to do it fast. I have to do it without glancing up, in case his gaze makes me lose my nerve.

When I accidentally do, however, the near-smile hasn't spread. He's not laughing. If anything he looks even more intense than he did before. He's leaning forward a little now, with one hand on the arm of the chair, and as I slowly restart this clumsy strip, his eyes follow my hands.

He watches me slide the wool down over my knees, occasionally tilting his head this way or that – as though to get a *better* look, I think. He wants a better look at something so completely ridiculous.

And I don't know what to think of that.

I know it makes my breath come in shaky bursts, however. I know it makes me even clumsier. For a long moment I can't quite get the tights over my ankles, and I wrestle with them briefly before finally giving in.

I'm going to have to sit down to do it, though God knows what kind of striptease that is. The truth is, I suppose, it isn't any kind of striptease at all. It's just me removing my clothes, in blundering fits and starts. First the shoes, then the tights, and now my shirt. Oh God, my shirt. Why is it so much harder with the shirt?

I guess it was just easy to pretend, with the other things. But I can't with something that covers most of my upper body. Once the material is off he'll be able to see secret parts of me that usually stay covered up, and the idea makes my hands tremble. I fumble my way through the buttons, random thoughts flitting through my mind as I do: what will he think of my frayed bra? What will he think of my weird breasts?

But in one way, he answers all of my silly worries.

He still isn't wavering. He doesn't look away when I slide the material off. He just keeps staring and staring, until it almost becomes a kind of challenge for me. Go on, go on, I think at him. Glance at something else. Here I am, with my tights and my worn underwear and my mannish shoulders.

Be bored. Be disgusted.

And when he refuses to obey I go faster. I get a little braver. I fumble the zipper down on my skirt and let it pool around my ankles, and once I've made a fist of my nerves my bra follows. It's really quite easy with him looking at me like that, because his look makes it abundantly clear.

He likes what he's seeing. Somehow, impossibly, he does. His eyes are almost fondling me, and when I finally bare my breasts that feeling gets stronger. I get that same spark of sensation thrumming down from my taut nipples as I did when he was actually touching me. My back arches and my shoulders straighten – like I'm proud, I think, like I'm proud to look like this and as confident as he said I could be.

And I am, really. In that moment, I am.

I feel all raw and ripe, and so aroused. My sex is a swollen fist between my legs, just aching for me to take that final step. The material of my panties is practically a prison by this point, and it only gets worse as time ticks on. I think he's looking now. I think he can see my wetness seeping through the cotton, and after a while I know he can.

He gives me this hooded look, near feverish and so greedy. *You're making a mess, you bad girl*, that look says, and I'm sure it's only a matter of time before he tells me to take them off. I can almost hear him ordering me, in fact.

'Just remove them before you sully the material any further,' he'll say, while I come close to collapsing on the quicksand carefuuicksanpet. Or maybe he'll simply tear them off with his teeth, as I swoon dead away. He certainly looks like he wants to do that.

He's baring those pearly whites right now. And he keeps licking his lips in this lovely, lascivious manner, like he's thinking what I'm thinking even though I haven't the slightest clue about anything in my head. I'm too busy enjoying the sensation of someone not actually touching me to get as far as what it might be like if he did.

Will it be as good as him watching me awkwardly easing my panties down my legs? I doubt it. He seems to flash fierce when I snap the elastic and softer when I get things right, and everything is so backwards I can't bear it. Why does he like it when I blunder? Because it's clear now that he does.

I almost trip when I get to the last hurdle, vacillating wildly between sureness and a fumbling lack of grace, and it's then that he moves. I hardly even hear him, or see him. I'm too busy tutting at myself for being clumsy, and then suddenly his hand is on my shoulder. His big, broad hand, as firm as I imagined it.

Only this is more than my mind could offer. My mind is thin, compared to him. It suggested a poised and professional man intent on a particular goal, but that isn't what I get. I get a man possessed by a raging demon. He pushes me back onto the bed without saying a word, all questions and answers and truth and lies forgotten.

This is the truth:

His hand making a hot stripe right down the centre of my naked body. My body arching to meet that sizzling touch. I feel as though I've waited for ever, and yet somehow it's no time at all. It's too soon, it's ... wrong. He didn't mean to do this, I think, though, God, I'm glad he does.

It's like getting early parole.

No more languishing in a prison of my body, afraid to be seen and touched and handled. There's just him and his hands on my thighs, and then the electric sense of him kneeling down somewhere just past the edge of the bed.

So he can look, I think.

But oh, it's so much more than that. I was wrong about him and his restraint, his clinical approach, his ability to be aloof. In one sudden swoop he's an animal, wanting me to spread for him, wanting to see, wanting to touch. I feel his thumbs press deeply into those sensitive spaces that surround my plump sex, and I know this is going to be too much.

He's going to take me apart with his hands, clearly. He's going to map out every part of me the way he mapped me out with his eyes, so he can use the information at a later date. He'll probably put it in his little notebook of me: she likes having someone run a finger down through her wet slit, so everything is nice and exposed.

Only *finger* is the wrong word there.

He doesn't do anything with his fingers, the way I imagine. I guess that would be too easy, really, to attribute to someone like him. You can clearly imagine him searching all over someone with those strong, forceful hands, maybe while wearing a pair of leather gloves.

But you can't see him pushing his face between someone's legs.

I can't see it. I don't expect it. I'm waiting for something else, and I get the sudden jolting press of his hungry mouth against my spread pussy. And when I try to sit up – more out of shock than anything else – he puts the finishing touches on this tableau.

He spreads a hand over my stomach, and pushes me back down.

I won't lie: it's possibly the most arousing thing to ever htrang to eappen to me. Not the press of his lips, or the idea of him doing it. Just the feel of that hand on my stomach. The way it looks spread out of my skin, fingers splayed and arm tilted – like he's about to exert some serious pressure, or at least wants the option of it.

He wants to keep you here, my mind whispers, but oddly my body doesn't revolt at the thought. Far from it. My body revels in the idea of him wanting something so badly – and after something so pathetic, too. I offered him a striptease a clown could have done, and his response is this.

I can't get over it. I'm still processing it when my body suddenly reminds me: someone is going down on you. That's what this is: he's licking your pussy, and you know what? You're loving it.

And oh, I am. Ohhhh, man, just the long, slow stroke of his tongue through my slit. Just the feel of him kissing and rubbing and making a mess all over his face ... it's more than enough to make me crazy. I squirm beneath his hand and almost let out a sound, even though I've never made sounds before.

I suppose I've never needed to.

No one's ever gone down on me before. Or at least no one's ever gone down on me like this. I've had a couple of guys almost graze my thighs with their lips, and once I think someone got a little lost on his way to my belly button. But nothing so intimate and obvious and nerve-jangling. I can actually make out the shape of my own clit, just by the way he slides his tongue around it.

And I know why he's urging my thighs wider with his free hand.

It's so he can get at me. It's so he can lick right into my hot, wet sex, while I pant and wriggle and half beg him not to. 'I can't bear it I can't bear it,' I tell him, and in response he goes after everything even harder. He devours my pussy, teeth grazing over skin so tender it could be made of tissue paper. I actually worry about it, until I realise how it feels.

Divine.

The spark of pain is like throwing a firework into a tank of gasoline. It shoves everything higher, makes everything sweeter, pushes the pleasure to new places. Once he's made a faint mark he licks over it with that soothing, slippery tongue, and my body can hardly keep up with the switch.

I'm electric with sexual confusion. Wires cross and

nerve-endings misfire, and though I want to be calm and cool and composed I can't be. I'm going to come, and so quick it's embarrassing. It's barely been a minute, but my thighs are starting to tense. My breath is starting to catch in my throat.

I'm going to do it all over his face, and there's just no way of stopping it. Not even the humiliation can hold me back – in fact I think the humiliation makes it worse. I imagine him telling me off for being a teenage boy, tumbling into orgasm while he's still standing on the sidelines, and my clit actually jumps against his sliding tongue.

I'm so wet I can hear it, as he laps at me greedily. And everything is so hot down there, so swollen and soft and ready. He could fuck me with very little trouble – just keep me pinned like this and unzip, then slide right into me. And in the state he seems to be in, I think he could do it. He's actually making noise into my slippery flesh, rough and close to grunting. It makes me wonder if he'd let me hear if I was doing the same for him, and it's this thought that puts me over the edge.

I think about him moaning as he takes me, and I just crumble completely. My body tightens like a fist, sensation ebbing and flowing through parts I barely knew existed. I feel it on the insides of my elbows and just under my ears, bent my earfore it finally, finally gets to the hot spots. My clit pulses once, heavily, beneath his still working tongue, and I'm just gone. I fly away. I no longer exist.

The me I was prior to this sits on one side, watching me writhe and gasp and make a complete fool of myself. Surely he must think I've made a fool of myself. The second this fizzing, insane sensation dies away I have to check, only to find him staring up at me with those midnight eyes. He stares and stares like I just did all of this to him, instead of him doing it to me. I've made something happen that I didn't even consider.

And I know what it is, too.

I made him want to do that. I somehow pushed him into this panting, slick-mouthed disaster, so fierce he doesn't know how to check it, so greedy for me he can't stop himself. And when I doubt myself on this he makes me believe.

He says:

'You are more than I dared imagine you'd be.'

As though there was already a fantasy version of me in his head. There *was* already one, and apparently I just surpassed it. I stumbled and fumbled and spread myself out naked in front of him, and none of it was found wanting. In fact, he found all of that better, greater, more. Different, I think.

The way that he is different to me.

He's assertive without being aggressive, sure of himself without arrogance, and kind in a way I could never have imagined. I thought he'd be sexually demanding, and instead he did something no one else has ever done before: he kissed my sex before I kissed his. He made me come before I did the same for him.

And for a moment all of those ideas are so over-whelming I just can't help myself. I wait long enough for him to stand and then I just do it: I grab hold of his perfect, expensive shirt, only slightly rumpled and so soft to the touch. I grab it, and him, and I haul his mouth down onto mine.

I *have* to have his mouth on mine. He's just done all of those things despite the fact that we've never actually kissed, so really I don't even need to think about it. I don't think about anything until I taste myself on his lips, and feel the amazing shape of them against mine – though I wish I had.

I can already tell where I've gone wrong. I can sense the sudden stiffness in his body, and the lack of effort in his response. In fact, there isn't any response to speak of. It's like kissing a marble likeness, smooth and perfect but completely inert.

Or maybe inert is the wrong word. He isn't still, after all. He's vibrating just a little with a strange tension, and it's this strange tension that finally makes me pull away.

I do it slowly, slowly, half-embarrassed and half-wondering. Is he really so averse to a kiss? Can it be possible, after everything we've just done? It doesn't seem right somehow, and yet there it is. It's in his expression, as flat and still as a glacial lake. And it's in his eyes, as they ask me *why, why did I have to spoil things?*

But I can't answer. How could I possibly? I filled my kiss with all the happiness in the world, and all the pleasure he gave me, given back.

And somehow poisoned him instead.

Chapter Six

I suppose I think it's over. That's how it seems, anyway – like something is done. He didn't really want to do anything after the kiss, and I don't blame him. I didn't want to do anything either. I couldn't even speak. The weight of hi, sos strange expression and his tensing body just sank me down, until it was time to leave.

Of course, he was a gentleman about it. He called me a taxi, and bid me a formal goodbye. It was all oddly respectful ... but oh, it was the painful sort of respect. It was the excruciatingly polite kind that only served to remind me of the bad thing I did. I kissed him on the mouth like the cruel witch in a fairytale, and he duly fell down dead.

I just don't know *why*. I don't know why, damn it – but God, how I want to. I'd do anything to understand. I keep thinking about his stony face, and what it would take to get a chisel underneath the top layer. What question would work on him? What words could possibly unlock his hidden secrets?

I can hardly imagine.

And that's probably my flaw. I'm not good enough for a puzzle like him. I don't have his preternatural ability to ascertain every lie, or work out every problem. Instead I have to settle for answering the questions on this week's edition of Mastermind, and I'll be perfectly honest: it's a very hollow substitute.

I've had a taste of something more, and now I don't know how to be satisfied with my life as it was. My microwaved meal seems bland and pathetic, like something only an idiot would eat. I feel trapped inside the confines of my L-shaped apartment, too restless to sit and too annoyed with my surroundings to pace.

I keep noticing things I didn't before, like the peeling paintwork in one corner and the narrowness of my neatly made bed. Why did I think it was a good idea to buy something so small? You couldn't fit a couple into it, though I know what I really mean when I think that. I really mean: you couldn't fit me and him in it.

He'd be too big. He'd spill over the edges and hang off the ends, crowding me into corners I don't want to be in.

I don't want to be in this one, obsessing about him. It's not healthy to obsess about a man, it's not right. Normal girls don't do it, and I should know. I was normal, before. I was eminently, perfectly normal, and now I'm changed in some way. I don't want to go to work in the morning, and take to some strange notions instead.

Maybe I should just go for a run. A big, wild run all the way down the road, then through the park and over the hill to the open fields beyond. Or what if I just decided to fly somewhere without telling anyone – the way Lucy did? Hell, maybe this is exactly why Lucy did it. She met someone like him who turned her world upside down, and suddenly she could no longer stand London.

She had to leave, and so do I. I need to get out of this apartment at least, though unfortunately I don't get any further than the hallway outside my door. I'm stopped by a box someone has left on the floor, and for a moment I'm flummoxed. I almost kick it down to the next apartment, thinking it's for the cute girl I sometimes see coming out.

And then I catch the edge of a curling S, and I understand. I pretend otherwise for a little longer, but I understand. The box is for me, bought by someone I'd pegged as out for the count a little while ago. In fact, I spent all night thinking he was out.

Now he's right back in again, too quick for me to process. I think I have whiplash – or at the very least, I'm suddenly unable to pick up mysterious gifts from enigmatic strangers. That gene is missing in me.

I've got the gene that tells me he's secretly sent me a bomb.

I can't even open it at first. I just set it down on my rickety little dining table, and let it fester. If I leave it for a whime it fohile, any hidden booby traps might reveal themselves. The fog of evil will start oozing out from between the folds of the wrapping paper, and I'll have a chance to get it to the bin and maybe seal it in.

In truth, I picture myself doing that anyway. What good will possibly come of this? It can't be a present, it just can't be. It has to be some final divorce settlement, for a marriage we don't have. There's an assignation contract in there that I didn't know about, and when I open it I'll find the price.

The dirty talk was twelve grand; the kiss for my pussy an even twenty. And as for the arm around me in the lobby ... oh, well. That one was priceless. That was beyond all measure. Just the thought of it makes me glance across at the bow-wrapped time bomb on the table, but I promise I quickly look away.

And then slowly, slowly, I start to give into its pull again. My head is on hinges, and the box has no problems making it turn. Soon I'm staring and staring, unable to think about anything else. What if it really is some kind of contract? I've read enough books about men like him to know that this is not beyond the bounds of possibility.

Maybe he read the same ones, and started getting ideas.

Or maybe I should cut it open and put myself out of my misery – which I do. I get a paring knife and slice the thing up, ripping through this and tearing that. The paper's probably worth more than my annual salary, but

I don't care. And I don't care about the bow, either. I toss it aside as though it isn't the prettiest thing I've ever touched, and then I open the box like I just brought it home from a phone store. There's a piece of plastic inside, I think. There's styrofoam and instructions in Japanese.

And that idea helps when it comes to touching the actual contents. For some reason, I'm finding it hard to do it. I see what he's put in this little box for me, and I consider that bin option again. I think about burning, though I don't really understand why.

It's just a snow globe.

There's nothing threatening or confusing about a snow globe. They're pretty and decorative and sometimes they hold down your flyaway pieces of paper. There's no hidden hurtful meaning in them, or suggestion of a contract I didn't sign. I don't even think the thing is so expensive that I should be offended, in some way.

Our little dalliance ended, so here's a parting pay-off, my mind says, but it isn't that. He could have got this from Hallmark, and when I lift it out that suspicion is confirmed. There are no diamonds, no crystal domes. It's just glass.

And inside …

Inside is an island. It's an island, like the one we talked about. There's a strip of dark jungle on one side and an ocean on the other, everything so simple you could almost call it crude. The whole thing reminds me of those creaking Plasticine kids' programmes I used to love, with thickly made figures that move awkwardly around on their doughy, basic limbs.

That's what the people on the beach look like.

But I can also see that they look like me, and they look like him.

He's had this made, I realise, and suddenly all thoughts of it being inexpensive and not a concern fly right out of the window. I don't even know how much it would cost to create something like this – and on such short notice, too. Even if he did it right after we first spoke about the island, that's still a remarkably small amount of time to craft glass and wood and something like modelling clay into this beautiful little thing.

Obviouslougfy">Obvy he's rich. And obviously this is a rich man's gift.

So why doesn't it feel like a rich man's gift? I don't feel bought, looking at it. I feel something else instead. There's this fluttering in my chest and my palms are all sweaty, and when I let my mind go it takes me to that beach. It shows me what it's like to have a secret story with someone, and when it does I know I want more.

I don't care that he couldn't kiss me. That he may be averse to intimacy, or something like it. I'd trade a thousand intimate kisses for this – I would, I would. In its own way, this is more. It tells a thousand tales about the world behind his eyes, lonely as that distant shore, dark as those forests, sharp with jagged rocks and so dangerous.

I should really beware, I think – but it's not a surprise that I don't.

If he's still in this deep, then so am I.

* * *

I jump every time the phone rings, despite the fact that a ringing phone is practically in my job description. I have to keep reminding myself that him calling is the unusual occurrence and everything else is reality: some woman wants to change her policy, someone else has an enquiry, a third person wants to know if he's speaking to his wife.

Stay cool, I tell myself, but it's hard to.

He didn't stay cool. He went all weird then sent me an amazing gift, and now I'm on tenterhooks for whatever comes next. I have questions on the tip of my tongue and all of this fizzing excitement for more of that unspeakable pleasure, and waiting is agony. It's like counting the days until Christmas, if Christmas was heaven and my workplace was hell.

My workplace *is* hell. My boss comes over to me after I've made myself a cup of coffee, and I can tell he's not going to say anything good. I don't even know why I expect him to, in all honesty, because he *never* says anything good.

He always looks the same: deeply suspicious and unaccountably angry. He has this permanent line between his brows, so deep and strange he could have made it with a marker. And he's always so … so full of this uncomfortable energy. Michaela says it's because of the stick up his ass, but that's not the impression I get.

A stick would probably improve his mood.

As it is, his mood is this:

'Is that your third cup of coffee?'

It's actually my first, but there's no real sense in saying that to him. He gets these ideas into his head, and they don't go away. I'm not even sure if he wants them to go away. I think he clings to them, the way I'm clinging to the idea of some different life I could be leading, if I was brave enough to call him instead of waiting like a drip for him to call me.

'I don't have to drink it,' I say, and he nods once, sharply.

'You shouldn't be drinking it at your desk, anyway.'

I glance around at the dozens and dozens of people who are doing just that, but as always he doesn't catch my drift. He never catches anyone's drift, but if you spell it out for him he nails you for it. Suddenly you don't get that day off you wanted, or there's a problem with your bonus this year. Maybe you don't get invited to the Christmas party, accidentally on purpose, and then he behaves as though you really care.

Oh, how sad for you that you missed it. I don't know why you didn't get the email …

'I'll pim >'Iour it down the sink, Mr Henderson. It's not a problem.'

'No, no. You can have it, this time.' He laughs in this big, false way. And I know it's a false way, because the line never leaves. His eyes remain as flat and grey as always, like he's a robot mimicking human emotion. 'I'll look the other way!'

He's so kind I can hardly stand it.

I can hardly stand *any* of this, in truth. My skin feels as though it's about to crawl off my body. It's all I can do to stop myself grabbing my pencil and stabbing it deep into his right eye, and to be honest I doubt I'd stop there. I can see myself smashing the copy machine. I've got a deep desire to pour this coffee somewhere other than the sink, and the longer this day goes on the worse the weird feelings get.

By the time it's over I'm almost beside myself, walking with pins pricking into the balls of my feet, unable to stay inside my suit jacket. I rip it off in the elevator, even though I know I'll be cold outside. We're running at a pace towards winter now, and the day outside is bristling with frost.

Darkness is coming already, and it's through this darkness that I see the car. Everyone sees the car. You couldn't miss it if you tried, in a parking lot filled with Pintos and

Peugeots and that moped of Mike Riley's. This car takes up the entire entrance – enormous and slick and so obviously him it might as well have his name painted across the side.

Though I still pretend otherwise, for a little while. I have to. Michaela nudges me and says, 'Check out Mr Big Shot,' and when she does my insides go all funny. Is that who I'm associated with? Mr Big Shot?

'I know, how awful,' I say, but doing so only makes me feel funnier. I'm going to have to eat my words in a second, and I know it. I can see someone getting out of the car – someone with a cap and a uniform and oh, God, he's an actual *chauffeur* – and even though I'm still pretending I'm not looking, I can feel him lasering in on me.

One side of my body prickles as I pass him, just waiting for the words I know are coming. They're definitely coming. Oh, no, are they not coming? And if they're not, why on earth am I panicking about this? I should be more worried that Michaela is going to think I'm a hypocrite, and that everyone's going to see.

But I can't be.

'Miss Layton?' the chauffeur says, and my first instinct is to almost die of excitement. Later on I can be affronted or aggrieved or disgusted by excess. Right now I just want to revel in something so insanely different it makes Michaela grab my shoulder and shake me.

'I think he's talking to you,' she says, because apparently she also forgets her contempt for all things big-shotty when it's someone she knows who might reap the benefits. It's not a CEO, lording it over the rest of us. It's not something Mr Henderson did, to show off in front of his staff. This is something else, and she immediately appreciates that.

Or at least she's immediately curious about that.

'What are you into?' she asks, as though it might be drug deals or international cartels or something. I suppose for all I know it could be. Maybe he's the head of some League of Evil, and the only reason I don't know it is because I'm blinded by my own silly feelings. Be rational, I tell myself, but it's almost impossible to maintain that state when the chauffeur is saying, 'Mr Kovacs requests the pleasure of your company.'

My mind just hears 'pleasure' and 'company', and all other considerations are rescin evs are rded.

'Oh, it's just a friend of my dad's,' I say to her, absent-mindedly. I don't even really care if she knows I don't have a dad, or that no father of mine could possibly be involved in anything like this. All that matters is moving towards that car, on slow solemn feet that seem as if hypnotised. My whole body is hypnotised.

I barely feel her hand leave my shoulder, or hear her slightly confused goodbye.

This could be my real life now, I think.

And the second I slip into the leather-lined confines of the car, it is.

Chapter Seven

I can't help noticing that he's arranged the chairs differently this time. His seat is still by the table, and in front of the double glass doors that lead to the balcony. Mine is now all the way across the room. We're going to have to shout at each other like passing acquaintances on the street, though maybe that's the point.

He can be intimate with me in the abstract, but not while we're in the same room.

When we're in the same room he stands at the glass, looking out over the city. Back to me, body language relaxed – on the surface at least. To me, there's something a little false about the hand he's put in one pocket. He's done it a little too jauntily – suit jacket ruffled up to accommodate his hand – even though he's not the jaunty sort at all.

He's the sort to find kissing distasteful.

And the sort to not speak for a thousand years.

I have to do it, in the end, though I really don't want

to. I have too many questions crowding out all sensible thought, and the one that wins isn't going to be pretty. I can tell it isn't. It practically rattles on the way out.

'Well, you summoned me. And here I am.'

I know it's unfair of me to say. I didn't feel summoned at all. I felt valued and excited and disbelieving, and still do in all the places that matter.

But I can't let him know that. He already has so much power, and I have so little. There needs to be some redressing of the balance. At the very least I want to make him look at me, and I succeed. He turns at the sound of my voice, nonchalant as anything, face as unreadable as ever.

However, I definitely think he's giving off other signs of … difference. They're small and insignificant – like the too casual hand in the pocket – but they're definitely visible, to someone who can't stop looking. I can barely resist when he's not actually around, so it's no wonder I'm noticing tiny details.

Like the way his hair is parted today. It's just a touch more severe, as though he wanted to make extra sure something on him was completely contained. The last time we met, there was a hint of curl just hanging down over his forehead.

But now there's nothing.

And is it my imagination, or is this suit a little tighter than the one he wore the other day? It seems to nip right in at his waist, and there's just a touch of strain around his burly chest. I think, unbidden, of the word 'caged', and the impression gets stronger as I watch him pace back and forth.

I'm sure he thinks he's strolling.

He isn't.

'Is that what you think I did? I summoned?' he asks, and I'm sure he thinks his question sounds like a walk in the park, too – light and breezy, with an edge of aall0musement.

It doesn't.

There's something else in there, alongside the slant of humour. Something a little brittle … something that scares me a tad. He doesn't seem like the sort of person who could ever be wounded, but I think I got him in the gut then. He's been so careful, so far, to respect what I want and not push too hard.

And I think I just accused him of pushing too hard.

'Maybe "summoned" is a little strong.'

'I wasn't asking you to moderate your words.'

'No? Then what were you asking for?'

'The same thing I always do: only what you really want, and honestly feel, and truly believe. If I summoned you then I don't wish you to take your words back. I wish you to say it, so that I might apologise.'

Damn him. Damn him. He makes it so hard to lie.

'It wasn't the idea of being summoned. It was the car.'

'You didn't like it?'

'It felt extravagant.'

'So you imagined you were being bought?'

'Not exactly.'

'Then tell me exactly.'

God, I love how greedy he sounds when he's close to some revelation of mine. He actually clenches a fist, too, and it's the sight of this that urges me on. I blurt words out without really thinking about them.

'I was worried you thought you had to buy me.'

I blush once I've said it, but only because of the assumption that he wants me in there. In all other ways the words are real, and honest, and loved by me.

'I see,' he says, and then I get another little flash of *as though he could ever desire you that much,* before he finishes the thought: 'And if you are partially right, what then?'

'Then I'd tell you that you don't. You don't have to send cars for me; you don't have to buy me gifts. Your arm around my waist meant more than a ride in the back of a Bentley did, and it will always be that way for me.'

He glances away after I'm finished, that near-smile slowly drifting over his lips. If I could see his eyes I suspect they'd be the same way – warm, like someone remembering something good that happened once.

'I'm afraid it's a flaw of mine.'

'What's a flaw of yours?'

'The need to express things with money, instead of with words.'

'And if you'd been forced to speak, what would you have said?'

'Can't you tell?'

'Well, the car definitely meant *I can't wait for you to be with me.* And I'll admit, I did enjoy that element of it.' I pause. 'Unless I'm wrong.'

'You're not wrong. Stop doubting yourself.'

'I'm trying to. And I think I'm getting better at it too.'

'I think you are as well. Soon you'll be like me.'

'What? Emotionally unavailable?'

For a second I think I've gone too far. He takes a short breath that almost sounds like something is catching inside him, and really that can only mean one thing: I've struck a nerve. But then he quite suddenly snaps open the single button on his suit jacket, and sits in his seat in the same way he did before.

It's a relaxed pose, I think.

And his deepening smile only strengthens that idea. Somehow I said something to make him ease back down, instead of wind back up – though I've no idea how. Shouldn't someone pointing out your cool aloofness make you defensive about it?

Apparently he doesn't know what defensive is.

'Oh, as much as it makes me a hypocrite, I'd hate to see that happen.'

'So you like me emotionally available.'

'I like you showing every feeling on your face. I like your willingness to put aside your fear and fumble your way towards something anyway.' He pauses, clearly considering whether to say more. I can almost see his jaw working around the words, as he debates whether to let them out.

And I'm so glad that debate ends on *yes*.

'I like that you kissed me.'

'Do none of the other women kiss you?'

I can't keep the incredulity out of my voice. Surely some of them must have been overcome by his face and his body and his manner? Not to mention his oral sex skills. To be honest, nothing could get in the way of my lips, after head like that. He's lucky I didn't try to cuddle him too.

'Not typically, no.'

'Oh. Sorry. I didn't have the assignation etiquette guide-book to hand.'

The smile he gives me for that is his best one yet. I think I actually see teeth, before he realises and reins himself back in.

'Yet another reason why I so enjoy your company.'

'You know, there *are* other women like me. You could probably find them by just … you know, dating. Instead of being a member of a sex club.'

'So there's something wrong with being a member of a sex club?'

'No, I didn't mean –'

'And you somehow believe I haven't dated in the past.'

'Well, of course …'

'Not to mention that this whole premise is predicated on the fact that there are indeed millions of women just like you, everywhere, constantly.'

I have no half-sentences to stutter out in response to that. Mainly because I know what he's suggesting here, and it makes all of my words fall down inside me. They congregate at the bottom of my body, writhing and rattling around the same concept: I am somehow rare, to someone like him. I am somehow special.

And for once in my life I actually believe it. I've seen the evidence of how different I am all over his face. I've heard it in his words. He's used to one thing: no kissing, no negotiations, no problems with his probable wealth.

But I am another matter altogether, on all fronts.

'So what would you like to do now?' he asks, after a moment of near stifling silence. I'm practically humming by the time he breaks it, and I think he knows. I can hear the teasing in his voice when he adds: 'Maybe take a walk in the park? Do a little light shopping?'

I picture us linking arms, as we wind our way through the men's section of Marks and Spencer's. Somehow I'm sure that's not what he's suggesting, however – and not just because he's pulling my leg. His idea of light shopping is probably flying first class to France for the Monet that caught his eye last week.

'Sure. Sounds great.'

" aÀ"justifWe could take in some sights.'

'Absolutely.'

'Maybe stop for a spot of dinner.'

'Well, why not? We'll probably be hungry by then.'

'And afterwards ...'

He lets the word linger, like a promise.

A promise that makes me too eager.

'Yes, afterwards,' I say, with just a hint of breathlessness. Just a touch. Not enough to give me away to anyone else, but certainly enough for him. His eyes gleam like onyx, that smile of his so voracious. How could I have ever thought it was faint?

It's as fierce as a burning fist.

'Oh, afterwards ...'

'Go on. Go on.'

In my head he's already tearing all of my clothes off with his teeth, as we roll around on my living room floor. Of course I know that he would probably never do anything of the sort, but that just makes the image all the more compelling. His imaginary hands burn my skin; his kisses are like something forbidden. We'll be stoned to death for daring to do it, by the President of the Assignation Society.

Or at least, that's what I'm *hoping* for.

He has something far less exciting in mind.

'I take your hand, and bid you goodnight,' he says,

in that teasing tone of his. I think he knows the thing I was picturing, behind my eyes. He can probably see it written all over my face – from the half-bitten lip to the foggy, unfocused gaze. I was just getting to the part where we run from our accusers in torn and bloodied clothes, clinging to each other desperately.

And then he goes and spoils it all with ordinary, everyday life.

'That's not how it ends!'

'It isn't?'

No. It ends with us stowing away on a cargo ship, making love between large containers of tropical fruit.

'You know it's not.'

He picks an imaginary piece of lint from his always flawless trousers, eyes studiously on something other than me.

'I'm afraid I know nothing of the sort. To me, that sounds like the perfect end to an evening: a chaste kiss upon the back of your hand, followed by a fond farewell.' He actually sighs, just to make it extra convincing. 'Bliss.'

'So that's what we're going to do here, is it? I'm going to come over there and give you my hand, and you're going to kiss it,' I say, voice as deathly dull as I can make it. 'And then I leave.'

'Well, we could do those things, if you wanted to.'

'You know I don't want to.'

'How could I possibly? I haven't heard you say.'

His expression is now so sharp and sly I could use it to pick a lock. After all, that's what he's using it for. That devil's smile has already levered its way beneath my skin, and now all he has to do is wait for it to slide straight on through to my heart.

'You don't need me to say,' I tell him, but my voice is thick and heavy – so full of uncertainty. And that pain I can feel just under my left breast … it's definitely him, slowly sinking his way in.

'We've already established that I do. Or at least, we've established how much I enjoy it when you admit all the things that you don't really want to.'

'It Custmuc's not that I don't want to.'

'No?'

'It's just that it's difficult.' I pause, lip still between my teeth. 'It's difficult to know what the right answer is.'

'And you think that's what I want? The right answer?'

It's clear what I should say, here. 'No', I think. *No.* He wants my answers, my true answers, whether they're right or wrong. In fact, I don't think there *is* a right or wrong with him. I could tell him about my torn and bloodied daydream, and he wouldn't hold it against me. I don't think he'd hold anything against me.

And oh, that thought is very freeing. There's something almost electric about it, like I've put my finger in some socket I didn't know about. All the hairs on the back of my neck prickle and bristle, and for a moment I'm so restless I almost stand.

I need to pace – like he did.

Oh, God, it's *just* like he did. Was that why he did it? Maybe a sudden streak of unadulterated freedom went through him, too, and he just didn't know how to contain it. He still can't contain it, because after a tense moment of silence he gets up and goes across to the bar – like he can't help himself. Something just spasms and he has to move, without a word of explanation.

Not that he needs to give me one. In truth, the lack just makes everything more exciting. I find myself leaning to one side to get a better view of whatever he's doing, and when I still can't quite see I actually lift my bottom off the seat. I'm an elderly gossip, suddenly, trying to see around the neighbour's wall.

Though the wall in question is much more man-shaped than it would usually be, I'm sure. This wall has shoulders like boulders and a back that could bar the way to the lost city of gold, and all of this heavy grey blankness is keeping me from seeing what he's doing.

He's rummaging through his briefcase, I think. But what does that really tell me? He could have anything in there. He probably *does* have anything in there. Somehow I can't see him carrying around three files and a pencil, which only leaves me with a very scary set of options.

Pliers, my mind says, for some reason.

Some terrible, terrible reason that kind of makes me hate my mind. What on earth would he be doing with pliers? Why is that the place my thoughts go to? He's not a mobster, on the verge of plucking out my fingernails until I tell him what I prefer.

No, no, that's ridiculous.

So why am I sweating? Why is my heart hammering hard enough to make my skin vibrate? I can actually see it when I glance down, thrumming slightly beneath the pressure. And it gets worse when he turns.

Of course it does.

He has some items in his hands, and suddenly that fear is threefold. It leaps through me, sharp with the memory of the first time I saw him. He put things on the bed then, too – or at least, I assume he did. They're the same things he puts on the bed now, so it's a reasonable theory. There is the red scarf, and the pair of handcuffs, and that damnable silver cane.

Oh, God, that silver cane. I can hardly stand to look at it, but of course he can see this happening. He can see me avoiding that one item, while my cheeks heat and my whole body refuses to keep still. And he knows what this means before I've even said.

So I blurt out the truth, like some sort of pre-emptive strike. I force it out of myself, raw and reeling, and in return he gives me C hee prothe smallest nod. He doesn't call me a liar, because how could I be? I said the most powerful thing – the thing that lots of women secretly want – and he accepts it without another word.

He just takes my hand and leads me over to the bed. Of course I'm still shaking when he does. I'm shaking so much that he puts his two big hands on my shoulders and smoothes over them again and again until I'm close to calm. My breathing evens out, at the very least. And I don't try to run for the door, the way I wanted to about a second after I said it. I'd only be running from myself, anyway, because this is almost definitely what I want. I've dug deep, and found the truth:

I'm a secret masochist.

I *must* be a secret masochist. That's why I'm trembling, I think. That's why I'm so hot and heavy between my legs, as though someone replaced my sex with a swollen heart. It has absolutely nothing to do with the way he's touching me now, because oh, he's touching me far too softly. He slides a hand over my belly, until it's beneath the material of my jacket. Then all he has to do to spread it open is ease that hand up, until the buttons pop beneath the pressure, one by one.

Of course this method of undressing me has two benefits: the first being its efficiency, and the second being the *sensation*. Oh, Lord, the sensation of his palm stroking its way up over my body, as it parts my clothes. It's almost more arousing than the oral sex he gave me the day before, and I haven't the foggiest clue why.

Because he's undressing me? Because he's almost fondling me, but not quite? He gets to my breasts but doesn't squeeze or grope either of them. He just carries on with this slow denuding, every move more deliberate and interesting than the one before it.

He turns me around in the same way I imagine tailors turn people to measure them for suits: thumb and forefinger pressing lightly into my shoulder, one hand just brushing my hip. If you would, madam, I think, and for some unfathomable reason that makes things worse. A little sound comes out of me, before he's even really done anything.

Though I think he imagines he has.

'The safe word is "island",' he says, as oddly clinical as anything else that's happening right now. We could be in a doctor's office, in the centre of a sterile space station, in a system made of perfect plastic. That's how clinical this is.

And yet I'm still gasping for air. I'm still feeling everything all at once, in a rush. I can hardly get up the wherewithal to nod, but I do it.

Because if I don't, he'll stop.

He'll stop touching me this way: one hand firm on my hip, clasping me, while the other works the zipper down. And once the skirt is in a puddle on the floor, he stoops to collect it. He helps me to step out of it.

Then folds it neatly before placing it on the chair I vacated.

I swear, by the time he returns I'm a wreck. He just folded an item of clothing in the middle of the most intense sexual experience of my life. And he does the same with my shirt, too. He loops an arm around my body to get at the buttons, in a way that's almost aggressive. It's almost like being held captive, and for a moment I thrill and fear all at the same time.

But then he steps away to make a laundry pile of my clothes, and I just don't know what to think. The contrast is mind-boggling, between the overt and almost brutal sexuality and the deliberate undressing.

Though I suspect that's where the excitement is coming from.

It's not that he's being clinical.

It's that he's giving me one thing, while I wait for another. I'm panting for it; I'm gagging for it; I think I sob when he finally gets to my bra. I'm so sensitive there I almost don't want him to take it off, though I'm glad he can't hear this transient panic.

The feel of the air on my bare breasts is worth every bit of uncertainty – as is the tender way the straps slide down over my arms. He just lets them fall, and every second is blissful. I had no idea such small things could be so significant, but they are.

Like the way he crouches down behind me.

On the surface, it's not that big a deal. He could be stooping to pick up a pen, or maybe his lace needs tying.

But when he does it every muscle in my body tenses, in response to what he's really doing: getting low, so he can ease my panties down my legs. Slowly, I think, so unbearably slowly, and still without a hint of anything truly sexual. He avoids all contact with my aching sex, and makes no comment on how wet I am.

Though I know he must be able to see it. The material feels nearly soaked through as it slides over my thighs. It's almost a relief when it gets to the stocking-covered portion of my legs, so I can't feel it. I don't want to feel it.

But I don't mind if he does.

Oh, God, I don't mind that at all. I'm almost certain he's doing something with that scrap of wet silk, and when he doesn't fold them and put them on the chair I know for sure. He's keeping them for himself, I think, and then it's all I can do to stay on my feet. He has to steady me, which really only intensifies the sudden rush of arousal.

By the time he speaks I'm almost over the edge.

And then his words just push me over.

'Put your hands on the bed,' he says, in the exact same tone as everything else he's done. It's low and soothing, with just a hint of *if you would, madam?* And it's followed by even more insanely awesome stuff. 'That's it, palms flat, arms straight.'

I never realised how good specifics could be until I met him. They were interesting earlier; now they're downright exhilarating. They make me think of innocuous things like assuming the position, while the reality is me bent over the bed, in the lewdest way imaginable. He even asks me to spread my legs a little, just to complete the tableau.

Christ, I bet I look filthy. I bet he can see every-thing. *I* can almost see everything, and I'm facing the wrong way while inside my own skin. The image is just that strong – me with my stockings just skirting my upper thighs ... the slippery seam between my legs, all soft and swollen and so obviously ready. The curve of my bare ass, the bend of my body ...

I'd kill to know what he's thinking.

Or maybe I wouldn't. Maybe it's better if I don't know. He's reaching for something now, and although I told him what to choose I kind of don't want to look. I have to close my eyes and pretend I'm somewhere else, doing some other thing that isn't this. I'm on the island, I tell myself, and then it's easier.

Yet still I flinch when he gets too close. The back of his hand just brushes my bare hip, and I skitter away – but once I have I'm not so sure. Was that his hand? It could have been something else. It could have been the Thing, I think.

And then I shiver all over.

Can he see that I'm shivering all over? He must be able to. He must be able to see the g C toght oose bumps up and down my arms, and even if he can't I'm sure he saw that slight sway I did. It's probably putting him off. That's why he's gone so still and quiet, in this already completely stifling room.

Or is it something else?

Maybe he likes a girl who cringes before him and his masterful ways, and that's why he's currently suffocating me with silence. He wants me to stew in my own juices until I go mad, but I'm not going to let that happen. I resolve to control myself in every single way possible, from the tips of my toes to the roots of my hair.

And I'm almost successful. I stand my ground, which is definitely an improvement. But the tensing isn't. I know what the tensing looks like. It looks like I'm bracing myself for a blow, quite obviously. My eyes scrunch shut and my fingers curl reflexively around a fistful of duvet. I can feel the muscles in my thighs snapping to attention, and all under his ever watchful gaze.

It's no wonder he doesn't bring the cane down. He must think I'm mad to want something and not want it all at the same time. Or is that the state he's aiming for? Perhaps that's why he's waiting and waiting like this, hinting at a touch he never quite gives. And a blow he never quite strikes. He wants me to go mad before it happens, torn between wanting it and not. He wants me to sweat and shake and foam at the mouth, and it's not as though he'll have to work very hard for any of it.

I'm already sweating and shaking and foaming at the

mouth. His hands now feel like fire every time they glance against my skin, and the burn is nearly too much to bear.

And then I feel it.

I feel something else … something that isn't his hand. There's no flaming fiery heat from this thing, as it draws so slowly along my side. It's ice-cold and barely there, like he's caressing me with an icicle – or maybe a knife he sometimes stores in the deep freeze.

Yes, yes. That's what it reminds me of: the cold edge of a blade that doesn't quite cut, just ever so slightly suggesting violence. In a second he'll lift it, I'm sure, and then whoosh and crack … followed by the split of my skin. I even hold my breath for it, eyes so tightly squeezed shut I can feel tears forming in the corners. It's here, I think, it's coming, it's now now now.

Only it isn't. I hold my breath for so long I start to see spots, but no blow falls. No sharp sting comes after it. That sharp suggestion of a knife's edge disappears, as though it was never there at all. In fact, I'm starting to wonder if it wasn't. Everything's so tense and taut I could have imagined it. I could be imagining all of this. Maybe I'm bent over in my bedroom, dreaming of a man with a face like granite and a teasing hand like the side of a knife, and in a moment I'll wake up.

Is it OK if I want to wake up? This is far too much for me – I was wrong, I was wrong. I'm not a secret masochist at all. I'm something else, though I've no idea what. And I keep on having no idea until the sensation suddenly shifts, from cold metal to something far softer, and finer.

At which point, I start to understand. It's easy to, when every muscle in your body suddenly relaxes as one. Relief like running water floods through me, so sweet I could weep. This is what I want, I think at him. This is exactly what I want.

But he already knows. He probably knew all along. Why else would he raise the stakes so high, then let them drop just as I'm dying for them to? Just as I'm crying for them to? I bet he saw the shake in my pointing finger, and decided then.

He's not go CHevioleing to cane me.

He's going to *tease* me until I go *insane*.

But if so, he has to know: I'm halfway there already. All he has to do is whisper that silk scarf over my skin, and I squirm and twist like a creature caught on a hook. I need more of it, I need more. Or am I trying to get less? I don't know – but I do know that he doesn't care either way.

'Stay still, Alissa,' he says, and somehow it's better than every sweet nothing I've ever received. His voice is as firm and smooth as a newly planed surface, with just a hint of that insanely good accent around the edges.

It's no surprise that I struggle to obey. But it is a surprise that I want to. Oh, I want to be firm and resolute; I want him to be impressed by my ability to be both. And the more I fail the keener this need gets, until I'm mired in it. I'm up to my neck. My body trembles with the effort of resisting, even as it strains to give in. Move towards the feather-light stroke of that scarf, my body demands.

But when I do he simply whispers the silk away – like some secret message. Stay still, and I will be rewarded. Move, and I'll get nothing.

Though following this set of rules is easier said than done. I manage to remain motionless for a full thirty seconds, as he dances it over my side – so deft and sure it's like being stroked by a third, achingly soft hand. Then he just barely lets its trailing end ease down, over the curve of my right breast ...

And suddenly I'm a mess. I fumble towards it without even meaning to, too greedy for more. The very tip of the scarf almost catches my stiff little nipple, and I just can't help myself. I react instinctively, like a flower seeking the sun – only violently. Oh, God, I jerk and stutter towards him so violently, oh, Jesus can't he see how much I need it?

If he can he doesn't care.

He does the same thing again on my left side – only this time it's worse. This time he gets so close to that one swollen bud I can almost taste the sensation. It clogs the back of my throat with sounds I don't want to let out, and warms through my insides in so intense a way I hardly realise he's stopped.

And then it hits me in a rush, and oh, the absence of that sweet feeling is brutal. A space opens up inside me where it was supposed to go. I actually attempt to claw it back with both hands, though rationally I know the duvet isn't going to make anything happen. If anything, me tearing at it like an animal is only going to make things worse.

He's laughing at me now.

He's laughing, but I find I don't mind as much as I should. I can't mind. I'm too preoccupied with the other sound he's making – the one that nearly makes me turn around and grab him.

He's taking a couple of steps backwards. I know he is, despite the soft carpeting and my position and this insanity I seem to be suffering under. I can hear it as keenly as I would a giant's footfalls on a stone floor. It's almost like the coming of my impending doom, though I know that's kind of the wrong way around.

He isn't coming *towards* me.

He's moving *away*.

And I have to do something about that. I have to lift a hand or make a protesting noise or just anything, anything to make him keep doing this. But, of course, the second I make a real move, that smooth voice comes out again, like he's pulling a gun.

'Remember what I said. Hands on the bed at all times, please.'

I think the 'please' is the most upsetting part. It's completely sincere, but there's something about the clipped, cool nature of it. Something that reminds me of that student-and-professor feeling I had when I first saw the cane. It's a 'please' that expects no refusal, polite in its own way but so definite you can't really refuse.

And, dear God, I want to clutch it to me. I want to write poems in its name. Ode to a please, I'll call it, and everyone will understand. They'll get why I obey him so quickly, palms flat again before I've even had a chance to think.

I don't want to think. I just want him to do all of this all over again – and he does. After a moment of my patient waiting, he comes in for another pass.

Only this one is so much sweeter than all the others. This one is my reward for following orders. It has real substance and real weight to it, heavy with the hint of his actual fingertips. They just hover by my side, close enough that I can sense a presence but not close enough for me to be sure.

The heat could be emanating from something else. He might have found another toy to tease me with, more diabolical than the items I've already seen. This one has the power to make me bite my lip and wriggle around, too tense to look. And when I do, I'm not sure what to think. There's nothing new in his hands – he's just threading the scarf beneath my body, the way someone might do if they

119

wanted to dress me with it. He's going to create a sort of makeshift bra, I think, then I almost laugh.

Until I realise that's exactly what he's doing. He's letting the material bow beneath my breasts, the ends clasped tight on either side of my body. And as soon as I understand this, I understand what the intention is. He's going to raise the scarf until it's touching my most sensitive places – or else he's going to tease me until I beg him to.

And I suspect he won't have to wait long for the latter. My arms are already shaking with the need to bend, because bending them will give me what I want. I'll get to feel that bright length of silk against my breasts, if I just lean down a little.

But I can't, I can't. He'll take it away if I do. I know he will. I have to be patient, and wait for him to do it his way – even if his way is absolute agony. He raises that material slowly, so slowly, inch by excruciating inch, drawing out the tension until I'm a plucked string. Until I'm moaning and rocking and oh, God, I can feel my own wetness sliding down the insides of my thighs. I can feel my clit like a second heart.

And then the silk just barely grazes my tight nipples. Just barely – nothing much, when you break it down. It isn't as firm as a fingertip, or as insistent and slippery as someone's lips. It's probably the same thing I feel every day when I pull on a sweater or hook my bra together.

So it's a shock when the sensation hits. It almost swallows me whole, intense enough to qualify as an orgasm but without the crescendo. I get one thick burst, and then nothing. No peak. And more importantly: no relief.

I can't sink into bliss just yet, apparently.

He's got more of this torture to carry out.

He lets the silk drop the second I cry out, then just as I'm sobbing with frustration I feel him start to lift it again. I feel it inching closer and closer, almost touching but not quite, before finally, oh, finally, oh, thank Christ … he actually allows it to touch me. He brings it up tight to my too sensitive breasts – so tight it's a kind of shock. I expected a softer touch, and suddenly he's giving me full-on fondling.

And he follows it with something even more startling. I'm sure he's about to stop it there, but instead he slides the material back and forth – the way someone might if they were positioning a ribbon around a gift they wanted to wrap. He's going to tie me together in a second, which I suppose is a rather unpleasant idea to have.

But it's also an idea that sends me insane. I think of myself all neatly bound – with that silk for ever rubbing over my stiff nipples – and I say his name. I say his name even though I've hardly said it before, and I don't stop there. I rub myself back and forth against the silk, other words bubbling up to follow that first verboten one.

'Yes, please,' I say, 'yes, yes, go on.'

So he does the opposite. He drops the material as abruptly as he brought it up, cruel enough to almost make me shout. I turn my head, all this sudden rage and frustration forming a kind of bottleneck in my throat. I can actually feel something thick and heavy forcing its way up, ready to kill him for his coldness and his calm and his endless rules.

Only to have the feeling die as quickly as it came.

Of course it dies. I can see his face now, and his body language, and neither of them inspire anger. They inspire a sharp dart of lust – and maybe some other complicated emotions – but not anger. How could it possibly be anger?

He isn't aloof, like I thought he'd be. He's not some cold, implacable statue. His shoulders are going up and down with each breath he takes, the way mine are. His lips are parted, showing teeth. And oh, his eyes ... they're like dark fire. They burn right through me, destroying any words I might have wanted to say. I was planning on something like 'Just fuck me, you fucking fucker,' but I end up with a kind of dying whimper.

And I don't care. I'd sacrifice a lot to see him like this – as lost as I am. I'd give up my dignity if it meant he let go of his at the same time, and suddenly ... suddenly I know what I have to do. I know how to get what I want, without endless hours of relentless agony. He's going to put me through it, I can tell.

But I can stop him. I can make him.

I might actually have some power over him. In fact, I'm sure I do. I think back to the first time we were together, when he'd seemed to reach a certain point before falling into absolute chaos. He hadn't meant to pounce on me like that.

I pushed him over the edge.

And I can push him over the edge now, too. All I have to do is watch for what he likes, the way he watches me. It can't be that hard, when he's already halfway there. He's actually a little red around the cheeks, even though he's the sort of man who scorns things like blushing. And his hands are definitely trembling a little as he reaches for me again.

It should be a cinch.

But oh, it isn't, it isn't.

How can it be, when he doesn't like the things other men like? I lick my lips at him and get nothing but a sardonic smile for my trouble, and when I give him my heaviest, most sultry stare he goes one better. He takes a step back, like he knows what I'm trying to do and is intent on heading me off at the pass.

Either that or he thinks my efforts are pathetic.

Oh, Lord, I bet he thinks my efforts are pathetic. I have the seductive capabilities of a peanut, and now all of my shortcomings are on show. I can't be sexy, and I can't seduce, and I don't know how to persuade. All I can do is blush and shrug around inside my own embarrass Cownhated skin.

But apparently that's all it takes.

He doesn't even wait for me to try my next move. He just steps forward again, so close this time I can feel his suit purring against the backs of my thighs. No fussing around with the scarf beneath my body, either. Now it's his hand on the small of my back, and the material trailing down from that one point of connection.

Like a tail, I think.

But I'm only doing it so I don't have to consider what that tail is touching. I can't bear to think about what that tail is touching. I need to create a separate body for all the feelings that spread out from that one soft, wet place, and when the laws of physics refuse me I'm forced to choose some drastic measures.

I have to try to escape, for a start. I can't stick around for this. I thought I wanted it, but wanting and getting are two different things. Wanting is something far away, abstract, based on seduction techniques I don't know how to do. Getting is the almost unbearable sensation of that silk dragging over my swollen sex.

And it's not just the sizzling feel of something touching me there, either. It's his hand on my back, slowly sliding upwards. His fingers are all spread out so I get the most benefit from each and every one, and oh, that benefit is *glorious*. My spine is on fire. It keeps sending flaming messages to my brain, like *He Is Touching Us With His Bare Hand* and even better:

He did this because you blushed.

It's obvious, I think. But its obviousness doesn't make it any less exciting and strange and unfathomable. He should prefer a sophisticated woman who knows exactly what she's doing, but it always seems to be the opposite. He likes it when I'm clumsy and awkward and all over the place, fumbling towards feelings I've no name for.

When I do the silliest thing possible – rocking back and forth to get a little more contact – his hand tightens on my back. It makes a near fist and, when he speaks, his words suddenly seem to mean something else.

'Stay still,' he says, just like he did before.

But now the sentiment is brand new and really wide open. He's not saying it for me, I realise. He's saying it for himself. It's what he needs, to negotiate his way through the tangled tension between us – my calm, my composure, my resistance to this onslaught.

And when I am none of those things, he isn't either.

I squirm with abandon, and that hand gets tighter – before leaving altogether. Only now it's not a punishment for my disobedience. It's a challenge. He's thrown down the gauntlet and I have to come back with something new.

And I do.

I keep wriggling, full of self-consciousness at first but gradually growing more and more uncaring. What does it matter if I look silly? He *likes* silly. He likes it enough to let out a soft sigh when I get bolder, even though a

125

soft sigh from him is practically a shout from anyone else. It strikes a spark inside me, bright enough to let me ignore him when he says those unbreakable words: 'Palms flat on the bed.' He even repeats it, with my name on the end.

But still I don't obey. I'm right down on the duvet now, the aching tips of my tits finally finding relief against something. If I rub just so, I'm almost sure I could orgasm, though I don't think I'm ready for that quite yet.

I think something better is coming.

In fact, I can almost feel it building behind me. 'I'm warning yo Cm se.

not giving a fuck, and if his panting breath is anything to go by he's close.

Though now I'm wondering:

Close to what?

Close to burying his face between my legs, again? Close to touching me with his hands? I don't think I could take it if he did. I'm so sensitive I can't even rub my pussy against the bed the way I want to. The tiniest brush of the covers against that smooth glossy swell is enough to make me jerk and stutter like a broken puppet.

Yet still I keep squirming. I must look absolutely shameless by this point. I feel absolutely shameless. I've never been so willing to be so bare in front of someone, and certainly not at my own behest. He doesn't tell me to turn over.

I do it. I sprawl out on my back, legs spread for him. Hands all over everything I can bear to touch – which is mostly my elbows and some space I didn't know I had behind my right ear. However, he doesn't seem to care what kind of innocuous places I'm touching. His expression is still a flame, and it burns more fiercely by the second. It licks over my hips and my tits, devouring greedily as it goes.

I should really know what's going to happen next.

Only somehow I don't. I don't expect him to grab me. I close my eyes for the briefest of moments and suddenly his hand is around my ankle – though that's not really the startling part. He's grabbed me before, after all. And this *is* what I was aiming for.

It's just that I'd forgotten. I'd forgotten what it's like to see him being so intense. I've started to form a standard image of him in my mind, great and grey and immovable. And when he shifts right in front of my eyes, it's always unsettling. It's like watching a wolf shedding its sheep's clothing.

Only much more exciting than that sounds.

Oh, *so much* more exciting.

His hand is almost a cuff around my ankle. And he doesn't just use it to restrain me. Restraining me would be bad enough on its own, but he goes one further. He actually yanks me down the bed, hard enough to make me gasp, smooth enough to make the gasp a delighted one. In fact, I think it might qualify as a squeal.

Though he's kind enough not to comment on it. Instead he simply plunges on into this feverish chaos, hands running and running all over my spread legs in a way that nearly makes me weep. I was starting to forget what ordinary human contact was like, and now I'm getting some my body doesn't know how to process it.

Does skin usually prickle like that when someone strokes it?

I didn't think so, but apparently it's true. Every nerve-ending is firing, and that's before he starts in on something I can't quite believe. I see his hand go to his belt, and am sure I'm hallucinating – but then I hear it too. I hear that familiar clatter of metal and leather, so dull at every other point in my lacklustre life.

And so electric here.

Is he really going to fuck me? I think he is, though I've no clue why the idea makes my eyes go wide and my heart pound hard enough to break out of my chest. It's just sex, I remind myself, but reminding does no good. I still moan excitedly at the sight of his greedy gaze and his frantic, fumbling hands.

Then louder, for his gorgeous cock.

It's just like the rest of him: too big and too solid and too everything. He could probably beat me to death with it, if he was so inclined – and, judging by the look of him, he might well be. He's still breathing too hard and moving in that jerky, frantic, unfamiliar manner, but none of it scares me.

I'm too excited to be scared, and I know exactly why.

It's because of the grip he gets on me, close to a kind of manhandling but without the brute force. He hauls me over onto my stomach, sure enough. And the move is firm and quick, riddled through with his new eagerness.

And yet it doesn't hurt. He strokes me through it, hands roaming and spreading out over various parts of my body. He has to cup my hip to make the move possible, and I feel his hand easing up into position. I feel it smoothing over me, exploring every dip and curve.

Before he arranges me on the bed.

Because that's what he's doing, isn't it? He's arranging me. He's preparing me for that thick, swollen-looking cock, so quickly I can barely catch my breath. So slowly I want to scream at him for it. *Hurry hurry hurry*, I want to tell him, even though I know we're already going at the speed of light. The turn took two seconds, and he isn't lingering on anything else.

I can hear the snap of rubber. I can feel the need in his grasping hands, and his panting breath, and oh, God, is that his cock stroking over my spread sex? I think it is, but it's hard to be sure when you've been on the edge of pleasure for a thousand years and suddenly something thick and hot is rubbing through your slippery folds.

It's like asking me to do algebra while upside down in a jug of spaghetti. I just can't do it. I'm completely focused on the slow, sweet pull of his cock, as it teases and explores my pussy – always hinting at something more but never quite giving it. He gets to the very outer edges of my stiff clit, before backing away.

Then just as I think he's sliding down to meet my wet and wanting hole, he glides right over it. He ignores it completely, like it's not even there.

He just can't help himself, it seems. He has to play this game to the end – this endless game of teasing insanity. Just when I think he's breaking he rallies again, and I don't have it in me to keep pressing for more. All I can do is lie there and take it, moaning occasionally under the onslaught.

But, thankfully, the moaning is enough.

I think it's because I'm saying his name, over and over. Or it is the way I move, every time I feel him sliding back and forth? I'm undulating into the sensation, hips rocking but just barely. Back arching for each sweet spread of pleasure.

And after a while of it, he just snaps again. He grabs at my hip, and I think: this is it. This has to be it. In fact, I'm so sure that I make a sound of relief, ready for that last little gift that never actually comes.

Instead, I hear the snap of rubber again. I feel his hand pressing down on my back, like a command – stay where you are. I'm not even sure if I'm allowed to look, though I don't really have to. I know what he's doing. I can feel what he's doing. He's breathing harshly and the back and forth of his hand on his cock is as clear as day – almost violent, and oh, so slippery sounding.

It's that slipperiness that excites me, I know. I can almost see it in my mind's eye: that glimpse I got of the glistening tip of his cock. It's probably all over his hand as he works himself, though I doubt it helps. He's going at it so hard it probably hurts – like h Cts ly e's punishing himself for something.

I can't say what, however. For almost fucking me? For nearly making me come with a strip of silk pressed against my breasts? Neither of these seem judgement-worthy. If anything, I want to judge him for not following through. I'm still standing on this ledge, waiting for an orgasm that's just out of reach. I'm still half-mad with desire, and all I'm getting is the unbearably hot sound of him masturbating over my bare back and ass.

Or at least that's what I get at first. He pushes it right until the last moment, still apt to tease even in the middle of whatever emotional disaster this whole thing is. I'm pretty sure he lets his knuckles graze my skin on purpose – and I know the hint of that slick cock is entirely intentional. He just dips his hand a little and suddenly I can feel it on the upturned curve of my backside: smooth and silky with pre-come, and so urgent against me.

Then, just when I'm about to protest, he does it.

He touches me, between my legs. He cups his free hand over my sex, in that good good way that tells me he would like to remain aloof but can't quite help it. And once he's there, he can't help other things, either. He wants to search through my slick folds and find things that desperately need touching – like my over-sensitised and far too swollen clit.

I swear, one stroke across its taut surface is enough.

Or is it the sound of his grating, throttled groan? He sounds like he's trying to choke the noise down, but I'm glad he's unsuccessful. For one long glorious moment I get every bit of him, unfettered and free. His body jerks against the backs of my thighs and that thick cock skids over my skin one final time.

Then finally, finally, I get the all too familiar slipperiness, pattering against my skin.

I think it's this that actually does me in. Not his stroking finger or the sound of his voice. Just that visceral sense of him giving it up like that, spurting thickly all over my back and ass. I feel it and my whole body seizes, as though it's resisting the jolt of orgasm as much as it's welcoming it.

I'm not ready, I think wildly.

But it's too late to back out now. The sensation gets me in its grip and shakes me right out of my skin. My clit seems to swell unbearably, and just when I'm sure it can't take any more the pleasure surges up, and out, and all the way through me – great breaking waves of unbelievable bliss, on and on endlessly until I'm wrecked. I'm wasted. I've been made to wait far too long and am never going to recover from this.

But I suppose that's a good thing, in one way. If I drift into an orgasmic coma now, I'll never have to face him and his obvious regret – the regret I know is coming before he's even backed away from me.

And then he does, and his absence is cold, very cold.

Though it's nowhere near as bad as what comes next:

The click of the door, as he leaves without speaking.

Chapter Eight

He doesn't call the next day, or the day after that. And by the third I'm starting to get the message. I got an inkling of it back there in the hotel room, when he decided to take a quick stroll after sex and then just not come back.

But now that madness is underlined: something has disturbed him. Something has disturbed him so badly that he can't even call me and pretend it never happened – which is very bad indeed for someon Fdily meon Fde like him. I'm sure he could explain away a random murder if he really put his mind to it, so the fact that he's struggling to come up with a credible response to this is ...

Unsettling.

It makes me wonder if it's more than that ... though how could I possibly know for sure? He's never said what his expectations are. They could be as small as an assignation and as large as a relationship, with a thousand different possibilities dancing around in the middle. And I've no way of picking out any of those possibilities, because he never really says. He doesn't talk about himself in any real way.

I don't even know where he works.

But I do have his number, if I feel like asking. Oh, God, I really *really* feel like asking, despite knowing that's probably the last thing you should do in a situation such as this. He walked out of the room. He did not come back. Now's the time for me to maintain my dignity, rather than rushing for the phone to ask him *what the fuck?*

Or at least I think that's what the dating guides say. Don't they usually have sections on the rules of interacting with a man, and how it's unladylike to call first? I think they do, though I'm not sure if the same thing applies in these circumstances. Most of the stuff I've read dealt almost exclusively with dinner etiquette and who should pay for a cab.

Almost none of them talked about kinky encounters. There's no subheading for being abandoned in a hotel room; no guidelines that discuss the ins and outs of sexual exploration. The best I can come up with are a few websites and a lot of porn, but even they don't tell you what to do in times of sudden crisis.

I'm going to have to decide for myself.

I've *already* decided for myself. I don't care if it's not ladylike – I've never been that sort of person anyway. And if I break a few rules of dating by doing this, well, what does that matter? We're not dating. We're doing something else instead, and if I have my way we're going to keep doing it too.

All I have to do is call.

Which sounds really simple until I'm actually doing it – and then I'm just a mess of chattering teeth and rattling heart palpitations and lots of sweat. Oh, Christ, I'm sweating buckets. I want to check under my arms to make sure I don't have any of those dark circles, and as soon as the phone starts ringing I forget every single thing I was going to say. The words *how dare you* now seem like something from another language, and I come close to hanging up. I have to hang up, so I can check my gibberish-to-English dictionary.

But I'm glad I don't, in the end. I'm not some little speck any more, too afraid to go through with a phone call. I'm something, now. I'm someone. I made him do things against his will and persuaded him into situations he didn't want to go near.

I can do this.

'Kovacs.'

I can't do this. He answers with his surname, for God's sake, like some slick character from a movie about making loads of money. He might as well add a little *you're turn to talk* on the end, but when he doesn't it isn't any better. I'm just left with silence instead. A long, aching silence that I'm supposed to fill with words from a language that's no longer mine.

I want to tell him that he's an ass, but the sentences in my head don't make any sense. They keep rearranging themselves, from gobbledegook to barely rational to something else entirely. Something else that I never want to say, under any circumstances.< Krcuep do/p>

You really hurt me.

Because he did – I can see that clearly now. The silence stretches out between us like a yawning chasm, filled with things I don't want to be feeling. He doesn't care about stuff like feelings. He doesn't care about anything at all. It's his defining characteristic: a complete inability to give a fuck.

Though that doesn't really explain the hint of sadness in his voice, when he suddenly speaks. And it certainly doesn't explain the words he chooses.

'I was sure you wouldn't wish to talk to me,' he says, so abrupt I do a double take. I jerk on my wheelie work seat – almost sending myself sliding across the aisle between the cubicles – and for some unaccountable reason my ear heats. In fact, the whole side of my face heats, as though the receiver has a small fire inside it.

Either that, or he's touching me through the phone wires. He's rubbing one finger against my cheek, and, God help me, I'm responding to it. That flame is already spreading from my face, down over my throat and chest and right on through to some other places that really need it.

I always need it now. I'm always aroused and always ready, primed in a way I've never really experienced before. Last night I woke up in the middle of an orgasm, so intense it probably qualified as stifling. I certainly felt stifled in its aftermath, too stunned to let out a sound but trying all the same. Oh, I'd done my best to scream out my pleasure.

But nothing had emerged. It felt like banging against a wall that isn't there, which feels kind of apt in the light of what he's just said. There's culpability in there that I definitely hadn't anticipated, and emotion that I can't quite grasp, and all of it adds up to one thing:

Me, unable to think what to say. All the anger and frustration die down, and I'm left with very little. Should I insist on an explanation? I really want to, but I realise now what the issue is: I think I'm afraid of what he might say. I can deal with him being bored, or even regretful about his loss of control.

But what if it's more than that?

'Perhaps my assessment was correct,' he says after a second. And though there's amusement in his tone there's something else in there too – a drifting sadness, like someone joking about times long past.

It's impossible to resist. It forces me to speak.

'No, I want to talk to you,' I say, and it's then that I realise how much I do. I thought I was so cool, keeping myself to myself for these past few days. I didn't so much as glance at the phone, and I spent every evening reading instead of thinking about him.

Of course my reading most often consisted of staring at the same page for half an hour, but we won't go into that. We'll just focus on right now, and all the thousands of things I suddenly need to say.

And all the ways in which I can't.

'I just don't know where to start.'

'You could try demanding an apology.'

'I don't think demanding is my style.'

'Are you sure? Personally I think you did very well at it, the last time we were together,' he says, and though I can't detect any approbation in his words, I'm not sure that lets me off the hook. At the very least I'm suddenly guilty, in my own head, of asking for something that he maybe couldn't quite give.

'I didn't mean to be.'

'So now youify" o now yre apologising to me? I think that might be the wrong way around.'

'OK then. You say sorry.'

'Is that another demand?'

There's laughter in his voice now, which is a comfort in one way. But it's also kind of a nerve-wracking, heart-thumping thrill ride. I'm starting to think I really shouldn't have made this call at work, but it's become a sort of groove now. I'm comfortable speaking to him while surrounded by other people. They're my safety net, in case I should think of saying things I don't really want to.

Like 'fuck' and 'me' and 'now'.

'It might well be.'

'I recommend taking out the "might".'

'OK. Then it definitely is. I'm demanding you apologise for abandoning me in a hotel room.'

He makes a noise like this: *sssstthhhhh*. It's the kind of sound someone makes when they've been told the cost of fixing something is far beyond what the item is actually worth.

'"Abandoning" is such a loaded word.'

'But true, none the less.'

'I did return later, if that ameliorates the situation somewhat.'

I love that he uses the word 'ameliorate'. I love how he says it, too – like it has seven extra syllables and needs to sprawl out all over a chaise longue. It sounds as though it means something else when he says it, like when something is so sweet you can't stop licking it.

You ameliorated *that ice-cream.*

'How much later?'

He hesitates, so tellingly. Even his pauses mean something extra.

'Maybe an hour … or two.'

'Two *hours*?'

'It could have been one.'

'And what? I was just supposed to wait around wondering, for that one hour?'

'I thought you might sleep.'

I think he knows he's being ludicrous now. There's a note of discomfort at the end of this explanation, as though he doesn't quite believe it either. He definitely knows me well enough to understand that I can't just snooze in a hotel I'm half afraid of, in the hope that he might return at some undisclosed point.

I mean, what if he hadn't? What if I woke up to find the cleaning lady dusting around me, or worse? Maybe that cool, snake-haired receptionist would have found me, and demanded to know what I was doing there, pretending to be a guest.

I see the way she looks at me every time I walk in the door with Janos.

It isn't a good look.

'And then what?'

He doesn't answer right away, which makes me think at first that he doesn't want to. He doesn't want to suggest that maybe he would have come back into the room and slept with me. Sleeping with someone implies an intimacy that we just don't have – and that he surely can't deal with.

But then I hear it: other voices, barging over his. Big, annoying, arrogant male voices, hacking away at a conversation I can't quite hear. For one awful moment I strain and strain, trying to determine if this is all some joke he's having at my expense. Maybe he has me on speaker phone, mewling like a child about my hurt feelings.

Though after a second I start to realise. The men aren't talking about me. They're no K Th one hour?t even talking to Janos, really. I get the word 'projections' and the word 'graphs', and then I realise with a little jolt: he's talking to me in the middle of a business meeting.

'Where are you?' I ask, before I've even had a chance to think things over. The words just blurt out of me, slightly and breathless and a little stunned.

'In the boardroom.'

He says it like it's nothing.

I can't believe he says it like it's nothing.

'You're *in* the *boardroom*. With other people there.'

'Well, naturally. You can't have a meeting without other people.'

'And you're just talking to me in the middle of it?'

'Of course.'

I wonder if he knows what those two words sound like. I wonder if he knows what they feel like. They're so simple, and yet they make me silent and still and so sure of his feelings. I don't think he'd ever say the words *'love'* or *'affection'* or even *'you're my friend.'* But he doesn't *really have to, when he can make the most innocuous little phrases sound like the sweetest compliments.*

His 'of course' is other people's 'I love you'.

Oh, God, what if he loves me?

He certainly feels enough for me to answer his phone in the middle of a meeting, to offer apologies and explanations and terms of endearment disguised as simple statements.

'Don't ... don't any of them mind you talking to me?'

'I can talk to whomever I please. I'm the boss. They're here to impress me, not the other way around.'

'You must look very unimpressed right now.'

'Ah, but there's an upside. They're working so much harder to get my attention.' He makes a little tutting sound, familiar enough for me to match an expression to it. Almost an eye roll, I think, followed by a dismissive glance away. 'One of them just disconnected the PowerPoint projector. I'm afraid he isn't very bright.'

'Can they hear you saying these things?'

'I don't believe so. My boardroom is rather large.'

'Now I'm picturing a palatial hall with marble pillars, and you at the head of a stone table like some ancient feudal lord.'

'You aren't far off.'

'Are you wearing a crown?'

'Metaphorically speaking.'

I can't help asking, at this point. If I let this go on any longer, I really will start to believe in his imaginary fiefdom. Next time we meet I might call him 'milord', and that just won't do. He has enough power without me giving him more.

'What exactly do you do?'

'You don't really want me to explain. It's too dull to bear.'

'I don't think that's a healthy way to feel about your job.'

'Ah. Because you enjoy yours so very deeply.'

His voice is so thick with sarcasm I couldn't cut my way out with a chainsaw, but for a second I still want to deny his claim. I even glance around, as though searching for something that isn't grey and awful and monotonous – but it isn't a surprise when I draw a blank. Michaela isn't here today to add a splash of colour to the cubicle next to mine. All I can see are bl Kan ing acks and whites, occasionally broken up by the off-green of the carpet.

The whole place is like a painting entitled Depression, and it doesn't get any better when some movement catches my eye.

Mr Henderson is by the water cooler again.

And he's looking in my direction.

'I think I should probably be going.'

'But we were just warming up.'

'I realise that, but my boss is headed my way and, unlike you, I can't just send him an icy stare and silence him for all eternity.'

'I thought your job was mostly answering the telephone.'

'It is.'

'Then what could he possibly have to complain about? I am an irate customer, calling to say how terrible I find your service. So terrible, in fact, that I might have to punish you.'

'I can't discuss that right now.'

'You can't discuss my complaint, or you can't discuss the possible punishment? Because I really think we need to go over the latter. I seem to recall that during our last encounter you indicated one item you wished to try, when in truth you wanted another one entirely. And that just won't do.'

'I see. Well, that's very serious.'

'Is he standing over you right now?'

'Absolutely.'

'How delightful.'

'That doesn't sound delightful at all,' I say, because it's the best I can manage. I've got to somehow answer him without seeming like I'm talking about something other than customer service – but he's not exactly making it easy.

In fact, he's making it harder by the second.

'So tell me, Alissa. Which one was it really? The scarf, the handcuffs, or the cane?'

'The first one.'

'Oh, that was a very good dodge. Does he suspect?'

'I believe so.'

'But he isn't entirely sure.'

'Not quite.'

'Well, perhaps we should convince him a little harder.'

'No, I don't think so.'

'Why not? Does he seem angry?'

'Yes.'

'Is he often angry with you?'

'Yes.'

'Because you always make personal calls.'

'No.'

I pause then, not sure if I should tell him or not. It paints a rather lonely picture of me, if I do. But then I realise: I don't have to tell him. I'm limited by customer-service-speak, and for the first time since this conversation started I find that, in a way, freeing.

'You're the only one,' I tell him, without flinching.

And for my troubles I get a long, slow sigh, of the sort people give when they're utterly satisfied. Apparently he likes what I've said. He's read between the lines – just as I read between his – and heard what I really meant. No one else was worth the trouble. No one else has ever been worth the trouble.

Just you, my Janos.

It's a strong and strange moment, fraught with those things called feelings and so ripe for something more. If we were alone now I'd Kne anprobably confess how much I like him, and maybe he'd even confess something *back, and then in this magical imaginary wonderland we would make love on a heart-shaped bed.*

But we're not alone. I'm in my office, with my boss standing over me.

And apparently my boss has something mood-killing to say.

'I know what you're doing, madam,' he snaps, just as Janos is about to speak. I can hear his words hovering on some electric edge, and then Mr Henderson interjects and the electricity dies. Instead of sweet nothings he clips out a couple of words – none of them romantic.

'Did he call you madam?' he asks, in a tone I hardly recognise. It's much lower than normal, like the words have to slip under some mysterious barrier. And he doesn't wait for an answer, either. After a moment of me trying to figure out how to speak to him without encouraging any further ire, he tells me that we'll talk soon.

And then he hangs up.

Not that I mind. If I'm honest, I'd rather he didn't hear the roasting I'm about to get for making personal calls. Of course I've only got the roasting he's given other people to judge it by, considering that this is my first transgression.

But I'm still pretty clear on how this is going to go.

He starts with disappointment – oh, he's so disappointed in me. And after that comes the dressing-down, with optional commentary on my clothes – which he's never thought were office appropriate – and some mild shouting, so everyone can hear him being a boss. He prides himself on being a calm, reasonable person, but sometimes his inexplicable rage just bursts through, brightening up most of his face and neck when it does.

It's a difficult thing to endure – though not because of the anger or the ranting or the way he leans right over you so you can feel the spittle hitting the top of your head. No, no ... the worst part is the way he won't listen. It doesn't matter how many times I tell him I'm sorry and that it will never happen again.

He's just not interested. He has to say what he's come here for, all the way up to the point where you know you're going to cry. In fact, I think he aims for that point. I think he relishes it. He's practically leaning on me now, in an effort to squeeze it out of me.

Which just makes me wonder: shouldn't it have happened already?

He's currently telling me how useless I am, over and over again. His face is like an angry tomato. And when I dare to glance a little to the right, I can see everyone in the office watching this little tableau. I should be bawling under this much duress.

Yet somehow I'm not.

In fact, I barely feel anything at all. It's like my skin has been coated with steel, and every silly, petty thing he says simply bounces off it. I find myself looking up at him as though he's an alien species, and I've only just noticed. I thought he was an important member of the human race, before.

But now I know he isn't. Close up like this he just seems somewhat ridiculous, to the point where I actually want to laugh. I can feel the corners of my mouth starting to tremble, and when he accidentally snorts I almost lose control entirely. I have to put my head down, just so he won't see.

Though the feeling is still there, burning away inside of me.

And once he tires and leaves me be, I suddenly realise what it is. My skin isn't made of steel at all. I'm not different in any particular way. It's just that I've spent my life think Kmy how ing all of these tiny, tiny things – the office, my boss, my colleagues who are all still gawping at me – actually matter.

When really I just didn't know what mattering was.

* * *

It's almost five in the afternoon when he calls me and asks me to come to his office. And if I cared, I'd probably find that very unusual. I'd probably be shaking in my boots, expecting a further dressing-down with letters and disciplinary actions and someone from HR pretending to take notes while Mr Henderson strips a layer of skin off me.

But as I'm this new person who doesn't give a flying fuck, I'm not thinking about any of that at all. I'm thinking about calling Janos again instead. It's almost like an itch now, and while I'm at work I can no longer scratch it. I have to sit still and act like it's not there, which is going to be interesting during this meeting.

How can I possibly feign interest when I've got this great big urge hanging over my head? He'll probably ask me where I see my future at the company, and I'll answer: 'With loads of phone calls to my semi-boyfriend.'

And then I just have the word 'semi-boyfriend' floating around my head to add to my lamentable lack of focus. When I walk in, that's what I'm considering. Is he my semi-boyfriend? Can the word 'boyfriend' ever apply to someone like him? Even with that mitigating 'semi-' in front of it, I'm not sure it can.

It's too childish. It's too basic. I need something more adult for our situation – like 'lover' or 'paramour' or another word that hasn't been invented yet.

He's my 'orinthian', I think, as I sit down on the chair Mr Henderson indicates. It's the one opposite his cramped and crap-covered desk – much more important than the seat I'm usually offered. Usually he makes people sit to one side like we're here to see the doctor. If he could get away with it, I'm betting he'd make us sit out in the hall.

But here he doesn't, and if I was paying any attention at all I'd probably notice that more. I'd probably notice how much he's sweating too, and wonder why his tie is askew. Typically he's as neat as a pin, and especially when he's about to give out an official disciplinary.

Something is wrong, though that fact isn't quite penetrating. Everything is still glancing off my steel skin, skimming over the surface of me like it's not even there. I'm looking to one side of Mr Henderson, my mind on newly invented words.

I barely register anything until he speaks.

And then I know. I know something has gone really bad.

'Well,' he says. 'How are you feeling now?'

I don't think he's ever asked me how I'm feeling. I didn't think he knew that other people have feelings. Mostly he just behaves like we're all interchangeable idiots, sent to test his patience.

But I can see he's not acting that way now.

He looks ... harassed. It makes me think that HR have had a word with him about his behaviour, though if they had I can't see him taking it this seriously. They're about as effective as a wet rag. Once, they told Michaela that they couldn't do anything about Mr Henderson, for fear of losing their job.

So I'm not quite sure what's happening here.

'I just wanted to say that I'm very sorry about our misunderstanding earlier.'

I'm real K'oesn'ly not sure what's happening here. Has

he ever apologised to me about anything? Has he ever apologised about anything to anyone? I don't think he has. The word seems to stick in his throat on the way up, and his eyes kind of bulge too. For a moment I'm sure he's choking, and almost get up to whack him on the back.

But then I remember:

He hasn't actually eaten anything.

He's just possibly gone insane.

'Our misunderstanding?' I try, but only because I don't know what else to do. This is completely outside the boundaries of our previous relationship, which was mainly him shouting and me cowering. Nowhere in our history has he tried to reframe an incident as a misunderstanding. He hasn't needed to.

He's got carte blanche to go postal on anyone whenever he feels like it.

'Yes, you know. The ... ah ... little conversation we had earlier.'

Little? Conversation?

What in God's name is happening here?

'You mean the argument.'

He laughs, but the laugh is too big. It's like he's in an enormous echoing cavern, and the sound is being reverberated back to me a thousand times. And his face ... his face still isn't right. He's no longer choking, but his eyes are almost popping out of his head.

'Oh, well, yes, I can see why you might think of it as an argument. But honestly, I meant nothing by it. I think you're a wonderful employee, Alissa.'

'You do?'

I can't help the incredulity in my voice. I think he once wrote on an evaluation that I 'failed to meet the minimum standards for mediocrity.'

'Of course I do.'

'Since when?'

'I've always felt that way, I can assure you.'

'I see. Well … I guess … that's good to know.'

'Excellent, excellent,' he says, then, just when I think he's calming down, he goes for a third one: 'Excellent.'

I have to ask. He's not only saying these insane things – he's also sweating so much I'm starting to wonder if he's having some kind of episode. Is that what the start of a heart attack looks like? Or maybe a seizure of some type?

'Mr Henderson … are you OK?'

'Of course, of course.'

'Because you don't seem OK.'

'Oh, no, I'm fine, truly. I was just sitting here thinking about the good work you do, and it came to me. Why not reward you for all your wonderful efforts on the company's behalf?'

'That sounds really nice, sir, but –'

'So what I was thinking is that you could take an extra paid vacation – let's say for a month – and when you *return there'll be a nice raise waiting for you. Because, as you know, it's company policy to reward exemplary employees.'*

It is not company policy to reward exemplary employees. It's actually more of a company policy to allow customers to try and kill employees over the phone all day every day until you want to die, while paying you a pittance for the trouble.

But, sadly, I don't think I can point this out to him.

I don't think I can point out anything to him.

I'm currently sitting there with my mouth hanging Kmous open and a noise coming out of my body like a balloon leaking all of its air. Did he honestly just offer me a month's paid vacation? And a raise? I've never had a raise in all my time working for the company – and after he berated me for being awful, too.

This can't be real.

'Are you serious?'

'Absolutely.'

'You're just going to give me a paid vacation.'

'If you'd like one. Would you like one?'

'I would.'

'Wonderful,' he says, and the relief on his face is so clear it almost makes me relax. I hadn't realised how tense my muscles were until I catch relief off him, and allow myself to sag a little in my chair. 'Well, that's all then.'

'So I can go?'

'You can go.'

'And I don't have to come into work tomorrow.'

'No, you don't.'

'Because I'm on vacation.'

'That's it exactly.'

He makes pistol fingers at me to emphasise those words, which really only makes me more nervous about this whole thing. There's just a strange hollowness about his every move, like someone pulled his strings and forced him to dance around for their pleasure.

In fact, that impression is so strong it's all I can think about as I stumble out of his office. It stays with me all the way down the hall and into the elevator, though at first I'm not sure why. It just buzzes on the edge of my consciousness, like that thing you know you were supposed to do but now can't quite remember.

What haven't I done? I think, as I push my way through the double-door entrance and out into the car park. And then I see the limousine, and I realise:

It's not something I haven't done.

It's something he has.

Chapter Nine

I almost don't get into the car. There's something satisfying about the idea of strolling past, like I can't even see this huge gleaming eyesore stretching out across the car park. I'm not aware that anyone is waiting for me, and even if I was I wouldn't care. I'm oblivious; I'm aloof; I'm completely cool.

I'm not the least bit furious about any possible interference into my life. I don't even believe he has interfered. That would just be the craziest thing anyone has ever done for me, and I'm not prepared to entertain the notion. It makes me too mad. It makes me too excited. And the two conflicting emotions are having a fight inside me, quite possibly to the death.

I'm going to die of not being able to decide how to feel. Does he know that he keeps doing this to my feelings?

I'm betting he does. I'm betting he's sitting inside that car as laid-back and louche as a lord from the seventeenth century, laughing about the brilliant act of puppetry he's just possibly done. Only he won't be laughing, naturally. He'll just be smirking with one side of his face, in that infuriating, smouldering manner.

And yet I still get into the car.

'Hello, Alissa,' he says, the second I've shut myself inside. It's like closing the door on a leather-lined cocoon, which doesn't make me any more comfortable about this situation. Nor does his greeting. Somehow I always forget just how good his voice so N meunds, until it's filling up my head and my senses and any remaining resolve I might have had. It just curls around my name like a lazy cobra, and I go completely limp.

Though I at least *try* to keep true to my course.

'You did something, didn't you,' I say, which isn't half as direct as I wanted it to be. I was aiming for *how dare you call my boss*, but I just have to veer left at the last second. There's still a strong possibility that he didn't. It could be that I'm crazy for even imagining he would do this.

And besides ... at least I get actual words out.

I'm proud of myself for getting actual words out.

'Define what you mean by "something".'

'You know what I mean by "something".'

'I'm afraid I don't.'

'You do.'

OK, the words are starting to fail me a little now. Somehow I've plunged into playground talk, which only serves to amuse him. His eyes are bright with laughter he's not quite spilling, and as I watch he settles back into his seat – the way people do when they're thoroughly enjoying a show.

I'm putting on a show for him.

And, of course, that idea only makes me angrier.

'Christ, you really *did* call my boss. You called my boss and scared the life out of him and made him do things like some … some … insane Svengali.'

'Why on earth would I do a thing like that?'

'Oh, I don't know. Maybe because you're a complete control freak?'

'I think "control freak" is a little strong.'

'You do? So you didn't mess around with my life and my job and my boss in a really frightening way? Because I have to tell you, Janos … he looked scared. What did you say to him to make him that scared?'

Instead of answering right away he examines and then straightens his cuff, even though his cuff doesn't need any straightening at all. Of course, I've seen him make a similar move before. He searched for lint that wasn't on his immaculate trousers – and once, I think, he smoothed his hair, despite there being no hairs out of place.

It's a stalling tactic.

But it's not going to work on me.

'Don't do that. Don't sort out things that don't need sorting out. Just tell me straight: what did you say to him?'

'Oh, I don't know. That I'd pull out his fingernails with a pair of pliers?'

'You did *not* say that.'

'No, I didn't. But I do so enjoy seeing that appalled shock all over your face.'

I do my best to rearrange my features immediately. It isn't easy, though. They seem to be stuck on open-mouthed horror.

'Well, can you blame me?'

'Of course I can. You honestly think I'd threaten someone in such a way?'

'I don't … that's not … I was just …' I say, stumbling and fumbling through all possible variations, until I suddenly hit on the right one. In fact, the right one explodes out of me. 'Hold on a second – we were talking about you, not me. You're the one who did a scary thing, whether pliers were involved or not.'

It's strange to see him look busted. It doesn't quite suit him, and I think he kn SI tse, Iows it.

The expression is gone as quickly as it came.

'I simply suggested to your boss that he stopped speaking to you that way. I'd hardly call that scary. And, in truth, I thought you'd appreciate the change.'

'I *do* appreciate the change. I do. You've no idea how amazing it was to see my awful boss actually grovelling – and you did that for me. You did something that no one else ever has, and you did it just because you didn't like

159

how someone spoke to me. That's an incredible thing, no matter which way you cut it,' I say, and I mean it. But I also mean the next part – the one that I kind of have to work up to. He's staring and staring at me with his midnight eyes, and I'm sweating in their glare. It takes a hell of a lot of effort to get the words out, and when I finally do my voice is shaking. 'But at the same time it's kind of crazy.'

'It's crazy to want people to treat you with respect?'

'No, that's the cool part. It's the other part that's causing me some problems – you know, the one that makes you think it's a good idea to mess around with my life.'

'I don't want to mess around with your life, Alissa.'

'OK, maybe you don't exactly want to mess. But you can't deny that you only like everything when it's precisely as you want it to be.'

'That's simply not true,' he says, but it's not the tone or the sentence itself that makes me spit something out. It's the way he shakes his head slowly, in this wise, paternalistic manner. *You're so silly*, that head shake says. *How could you possibly think such a thing?* that head shake says.

But I know why I think such a thing.

Because he's a –

'*Liar.*'

The word is like a gong ringing, inside the silent

160

cocoon of this car. We've started moving, but you can barely hear a thing through the tinted windows and the glass partition behind his head. We might as well be in outer space for all we can see or hear or feel, and I'm sure that adds an ominous air to my pronouncement.

Or is it his resulting expression that adds the edge to it? His eyes widen just a touch, which is bad enough on its own. But there's also the slight intake of breath, and the way he leans back minutely. All tiny things, and yet so enormous on him.

He doesn't like the game being turned around on him, quite clearly.

'Are you really so sure?' he asks, but I don't know what he thinks I'm going to say. A 'no' would fly in the face of every scrap of evidence he's ever offered me. I can't possibly give him anything other than this.

'You actually abandoned me in a hotel room because you didn't like it when things weren't perfectly within the boundaries you set. Everything has to be played by your rules, and at your discretion, and in the exact manner you think it should be done. Anything else and you run for the hills.'

Though I honestly don't expect him to be so blasé about it, once I've forced all of those accusations out. He seemed ruffled by that one little 'liar', so I'm expecting big things. I'm expecting an explosion, and at first it seems like I'm going to get it. He wrestles with himself for a moment, quite visibly – his jaw tightens; he sits up in his seat. It's akin to watching a boxer sizing up his opponent.

Only to have it all come to nothing.

'Perhaps you have a point. I confess, I S I . We've become very set in my ways,' he says finally, in a way that suggests the boxer found a sniper rifle, and decided to blow off my head before the match could ever take place. His expression even matches that rather unsettling assessment – it's all sharp and satisfied, like he's found his footing again.

He doesn't have to worry about little old me digging down to the heart of him. I have no weapons; there are no tools with which I might do such a thing.

Or so he thinks.

'Well, that's good of you to admit,' I say, as a seed of an idea begins to germinate in my mind. I can't come at him from that angle. But there might be another one I can work my way through. All I have to do is lead him in the right direction … 'And perfectly understandable.'

'I'm glad you think so.'

'And I'll be honest: I do like you taking the reins.'

'I had noticed,' he says, and now he's really comfortable. He leans back again in that deliberate, near-prowling way of his, sure and certain in his own strength. He's not really the sort of person to run for the hills – oh, no no no.

'Yet one thing is troubling me ...'

'Then please, share it. You know you can tell me anything that might be bothering you. In fact, I would prefer it if you did,' he says – so confident in himself. He has absolutely no idea what I'm planning, which of course makes it all the sweeter when I say it.

'I think you secretly enjoyed going to pieces,' I tell him, and then just let it linger for a fraction longer than is necessary. Just to give it a little more weight – though somehow I don't think I need it. That unsettled look crosses his usually so ordered features before I've even finished.

With a little flourish, of course:

'True?' I say. 'Or false?'

* * *

He is quiet for a long time after that. Though really he doesn't have to be anything else. He doesn't need words. His heavy gaze is enough, as it holds tightly to mine. We simply sit there in the strange silence of the car, staring and staring at each other like two kids playing chicken. Whoever breaks first loses.

So naturally I don't expect it to be him.

I give a little start when he suddenly speaks.

'I always knew you'd be the death of me,' he says – intending a joke, I think.

But it doesn't come out that way. It comes out like he really means it. I'm somehow deadly to him, as if my eyes are actually knives and my skin is suffused with arsenic. And though I have the strongest urge to reassure him on that score, something else comes out of my mouth instead.

Something probably poisonous.

'That's not answering the question,' I say, and that look all over his face deepens. It's impossible to describe – a study in contrasts and all of them clashing violently. His eyebrows are almost raised, but there's no surprise in his darkly gleaming eyes. And though he seems to be smiling ruefully, there's something pained about it.

Like it hurts to move his muscles that way.

'And you really think I'm going to?'

'You could try. I tried for you.'

'Oh, I see. And now the tables are turned?'

'Probably not. But the illusion of it is nice.' St i Th

'You're enjoying yourself.'

'I'm enjoying something.'

'Please – a little more specific.'

'I will be,' I say. 'But after you.'

He makes a sound, caught somewhere between a laugh and a snort of frustration. And he glances away when he does it, too – just to give it that extra edge of *I can't do this*.

'Very well then,' he says, in a voice like something snapped off. 'False.'

He looks back to me, but only to give me a challenging stare.

Go ahead, those eyes say. *Call my bluff.*

So I do.

'Liar,' I say, and oh, this time he can't smother his unsettled reaction. It's real and raw and all over him. His breathing speeds up in this almost animalistic way, like a bull about to charge. And when he leans forward a little, he doesn't do it normally.

He almost *lunges*. I feel sure for a second that he's about to grab me, though I don't know if I mind. My upper arms are burning, in anticipation of a reckless move he can't quite make. He can't quite give in to wild passion.

But soon, soon.

'How can you be so sure?' he says, and, though it seems like he's challenging me again, I can hear something else in his voice. It sounds like he's leaving the door ajar for me – just a little. From a distance you probably couldn't see it ... and maybe you'd even walk past without giving that tiny invitation a second glance ...

Only we're not at a distance.

He's leaning forward and I'm leaning forward, and if either of us moved an inch we'd be kissing. In fact, in a way it feels like we already are. The air between us is thick and tension-filled, taking the place of a touch he doesn't know how to give. And when he turns his head in this certain familiar way, I find myself following.

Just as I would if our lips were pressed together.

'The same way you always are. I watch you, and your face tells me tales that your words won't.'

'So what did my face tell you the other day?'

'It told me that you wanted me. That you couldn't wait for me. That seeing me behave like that drove you wild,' I say. 'The way it's driving you wild now.'

'And if I tell you you're wrong?'

'I'll call you a liar again. And I'll keep calling it until your debt to me is ten thousand feet high, packed tight with all the things you say you hate the most while inside I know you love it. You want to grab me now, don't you?'

'Absolutely not.'

'You want to tear off my clothes with your teeth, and ravage me right here in the back of this stupidly expensive car.'

'That doesn't sound like me at all,' he says, but each word is imbued with so much charge it's like he's saying something else entirely. He's pushing them all to the surface so I can see the opposite underneath, boiling away insanely.

'Then when you're done …'

'Yes.'

'When you're done fucking me and filling me and making me feel all the things you definitely don't want to, you do something even worse.'

'Yes, tell me,' he says, and now his hands are poised around my upper arms. I ca Ser

'I can hardly bring myself to say it.'

'You have to. You have to,' he tells me, but he goes one better than that. He goes one better than the brutal, cracking desperation in his voice, one better than his obvious longing and his need: he speaks to me in another language. 'You have to,' he says, and then he follows it with a stream of words I don't understand.

And yet oh, God, I understand them perfectly.

They're begging me to finish this, each syllable so obviously fraught with need I can't deny him anything. I have to lean in close, to give him the final perverted act. I have to put my lips to his ear and whisper, as soft as silk and so filled with delight.

'*You don't leave.*'

Chapter Ten

He doesn't quite savage me. But it isn't far off, either. The second I've said those subversive words, he makes me turn around. And when I say he makes me, I mean he makes me. There's no persuasion, no precise and deliberate commands. He just gets hold of my waist and manhandles me – like he did on the bed for that brief moment of absolute ecstasy.

Only this time it's much more obvious.

And much more forceful.

I suppose that's what happens when you jack someone up to force factor ten before things have even begun. Previously I'd only experienced his sudden storming desire from the mid-point onwards. Now it's right here from the beginning, and oh, Lord, it's overwhelming. It's like being mauled by a mad tiger.

His hands feel enormous. They seem to span most of my sides, from my hips all the way up to my ribcage. And he's gripping me really, really hard. I'll probably have bruises tomorrow, but oddly I find I don't care. Instead, my insides sizzle whenever I think about it. I'll be able to look in the mirror and see where he held me, I think, and then I just have to sag against the back of my seat.

He doesn't let me hold the pose for long, however. He just hauls me back up, until I'm on my knees. And once I'm in a position he likes – facing the rear window, arms on the back of the seat, legs slightly spread – he does something even better than the rest of this madness.

He shoves my skirt up.

There's no careful, inch-by-inch removal here. He simply yanks at anything that gets in his way, and that includes my skirt, and my shirt, and my panties. The first ends up around my waist, as I mentioned. But the second, ohhhh, the second one. I could swim around in the way he goes about that.

He gets a grip on one side and pulls – and most of the buttons pop. Then he simply slides his hand inside, roaming over my breasts in this really greedy way. By the time he's done, the cups of my bra are no longing covering me, and I'm shivering all over.

And that's before he goes for the third item on my list: My panties.

I think I expect him to really rip that item of clothing. He's getting progressively worse as this goes on, so it doesn't seem like a far-out assumption – and in fact I'm bracing myself for it. I'm imagining the pain of the elastic as it briefly digs in. I'm wondering if that will leave a bruise too.

And that's when he eases the material aside, and slides his fingers all the way through my soaked folds. Just like that, so smooth and sudden I can hardly accept it. Veter th andIs he really touching me there, or did I want it so bad I invented his hand on me?

I'm going to go with the latter, because oh, it feels so amazing it can't be real. There's just something about the way he did it that flips all of my switches. My panties were a minor inconvenience that he barely registered, on his way to getting what he wants.

And what he wants is my pussy, hot and wet in his hand.

I *know* he wants this.

He *tells me* he wants this.

'I can't wait to feel this slippery little pussy around my cock,' he says, while I quietly die of desire. I'm not sure if it's the 'slippery' or the 'pussy' or the 'cock', or a combination of all three. But they definitely do something to me.

How could they not? He's never really spoken like that before. Oh, he's said sexy things, sure. And in all honesty, he could read the phone book in that accent and I'd be melting. Yet nothing – and I mean *nothing* – beats him saying filthy words out loud. Nothing beats him talking about his own cock as though it's an actual part of him, instead of something he hardly acknowledges. Usually he pretends he has no desires at all.

But now he seems pretty keen on letting me know. Even if I set aside the hand on my breast and the fingers he's just sunk knuckle deep into my pussy, I can't possibly overlook what he's doing against the curve of my hip. He's rubbing himself over me, though really it's more than that. Rubbing suggests something fairly innocent.

This is not innocent at all.

This is him rutting and rutting at me like a bull in heat. I can actually make out the shape and length of his prodigious cock, even though he still has all of his clothes on. It feels heavy and solid, and somehow so much ruder for all the material around it.

Like it's a secret, I think. Like he's secretly aroused, and can only let me know through this long, slow insinuation against my body. He's not allowed to say, and he can't strip, so this is all he's got.

Though, God knows, it's enough. I think I almost come when I first feel him doing it – and I definitely skirt close when he finds my clit with his thumb. He just flicks over it, as he keeps up that long, slow roll against my hip. Never increasing the pace. Never showing me too much.

But always showing me just enough. He's really and truly excited, and he wants to do this, and he's happy to come apart for me. And all of those things make a swell of feeling rush through my body – almost an orgasm, but not quite. I'm right on the edge, and just need a little more to push me over.

Maybe a bit more of that stroking over my swollen clit. Or a kiss to the back of my neck. And oh, I'd kill for one of his thick, rough fingers sliding into my pussy.

So I suppose it's lucky, really, that he gives me all three. He presses down with his thumb over my stiff little bud, and when I shiver – that's when I feel his hot, wet mouth on the back of my neck. It's the first time he's really given me a kiss of any kind – if you don't count his tongue stroking and stroking through my wet folds – and of course the sensation is electric. I think I actually gasp over the feel of it.

But the gasping is a little premature. I should have saved it up for the third and final thing on my wish list, and not just because of the sweet, unbearable slide of something easing into my slippery pussy. There's also the shock, oh, God, the glorious shock of suddenly realising that he's not touching me with his fingers.

[fine

He's using his obviously condom-clad cock.

He's going to actually fuck me – though I don't know why that's so stunning. He did say he was going to. And I guess he came kind of close the last time we were together. Yet still, the idea overwhelms me. I say his name three times in a row, like I need to somehow grind the sense of him into me.

I need to know that it's definitely him doing this, despite knowing that it couldn't be anyone else. I can smell his cologne, light and rich at the same time – and that body couldn't belong to any other person. All I have to do is lean back a little and I can feel how heavy and solid it is. I can feel how it surrounds me, as he slowly pushes inward.

And oh, man, am I grateful for it. I can sag against him when the pleasure proves too much, which happens often. In truth it's already going on, because, good God, it is incredible to feel him sliding into me. He's as big as I remember and as thick, but he doesn't force his way in. He rubs and urges and insinuates, until the head of his heavy cock just parts the way.

And then rocks, ever so slowly, until he's all the way there.

It's blissful and agonising, all at the same time. Blissful because of the feelings – that thing opening me up, then pressing and sliding against a thousand different nerve-endings – and agonising because of how deliberate he suddenly is again. He's slowed right down, just when I want him to keep going, keep charging forward, keep using me like this.

I needn't have worried, however.

The second he's inside me, something shifts. It's like he knew he had to be careful at first. Anyone with a cock like his would have to be careful. But once I've taken him all and am obviously insanely happy about that fact – panting and mewling and twisting like a maniac – he returns to that feverish, frantic state.

His hand snaps up to grip the back of the seat – knuckles white with tension, one bicep so firm and hard next to my head. But it's a good thing he does, really. I need something to hold onto, when he finally cuts loose. His arm is my safety bar for this ride I'm suddenly on.

And I cling to it. I have to cling to it. His first thrust is so jolting my teeth snap together, and his second is even better. It hits places I'd only previously read about in implausible books, and a moan just gushes out of me – too loud in this silent space.

But I don't care. How could I? He's driving into me, and besides:

He's not being quiet now, either. He's breathing so hard it would probably qualify as grunting, if he was the kind of person to do something like that. And after a while of this fierce and furious pounding, he actually *becomes* the kind of person to do something like that. He makes noises – real and actual noises. They're all breathless and hard won, as though he has to strain and strain to get them out, or else strain and strain to keep them down.

And then he says my name, and I'm lost.

I'm already shaking. The hand I'm holding onto him with is sweaty and spasmodic, like it can't decide if it should grip him close to the elbow or further down towards the wrist. And I know I'm crying a little. I can taste the salt on my lips.

But there's still that other level of abandonment. There's still a place of complete pleasure, where I'm sobbing and begging and twisting against him, close enough to orgasm to almost taste it, but not close enough to get that relief. No, no, I need something else to get to that perfect point.

Something like him speaking.

'Ah, yes,' he says. 'Come all over my cock.'

And I do, I do, oh, God, I do. *Of course* I do. I can hear his gorgeous voice – fraught with his own pleasure and desire – and his gorgeous voice is saying things. He's talking about his cock again, and about coming, and most of all:

He knows I'm almost there. He can probably hear it in my newly urgent moans, and see it in each shudder and twist – or at least that's what I think until he speaks again. After which, I don't think anything at all. 'Oh, I can feel your sweet pussy tightening around me,' he says, and my brain goes on a much-needed vacation.

My body takes over, shuddering through an orgasm so intense I can hardly stand it. It's just like before on the bed – I try to get away. I buck and twist and attempt to climb the back of the seat, and the way he fights me just makes it worse.

His hands go to my hips, holding me in place. Then, just as I'm processing this sensation, he uses that grip he's got to pull me back and back and back onto his cock, until I'm reeling. I can't breathe. I can't make the sounds I want to make. They're all stuck, and when they eventually emerge they're too much like a throttled grunt.

I sound like an animal.

Though he doesn't care.

'Yes yes yes, do it, do it,' he says, in a tone that sends me inside out. It's as guttural as my voice currently is and almost too low to hear, like he can't expend too much energy on talking. He has to really focus on fucking me and fucking me, all the way through this orgasm and right into the next one.

Which comes as just as much of a surprise to him as it does to me.

'Oh, *szeretett*, are you coming again? Are you? Tell me. Say something to me,' he demands, but it's the desperation in his tone that really makes me want to answer. His voice almost breaks around 'say' and 'something', in a way that makes me wonder:

Has he been waiting all this time for that? Has he been waiting for my words? I think he has, but if so he has to know: I've never been much of a talker. I'm always at a loss what to say, or mired in worry that I'm saying the wrong thing. What if I talk about cocks when someone is wanting a pussy?

What if I go too far?

And then I realise:

There *is* no too far with him.

'Fuck my pussy,' I say, and he hardly flinches.

He does moan for me, however. And he grabs my shoulder, as though he needs something extra to hold onto. He needs to stabilise himself, just like I did – and oh, that thought is so very welcome. There's absolutely nothing better in this whole world than Janos Kovacs truly going to pieces.

And it's definitely happening now. He can't seem to stop himself moaning my name, though I know he wants to. Each syllable is thick and throttled, punctuated by an increasingly shaky thrust. He can hardly contain himself any more.

And I just have to lean on that a little.

'Yeah, that's it, fuck me,' I say, then bolder, and louder: 'Oh, God, I want you to come so bad, oh, I want you to fill me, yeah, fill me.'

Though I swear I don't expect him to actually do it. I thought it was just me who bent to the will of words, but apparently not. The second I've said it I feel his hand tighten in the material of my shirt, and his body stiffens.

But that's not the best part.

No, the best part is the sound he makes, oh, God, the *sound*. It's got this note of disbelief running through it, like he can't quite credit that this is happening. And when his body jerks and this orgasm really takes hold, he calls out my name. He draws it out like a plea, one sweet syllable at a time.

With that unknown word on the end: *szeretett*.

Though I don't need a lesson in Hungarian to know it's an endearment. I can tell it's an endearment from the tone of his voice, so soft, and sweet. And when I glance back – just to see how he looks when he comes, just to watch him give everything up for a second – I know for sure.

His eyes are dark with feeling, so obviously full of tenderness and love I couldn't pretend otherwise if I tried. I don't want to pretend otherwise. I want to revel in his honest-to-God emotions, and for a while I do.

Before I realise that there's something else there too. It's just flickering around the edges of all of those warm feelings, and at first I can't quite place it. It's lost amongst the stuff that makes my heart catch fire, though maybe that's more my fault than his. I want to focus solely on them for just a moment, despite knowing that I can't.

I can't because I'm pretty sure it's yearning. It's yearning, even though he has to know he has me. He has me so completely I almost say it then and there: *I'm yours. You don't have to keep reaching for something I've already given.*

But I know why he does, all the same.

It's not because of something I'm not offering.

It's because he doesn't know how to accept it, even when it's there.

Chapter Eleven

He doesn't seem to know what to do, in the aftermath. He manages to straighten my clothes, and follows it with straightening his. But his movements are not half as fluid as I'm used to. They're all jerky, like his arms and legs are suddenly independent from his body. They belong to someone else, who didn't just fuck the living daylights out of his semi-girlfriend in the back of a moving limousine.

And then I slowly start to realise what being in a moving limousine means. I forgot for a while – mostly due to all the overwhelming pleasure. However, once he's seated opposite me and everything is almost normal, it's hard to think of anything but. Did the driver hear us? He probably didn't, thanks to what I'm hoping is a soundproof partition.

But that doesn't solve the other problem:

Why are we still driving around? He must have told the driver to just keep going and going, and really there's only one reason why. There's only one reason why we're in this lavish car, too. He knew we were going to be doing God knows what in the back, and wanted to make that experience as pleasant as possible.

He's such a thoughtful guy.

Who can't actually express any of the thoughts he's having. For a long, long time he simply sits there, moving from trousers that need brushing to cuffs that need neatening to his hair, which is still barely out of place. You'd honestly never know that he just took me roughly against the back of this seat, if it wasn't still warm from our bodies.

Though, if I strain, I can almost feel the indentations where his knees went. And when I do, other things become apparent – like how warm and wet and over-sensitised I am between ^"1em" half amy legs. My body is still completely raw and ripe from my orgasms, and any kind of pressure proves problematic.

I think my clit actually jumps and jitters when I accidentally press too hard against the seat. And my nipples definitely don't like the brush of my bra over their tips. It makes this funny feeling buzz upwards through my body, before ending somewhere strange – like my teeth. I don't think I'll be able to walk when I get out of the car.

But he doesn't seem to have that problem.

He doesn't seem to have any problems. He just gazes out of the tinted window at nothing and no one, in a way that should seem completely cool and calm and at ease. In any other circumstances it would definitely give that impression – I can imagine him in the boardroom sitting like that, with one leg over the other and a faintly bored expression on his face.

However, in these circumstances it's a little different. He's not trying to get through another dull presentation. He's trying to present a perfect front – and he's failing quite badly. Everything just looks too poised and put on, like he slipped on a mask right after we'd finished. And though he wears it well, I can see the cracks around the edges.

Though I don't have to.

After a long, long moment, he quite suddenly says:

'I don't know why I am the way I am.'

'I was going to guess childhood trauma.'

'No, no childhood trauma. No terrible event in my teens, no sudden grief that forever formed me into this closed-off creature who doesn't even know how to talk after sex.'

He sighs, like it's some minor inconvenience. Instead of a terrible truth that makes me kind of ache for him. And I think he knows it makes me ache, because my voice goes all soft and funny when I finally speak.

'You're talking now,' I say, and he seems to like that. His mouth twists up on one side, at least, though after a second I realise it's actually ruefulness.

'Because we're trapped together,' he says, and then I'm *sure* it's ruefulness.

181

He really knows how to beat himself up.

'You could tell the driver to stop. You could get out.'

'And fail at the one thing you wanted?'

'I don't think it would matter all that much. I can hardly remember what it was,' I say, which is a complete and total lie, but never mind. It's more important that he feels better right now, because I can't bear him to be this strange and sad.

It's tearing me in two.

'It seemed important to you before.'

'Well, maybe it isn't now. Maybe it's more important to me that you feel comfortable,' I tell him, intending just that. But when he glances at me, his expression isn't the least bit consoled. His eyes are the same as they were when I looked back at him over my shoulder – shot through with this vulnerability that shouldn't suit him at all.

I'm used to him being impenetrable, implacable, unable to show feeling.

But suddenly the feeling is starting to spill out.

'Have I told you before how kind I find you?' he says, in this low, grave voice that makes me shiver. 'And it fills me with such pleasure, when I see all of these little gifts you give me, and all of these little allowances you make for me – but even with all of this, I cannot allow you such small matters. I cannot let c I the go without feeling cut loose of my moorings. And more importantly: I cannot stay.'

'And yet you're still here.'

He nods, but it's not the nodding I notice. It's those ever-shifting eyes of his, running their way from almost wounded to something like warmth. Oh, they're so warm I could sit by them, on a cold winter's night.

'That is true,' he says, and there's a short silence.

But this time it isn't the least bit uncomfortable. It spreads between us instead, a great and beautiful blanket unfurling. All we have to do now is sit in its centre and talk a few things through. Maybe soothe each other little.

If I'm capable of something like that – which I'm sure I am.

'It's not a crime, you know,' I say, and that seems like a good start. I can do this. I swear I can. 'To want to control things and be aloof – in fact, I often wish that I could be the same way. It sounds like you get hurt a lot less often.'

'Oh, I wouldn't say that.'

'Are you hurting now?'

I ask it only half seriously, but he glances away once I've spoken. And it's definitely not a dismissive move, either. It's a full-on avoidance tactic that makes me want to do some damage control. The blanket is being folded back up as I sit here, slightly panicking.

So really it's no wonder that I blunder my words out, searching in vain for whatever is making him suddenly suffer.

'Because you should know: if you choose to stay, I won't suddenly leave,' I tell him, fumbling towards more before I've even fully formed the first part. 'I won't let you down. I don't know if that's what you're thinking, but –'

He cuts me off before I can finish the thought, and I'm grateful. I've no idea what the thought was going to be, in all honesty. And besides, it's better this way. Everything is better this way, because he doesn't cut me off with some words of his own.

He does it by crossing over to where I'm sitting, so abruptly that my sentences fail me. Whatever was supposed to come after that just dies in my throat, and is replaced by something else entirely: a little sound, maybe, and most certainly a smile. Oh, I'm smiling so hard I fear my face might crack – mainly because it's obvious why he's done this. He doesn't even have to do anything else.

But I'm glad he goes ahead anyway.

He takes my hand, without looking in my direction. He just does it while staring straight ahead, as though it's nothing at all, really – even though it's clearly taking every bit of willpower he has. The palm pressed against mine is slightly damp. I think he might be vibrating just a little bit.

And then he tells me, in a slightly unsteady voice:

'Yes. I believe I will choose to stay.'

* * *

Things are different then, our meetings are different. Not hugely so, but if I look hard I can see the shift. Oh, he still likes to arrange everything, and be completely in control. And when he lets slip some hint of emotion or passion I can see that panic on his face. I can feel him vibrating with the urge to just cut out on me before things get too real.

But I can also see him resisting all of those impulses.

He's resisting them now, as I put him through the conversation from hell.

'There must cT I fear mbe something you want.'

'There are lots of things I want. I've done most of them to you.'

'Well … I can't argue with that.'

'So what more could there be?'

'There's plenty more, and you know it.'

'I know nothing of the sort.'

'Come on – share your deviant secrets.'

He snorts, and I suppose I should be offended.

I can't be, however. I know just what he means when he says:

'I doubt you could handle my deviant secrets.'

'I've handled stripping and semi-public sex and bondage.'

'That was hardly bondage.'

'So you want to twist me up like a pretzel. You want spreader bars and ball gags and blindfold and butt plugs?'

He snorts again and gives me a 'no', and sadly I can tell he isn't lying. He really doesn't want any of those things – though I'm hard pressed to uncover what he does want. Ever since we started playing the game the other way around, it's been less of a kinky trick and more of a battle of wills.

'Something worse, then. Something appalling.'

'Like pliers and fingernails?'

'I didn't really believe that, OK? Stop bringing it up!' I say, but I can tell he's teasing me before I've even finished speaking. He's got that gleaming-eyed look on his face that says he's come out of this triumphant. He's made me take a different path – just like he always does – and I hardly even know I'm lost until I glance around and discover I'm surrounded by gnarly old trees.

'I think you did really believe that. You think I'm secretly some sort of mobster.'

'I do not. And stop changing the subject.'

'This was hardly a subject change. It was just a little diversion.'

'Yeah, I know all about you and your diversions. Next thing I know I'll be sprawled all over the bed with your face between my legs, and then I'll hardly be able to think about any of this at all.'

'Oh, I don't think that's true.'

'No?'

'Absolutely not. I wasn't thinking of going down on you.'

'Well, good,' I say, and yes I'm aware that I sound

singularly unconvincing. My voice wavers all over the place, and now my head is full of nothing but the feel of his mouth on my spread sex. The problem is that he's just too good at it. He knows he's good at it. He can get me to concede anything just by talking about licking my clit or fingering my pussy.

I've never had oral sex that made me come so hard or want it so much. In fact, I've never really had much oral sex, full stop – and he knows it.

And he knows other things, too.

'I was thinking of taking you out onto the balcony, so everyone can see. And then ... maybe just lifting your dress a little ...'

'That's so ... that is very ...'

'Rude? Yes, I'm aware. So shall we?'

He puts a hand out, and I *almost* stand to take it. I teeter on the brink for about ten seconds, muscles tensing in readiness, body sliding forward to send me off the edge of the chair. In fact, my ass is actually off the seat, when I suddenly realise.

'You know, you almost had me there,' I say, and to my great delight he snaps his fingers. The way other, sillier people do, when their plans have been foiled again. Curses, I think, and then am filled with the strangest glee.

He's becoming a different person right before my eyes, and oh, I adore him for it.

'Damn, I thought I'd gotten away with it.'

'You'll never get away with it any more – you know that, don't you? I did learn from the master, after all.'

'I've created a monster.'

'I won't deny it. Now, where were we?'

'You were telling me all about the appalling things I might want. Apparently, exposing your pussy to the whole of London wasn't quite enough.'

'Well, it's probably enough for me. But I doubt it's enough for you.'

'And you're sure of that?'

'I'm absolutely positive. When I hit the truth, you tend to glance away.'

His eyes widen a little at that – but not in a way I've ever seen before. This expression is still ripe with shock, but there's something else there too. There's a hint of disbelief, as though he never imagined I'd guess. And more importantly, I can see he kind of likes it.

I think he might even be a little impressed.

'So you think I have a tell, like in poker' he says, but I'm certain he's just trying to deflect.

He *knows* he has a tell.

'And you often check yourself for flaws that aren't there,' I say, and he gives me the strangest look. I don't even know how to describe it. His eyes almost close, but I can see him rolling them through the little slits he leaves. And he lets out such a breath, too. It's almost a frustrated snort, but not quite.

If I was going to pin a label on it, I'd call it withering regret.

But the word 'busted' seems to suit, too.

'I'm going to have to stop doing that.'

'You really are. It's very revealing.'

'Yes, I can see how it would be.'

'I mean, it's not just the fact that you do it when you're uncomfortable or trying to avoid the truth. It's also the act itself – searching yourself for flaws, doing your best to remove them, making sure you're completely perfect ...'

'All right, all right,' he says, but he's smiling when he does. And his smiles are getting so much broader, too. They almost have substance, now. I see teeth on at least two out of every three occasions. 'You win.'

'I do?'

'Yes. And I can see how much you like it, too, so don't pretend,' he says, then, after a moment of the best sort of bliss, he goes one better. 'You are so inescapably lovely when you smile. I can hardly begrudge you it.'

I blush at that – though he needn't think he's off the hook.

I know he's still trying to get away from the main topic.

'That's really nice of you to say so. But I think we were discussing something else ...'

'Ah, yes. I keep forgetting.'

'Of course you do. But don't worry – I'm here to remind you. We were talking about the awful things I imagine you might want.'

'Oh, csti"1e they're awful now?'

'Terrible. Taboo. Completely forbidden.'

His lips part over his teeth, like a shark sensing dinner. He's just too easy. How did he get this easy?

'Still illegal in parts of the country?'

'Quite possibly. Certainly, you will probably think so.'

'So you really think you're going to shock me.'

'I've succeeded a few times now. It's not beyond the bounds of reality.'

'Getting confident, then?'

'I think that would be an understatement.'

'It doesn't pay to be *too* sure of yourself. You never know what might happen.'

'I know what's going to happen here.'

'Oh?'

'You're going to try and get out of it.'

'That bad, then?'

'It's bad. But I know you want it. You've said as much to me before today, though I don't think you knew you were doing it. You were just teasing me.'

His gaze goes a little flat after that – in a way that suggests he's running back through our every conversation, searching and searching for the exact right thing. Was it when he spoke to me about the island? Or did the need to see me strip give him away?

'It's going to be something non-sexual again, isn't it?' he says, after a second – and is it my imagination or does his voice sound kind of defeated when he does? There's something in there, at least. Something that reminds me of the feeling I get when stuff goes horribly, horribly wrong.

It's like a pocket of air dropping down through your body.

'It might well be.'

'Something that I no longer do.'

'Yes, I believe that's true.'

'And if I lie and tell you I don't want to ...'

'You know I'll know.'

'I can't hide from you any more can I, *szeretett*? You have me now,' he tells me, and I'm so overwhelmed by the sentiment and the sound of his voice and that word – the one he thinks I don't understand, but always do – that I speak in this big rush of emotion.

'I hope I do. Because there's nothing I want more than you,' I say, sure and certain in the feeling but bracing myself for his reaction anyway. Maybe he'll turn away from it, or tell me I'm foolish.

But he doesn't.

He looks at me with eyes so bright and soft, instead. And his voice when he speaks is almost unbearably tender.

'Then say. Say what it is,' he urges me, and I can't help smiling – slow like flowing syrup, and so completely happy.

'A date, of course. You want a date, with a kiss on my wrist at the door,' I say, and in response he gives me

191

a thousand ways to say no, and all shot through with laughter. 'No, nyet, never, non,' he says, 'impossible, improbable, I deny it with my last dying breath.'

But he only does it because he knows what I'm going to say.

There's only one thing I *can* say.

'Liar.'

Chapter Twelve

He's much calmer sitting in the limousine than he was in the hotel room – as though he's rearranged himself into the necessary shape to successfully go on a date. He's had a few days to let the idea sink in, and now he's completely on board. He's dressed to the nines in a suit that probably cost more than my entire life, and he smells so utterly divine I almost maul him right then and there.

But I resist. I *have* to resist.

I'm supposed to be poised and elegant, now – though I know I'm failing badly. I've put my hair up and can already feel it coming down. Little tendrils are kissing the back of my neck, which isn't a good thing on two levels. The first being how shabby I look, and the second is simply the sensation.

It reminds me of his mouth on my skin. It has me humming before we've stepped out of the car, and that doesn't bode well for the rest of the date. I'm not even sure if I'll make it through dinner, and I think he knows it.

I think he's leaning on it a little, in fact. As we walk into a building I've never seen before – with no sign on the door, just like The Harrington – he slips a hand around my waist. And it's not a casual hand, either. It's very insistent, and so tight against my body I could probably make out every whorl on his fingertips if I tried.

And oh, the way the fabric moves beneath his touch …

I shouldn't have worn this dress. I see that now. It's far too thin and much too revealing. He barely has to do anything at all to caress me and fondle me and make me go insane, which isn't the best position to be in while dining at a place like this. The entranceway alone is enough to put me on edge – all gloss and glamour, capped by a maître d' who fawns over Janos like he's the second coming.

'So glad to see you again, Mr Kovacs,' he says, while giving me a look that could strip paint. I actually see his nose wrinkle, but I can't let it bother me. I have other things to contend with – like the dining room we're swept into.

Oh, God, the dining room.

I think the walls are actually made of leather, and everything has this glossy glow that almost hurts the eyes. Even the patrons seem to glitter, to the point where I have to look away. If I see one more person dripping with diamonds I'm liable to lose it. At the very least, I want to take off the silly ring I have on my middle finger – just plain old silver, with a stone that probably came out of a plastic moulding machine.

And my dress ... oh, I shouldn't have worn this dress.

I can see people looking at it already. They're probably wondering why it doesn't have any interesting accents – it's plain black, with a little nip in the middle to give me an hourglass shape. And if they're not wondering that, they've got to be puzzling over the material. It's not silk or satin. I think you could most kindly call it a jersey-ish material, and I know that fact is showing.

I know I look drab next to Janos – but he doesn't allow me to linger on that thought for long. It's just too hard to keep up with those kinds of concerns, when the man you're with can't stop touching you. He takes my hand and guides me into my seat, then once we're sitting down he does something even sweeter.

He touches a finger to the side of my face and brushes away a hair that's fallen there.

I swear, it's the tenderest caress I've ever been party to – and not just because of the feel of it. There's something about his intent in touching me that way. Something about the way he looks at me ke l stone when he does it.

It's like only I exist, in this room swimming with sophisticated people.

And he wants to make sure I know that, above all other things.

'What would you like, then?' he asks, but he keeps

that hand on me as he pores over the menu. Now it's at the back of my neck, stroking and stroking, almost hypnotically. I can hardly pick up my own menu to look – I'm too preoccupied with him and his attentions.

But who could blame me? It isn't just the solicitousness. It's the whole of him, from the black of his hair to the cut of his suit. He's so handsome I can hardly stand it, and in ways I hadn't really appreciated before. I like the lines around his eyes – so deep below and yet fainter as they fan out – and the firm slant of his jaw. Just below his lower lip is a little groove, faint as a thumbprint.

It's completely compelling, and I can't help exploring it with my eyes.

Much to his amusement.

'Are you enjoying the view?'

'I wasn't staring that much.'

'No? Ah, well, that is a pity.'

'Why is it a pity?'

'Because I like the thought of you looking,' he says, and oh, I don't know what to feel after that. There's some embarrassment and a touch of indignation, swiftly followed by the sweetest surge of warmth that spreads and spreads through most of my body. He likes me looking. He revels in my appreciation, just as I revel in his.

It's wonderful – even if I still feel the need to explain.

'I can't seem to help it.'

'I wouldn't worry. The feeling's mutual,' he says, before

doing his best to prove it. He pulls me closer in one firm move, sliding me over the soft red velvet cushions of this booth we've commandeered. And when our bodies are almost sandwiched together – knee to knee and hip to hip – he puts an arm around my shoulders.

And that's not even the good part.

No, the good part is the feel of his hand on my back, spreading out to touch every inch he possibly can. It's the long slow rub he does, back and forth and back and forth and finally … there's the way he cups my face. He actually combs his fingers into my hair, and rests his thumb on my jaw.

And then he strokes me there, in such a familiar way it's almost as though he's done it a thousand times before. We sit like this all the time, with his hand on my face and his eyes exploring every facet of my features. There's nothing the least bit unusual about any of it, despite the pounding of my heart and the shaking and this overwhelming certainty –

'You want to kiss me, don't you?' I whisper, and though I don't intend it to be a game of truth and lies, I can see he takes it that way. He struggles for a second, mouth tightening. Eyes half-amused and half-frustrated – unable to say yes but knowing what no will mean. No will mean he's a liar, and liars have to pay the price.

Which leaves him stranded between the two, just like I always am.

'I didn't appreciate how hard this game was, before,' he says finally, and I can't help laughing. Just a little – more of an exhalation than anything else.

But it suits my words so well.

'You're damned if you do, and damned if you don't.'

'That's a good way to put it.'

'So should k‘

'You don't really need to,' he says, and then after the most excruciating pause of my life he says the rest. Oh, he says so much more. 'I want to kiss you. I want to so badly I can barely think of anything else. When you enter a room it's my only thought, and it torments me night and day.'

'Then don't let it. I'm right here.'

'It's not as easy as you make it sound.'

'Why not? You've held my hand, you've taken me out. You've stayed with me when I asked you to and now you're holding me in your arms,' I say, though I'm sure I'm not making any sense. My words feel all rushed and garbled, and somehow seared around the edges. They're probably burning him on their way out. 'I think you're doing OK with intimacy.'

'Maybe it isn't intimacy I lack. Maybe I've just grown too used to the way things were, and can hardly remember how to begin something like this.'

'Well, the hand on my face is an excellent start.'

'Is that so?' he says, but he knows it is. Every time he

198

strokes that thumb over the bone, my eyes try to drift closed. My entire body leans in. If he wasn't so effectively holding me here, I'd simply go for it.

But as it is I have to wait.

Oh, it's agony to wait.

'It's definitely so.'

'And what about the way I'm holding you?'

'Oh, there's nothing better,' I say, voice so breathless it's embarrassing.

Or at least, it would be embarrassing, if he wasn't doing the same right back to me. I can feel his warm breath against my lips, as rapid as a butterfly's wing. And that heat I was sure I was exuding ... it's rolling right back at me in great waves.

'We're not even going to make it through the first course, are we?' he asks, which is a pretty pragmatic thing to point out. I'd think he was back in the board-room, doling out tedious questions – if it were not for the way he looks and feels against me. He's practically biting the air between us.

And I'm biting it back.

'It's looking very unlikely,' I say, and that's all it takes. That's the tipping point – just those four innocuous words. I don't know why they are or what made them so special, but once they're spoken I just reach out and grasp his shoulder.

I just get great handfuls of his suit, hard enough to

pop the seams. I'm probably ruining something worth more than my apartment, but I don't care. I need to grab him. I need to clutch at him and tear at him and pull him close.

And apparently, he needs to do the same to me. That hand actually clenches in my hair – not hard enough to hurt but certainly hard enough to make me notice. This heated pulse goes through my sex the second he does it, and I know my nipples are stiff beneath this thin material. They must look obscene, but I'm hardly bothered by that either.

All that matters is the way he's angling my face up to his, thumb and forefinger still on my jaw and my chin. It makes me think of someone taking a drink, only the drink in question is my lips. He wants to taste me there, and oh, that's exactly what it feels like.

He doesn't press his mouth to mine, too hard and too frantic. He just dips in, getting a little of me on his lips before going back for something deeper and sweeter. It's so much sweeter I could cry. I feel like I've been waiting for this for a thousand years, a ksanelsnd, if his reaction is anything to go by, so has he.

In fact, I think he might have been waiting longer than that. The second he's gotten a feel for it he pulls me closer, as though he's never going to let me go now. He wants to kiss me like this for ever, and I have absolutely no objections.

Anyone would want to be kissed like this for ever. His mouth is as soft as butter and, instead of the usual press and slant and part, he just insinuates himself against me. His lips roll over mine, which is enough to make me melt all on its own.

But then there's the way he *watches* me.

I don't see it at first. I'm too busy closing my eyes, savouring every inch of this experience. However, after a while I have to look. This strange tension just takes hold of me, building and building until I can't do anything but.

And when I do, I see him looking, too. I see his eyes trailing all over my face, just like before. Only now it's ten times more intense. Now he seems to be actively searching for something – a reaction? A sense that I'm enjoying myself?

Though if it's the latter, he could well be crazy. I'm so obviously enjoying myself even the waiter can see it. His face is a picture when Janos briefly parts from me to wave him away, and I know it's mostly for me. There's a hint of disgust in there that only women get, when they seem like the sort who loves sex.

But I don't care. He *kissed* me.

And he's not finished yet.

He kisses me until my mouth is sore from his stubble, and most likely cherry red. Then, when he sees its ripe colour, he kisses me more to make up for it. He kisses me between courses and in the middle of them too, licking chocolate from my lips when I accidentally make a mess – so uncaring of whatever anyone in here might think.

I see them looking, from time to time. And there are moments when it twists something inside me – that little knot of not-good-enough, not smooth enough, not elegant enough. But I can't keep focusing on it, when he's saying things like 'Oh, I'd forgotten how good this could be.'

It just twangs a note inside me to hear him say that, and to see him being this relaxed and happy. He's almost smiling and he keeps shaking his head – like he can't quite get over this thing he's just done. And once we're outside he goes one further.

He actually lifts me off my feet, as though we're in some movie about romance and love and all the things I didn't think he was capable of. Hell, I didn't think *I* was capable of them. I watch films like that and roll my eyes, so certain that nothing of the kind ever happens in real life.

Men don't lift women up and spin them around, as rain starts to delicately fall and the music from across the street rises to a crescendo. They don't, they don't, and yet that's definitely what's happening here. He even sets me down in this slightly awestruck way that suggests he can't believe I'm real.

Maybe I'm not.

Maybe this is just a movie – a freeze-frame of total happiness, mine for a moment but soon gone. And if that's the case, well, I'm going to catch it while I can. I'm going to look up at him with all the love inside me, just like they do in those romantic scenes. And I'm going to let him lean down in this unbearably tender way to taste my kisses again.

I'm going to let him, because I know the credits are coming.

And I just want to hold on a little bit longer.

Chapter Thirteen

He doesn't take me to The Harrington. He takes me to some other place, and it's only when we're in the elevator that it slowly starts to dawn on me.

This is where he lives. I can tell it is, before he's pressed the button for the penthouse. The whole building is just so him it can't be anything but, from the burnished steel that seems to be almost everywhere, to the smooth, clean lines and minimalistic approach to decoration. There no pictures on the walls or unnecessary plants in the corners, and that lack of fussiness suits him to a T.

He fits right in – but I'm more keenly aware than ever that I don't. I can see my reflection in the over-polished surfaces in this elevator, and I look even worse than I did before. My hair has ceased any attempt to stay up, and is now making a serious bid for freedom – as is my dress. And my mouth ...

Oh, Lord, I look like I've been eating jam. I want to rub myself and get it all off, only there's nothing there to remove.

He's just kissed me into this red-lipped mess, and if he gets his way he's going to do it again. While I'm busy with my silly doubts and concerns, he's sliding a hand around my waist.

And then the hand dips lower – which wouldn't be a problem.

If someone else hadn't just stepped into the elevator.

He nods at Janos before turning to face the doors, and Janos nods back as though this is just an ordinary, everyday meeting. You'd never know he had a hand on my bottom, or that the hand is currently gathering up my dress at the back. In fact, he does it so subtly that I can't even tell when I flick my gaze to my reflection.

My legs are closed so you can't see it rising between them. And somehow, the material is barely stirring at the front. He must be doing the whole thing so delicately, so carefully – but it doesn't feel that way. It feels as though he's running white-hot coals along the backs of my thighs and the curve of my ass. My legs keep wanting to bend, and there's already sweat on my upper lip.

I almost turn to him and say:

'Are you *trying* to make me look worse?'

But the truth is, I don't really need to. I already know the answer: *yes yes yes.* He wants me to look worse – only to him it's probably better. I bet he loves me all sluttish like this, with my hair in disarray and my red, red mouth and my complete lack of underwear.

Though somehow, I don't think he guessed that last

one. Oh, no – he didn't guess it at all. His hand freezes the second he gets to the place where my panties should be, and I hear his slight intake of breath. The guy in here with us hears his slight intake of breath.

It's too loud for someone like him but oh, so welcome because of that fact. I don't think there's anything I like more than throwing him for a loop, and I've definitely succeeded here. His movements go from subtle and cautious to greedy and frantic in the space of a couple of seconds. I can actually see my dress stirring, now, though he hardly seems to care.

He just wants to fondle my bare ass. He wants to squeeze and grope and all the other good words that usually don't apply to him, and once he's finished thoroughly exploring the tame parts, he progresses to something much worse.

Now it's *my* turn to be shocked. I actually go up on tiptoe the moment he touches me there. Maybe doing so will help me get away.

But of course it do s corseesn't. He just follows me with his hand, pressing and pressing in a place that makes my cheeks flame. I can see the bright red colour in the glossy doors, and unfortunately so can our fellow passenger. I catch him glancing at the sudden bloom of colour, and then, horror of horrors – he looks back at me.

While I silently pray for Janos to stop. I'm very close to whimpering or shuddering or just something that will give the game away, and the pressure is getting worse by the second. At the moment, he's only touching that strip of skin just above the more important parts, but I know he's slowly working his way down.

And it isn't going to take him long, either. All the kissing has made a slippery mess of me, so really all he has to do is let the lubrication do the work. He barely has to push or squirm or work his way there. Everything just parts for him, and he glides down to the worst possible place he could touch.

Don't, I think at him, but it's too late for that. It's too late for anything. If I glance at Janos, the stranger will know – and the same goes if I make any kind of revealing noise. He's just paying too much attention now, though I think he's trying to pretend he's not. He feigns interest in something he doesn't actually have in his pocket, and after a second of this unbearable tension he lets out this little cough.

Like he's giving us a chance to stop, maybe.

Though if he is, he should probably know:

That's *never* going to happen. His only possible respite is the ding of the lift arriving at a floor, which seems to be taking a thousand years to come. Otherwise, he's trapped in here with a man who thinks nothing of stroking his companion's ass and pussy, and a woman who couldn't ask him to stop if the lift had a million people in it. We could be surrounded by nuns and I wouldn't say a single word, because the truth is:

I don't *want* him to stop.

Oh, sure, I might say I do. And it's possible I squirm, and seem like I'm trying to get away. But if I'm being honest, getting away sounds like a terrible, terrible idea. The pleasure will undoubtedly cease if I do, and I never want that to happen. I want it with me all the time, constantly, twenty-four-seven. I want to go to work with this pulsing ache between my legs, and sit in fancy theatres with it still beating there.

And the more he does this – the more firmly he strokes over my now slick asshole and my greedy, grasping pussy – the stronger that feeling gets. I'm on the verge of not caring whether the stranger sees and knows or not, when the lift dings at floor twenty-four. In fact, I'm so far past my own restraints I could rock against the maddening fingers. I could moan and beg him for more. I'm so stuffed with fizzing, searing sensation I've gone all mindless, and another moment would have seen me suddenly pin Janos against the wall of the elevator.

But, thankfully, I manage to wait until the doors are closed again.

After which, all bets are off. I lunge at him like a woman possessed, furious at him for teasing me like that but oh, so grateful that he did. Oh, God, he has no idea how grateful I am for the things he does and the feelings he gives me. It's not just the kissing, or this little slice of elevator kink – it's everything.

The way he held me outside, the sense of how serious things are becoming and how quickly they could end … it's all just too much. I have to take hold of him. I have to seize him by the lapels, barely thinking of the disaster I've made of his suit. The right shoulder is still oddly bunched from the grab I made in the restaurant, and a b sranisautton definitely pops when I do this. But it doesn't seem to matter to him.

How could it?

He's far too busy looking at me with wild eyes – eyes that seem so familiar. I've seen that exact stare somewhere before, and after a moment I realise where.

They were reflected back at me in the elevator door, about thirty seconds ago. They're the same as mine, right down to the way they widen when I run a hand down over his body, and darken when he realises what I'm doing. I'm going to stroke his cock the way he stroked my pussy, and I'm going to do it until he's so stiff he can't think straight.

Or at least that's the plan. But it's harder to enact once I get there and find him already solid beneath the material. Yeah, it's much harder then. I go still and my hand pauses mid-stroke, every single inch of me flushing with the knowledge that I did this to him.

Though I should have guessed.

I don't know why I find it so hard to guess. He makes it abundantly clear in so many different ways, from the looks to the words to the way he grabs me in return – because he does. He takes hold of me as though *I* was tormenting *him*, and clasps my face in his big hands. Then, once he has me, he reverses our positions. He spins me around until I'm the one with their back to the wall, and he's the one pinning me there.

And he really pins me too. He's not satisfied with just a little pressure – he has to gather up my wrists and hold them above my head, until it feels like I'm dangling there. My body bows and my feet seem to scrabble for purchase, which sounds like a bad thing, I know. It should be really uncomfortable and overly aggressive.

Only it isn't.

It feels so good I gasp a little, about a second before his mouth descends on mine. And though we spent the last seventeen years smooching each other's face off, the thrill is still there. It's still ripe inside me, bursting at the idea of him giving in like this, of him stepping over his own personal boundaries and just going for it.

And boy, does he ever go for it. He stops the lift with one bat of his hand, so I know he means business. But then his mouth connects with mine again – rough and soft and most of all *open* – and *business* upgrades to something like *red alert*. I can actually feel his tongue, stroking hot and wet over mine. His hands cup my ass; his body grinds against mine.

That's his stiff cock I can feel against my right thigh.

It's a wonder I can breathe or think. I can't breathe or think. I keep babbling at him to just fuck me, fuck me, fuck me, even though we're in an elevator in his expensive building. There's probably a camera in the corner, filming our every move. In a moment the lift will make a grinding noise and some security guard or maintenance man will burst in, rushing to the aid of one of their fabulously wealthy patrons.

But, strangely, the thought only seems to heighten my excitement. It makes me louder; it makes me more aggressive. I claw at his back with hands like talons, determined to finish the job on his perfect suit. By the time I'm done I want it in ribbons – or at least I want him to react to what I'm doing.

And he does. He gets hold of my wrists again and pins them back above my head. Then, just as I'm gasping over that, he murmurs words in my ear. 'Keep them there,' he says, in a way that makes my eyes drift closed. I could live inside that tone – so heavy with authority, and yet still shaky with need. It's the perfect combination of his commanding, controlling s, cng in side and that new need to just do and take and be.

He no longer has to stop and organise everything. He just shoves my dress up around my hips. He just makes me stand like that, with my hands against the metal and my heart going a mile a minute – mainly because I just don't know what he might do in this state. I'm sure there were limits before, but there aren't any more. He could fuck my pussy, or my ass, or my mouth, or some unholy combination of all three. He could take off all my clothes and make me stand in front of a camera that probably isn't there, or maybe … God, maybe he intends to wait until someone *does* come to our rescue.

Maybe he's thinking of some big, aggressive maintenance man, and what he might do to me if he finds me in here naked and on my knees. They could share me, I think, though the second I do I know who really wants these things.

It isn't him.

It's me. I want these things. I'm flushed with fear and so on edge, but I'm the one putting myself there. I like the way my heart races. I love the taste of adrenaline in my mouth, and the feel of it coursing through my limbs.

And most of all, I love him for giving it to me – this world of infinite possibilities. No man actually does come into the elevator, but it doesn't matter. It only matters that my head is full of that idea, when he spreads my thighs apart. It only matters that I'm thinking of servicing seventeen men when he grabs between my legs – mainly because my arousal is so intense by this point that I come the second he does.

I come in a wet rush all over his hand, bucking and moaning and saying all the things I probably shouldn't. 'Oh, yeah fill my mouth,' I tell him, but I'm not just talking to him. I'm talking to a group of strangers, as they take turns with me.

Not that it makes any difference to Janos. His face goes bright and startled the second he realises what's happening to me, before slowly sliding into that delicious feral need. Teeth bared, eyes hooded – God, he drives me crazy when he looks at me that way. And he drives me even crazier when he says in a guttural voice:

'Get on your knees, then.'

Of course I obey him. I have to obey him. My legs no longer want to hold me up, and even if they did I wouldn't stay standing. I'm too eager to fulfil this little fantasy, for all kinds of reasons. There's the idea of those men ... the thrill of doing what he says ... and finally, there's the act itself.

I've never sucked his cock before.

Oh, I've dreamt about it. I've lain in bed with my hand between my legs, and imagined him fisting a hand in my hair, grunting at me to do it, pushing past my lips in one hot thrust. But now I'm getting the reality, and oh, the reality is so much sweeter.

His voice isn't a grunt. It's this rough, gravelly groan, as he unbuttons his trousers. And he doesn't fist his hand in my hair – he guides me into position, slowly stroking through the strands in a way that sends electric shivers down my spine.

By the time he eases his cock out, I'm practically

drooling. I don't even stop for him to say anything more – I just take him in my mouth, sucking and licking until he's the only thing I can taste and feel. He's salt-sweet and smooth as silk, so hot he almost burns my tongue. And of course he's hard.

Oh, God, he's so hard I could come all over again, just at the feel of it. Just at the *sight* of it. The shaft is so stiff it's almost curving upwards, and the head is swollen enough to pose a problem. I can hardly get the whole thing se wme even in my mouth – though naturally I persevere. And when I fail – when I gag and strain too hard – I make do with a frantic licking and lapping that he definitely seems to appreciate.

'Oh, what a filthy little cocksucker you are,' he says, and although I should probably be offended my body just doesn't take it that way. Instead, my sex thrums and thrums to hear him say it, and my already flushed face heats even further. I'm almost a furnace by this point, burning bright enough to rival the sun.

If he keeps standing this close he's going to go up in flames, though I don't think he'd care. He's leaning over me now, one hand on the wall above my head, and the longer this goes on the more he seems to need that support. His legs are almost trembling and I can feel his hips rocking back and forth in this crazily exciting way. In a second he'll be shoving his cock past my lips, and I don't know what will happen then.

I might come again. I'm already close, despite the lack of contact. Just the taste of his pre-come is enough to make me ache between my legs, and the feel of him thrusting almost pushes me the rest of the way.

But it's the sound of him that really does me in. It's the rough note to his voice, and the low moan that runs beneath it. 'Yes, yes, take it, just like that,' he tells me. Apparently, the noises weren't enough on their own. He has to add words to the mix, to ensure my complete and total destruction – and he succeeds admirably.

My whole body blooms with sensation at the 'yes' and the 'take'. And then he lets out a long, low groan and I jerk as though struck. My hands snap forward of their own accord, to grab great fistfuls of his trousers. I have to grab great fistfuls of his trousers.

I need something to hold onto.

And apparently so does he. The hand in my hair suddenly tightens, and the one he had pressed to the wall comes down heavily on my shoulder – like he has to lean on me. He needs to prop himself against something, and after a second I understand why. I feel it thrumming through his body and hear it rushing out through those desperate moans.

And then his cock swells in my mouth, and ohhhh, yes, that's it, that's it. Flood my mouth, I think, and he does just that. His thick spend spurts over my tongue in long ribbons, so copious I can't quite contain it. I have to move back, but of course the second I do he simply finishes all over my face.

He makes a mess of me, and I have to admit:

I kind of like it.

I like the way he pumps his cock to eke out the last of his orgasm, swift and brutal and slick. And I like the look he gives me as he does it, too – every feature tense with pleasure, but shot through with a kind of wonderment. He didn't expect me to be this way, I'm certain. He had no idea that I'd be willing to kneel on the floor of an elevator, with his come staining most of my face.

But that's OK.

Neither did I.

And I certainly didn't know that I could stand with that slickness still all over me, and look right into his eyes. Then just when he's about to say something, just when he's about to reach up and clean me off, I go one better than that. I lean forward, on tiptoe.

And I kiss his shocked mouth, with my utterly filthy one.

Chapter Fourteen

He gets me on all fours, like before. Only it's not like before at all. Things have shifted between us, to this intense point of vof swt rus no return. His boundaries are down and he's no longer the deliberate, careful person he was before – though, in all honesty, neither am I. Of course I'm still fizzing with that thrilling fear, and part of me wants to jump off the bed and run right out of his apartment before anything insane can happen.

But that part is getting smaller all the time. It's being consumed by the desire to have him do anything, just anything, all at once and in a big muddle. I'm rocking on the bed and kind of mewling like an impatient child – and that's before he's taken all of my clothes off. After they've been stripped away I'm almost insane.

I can't even describe the sound I'm making. It's a keening, desperate noise, made worse by the little teasing passes he keeps doing. As he unhooks my bra he catches my stiff nipple between thumb and forefinger, and just plucks at a little. And when I squirm over the sensation, he wets his fingertips and repeats the action.

And it's obvious why.

Because it makes it worse. Oh, that hint of slipperiness makes it so much worse. I almost beg him not to do it, but the desire to have him continue fights back. I want him to play with my tight nipples until I come and come and come, and I'm pretty sure I could do it. Those odd, faintly blooming orgasms in the elevator tell me I can, but this time he doesn't let me get that far. He doesn't make any sounds to push me into it, and he stops short of anything like a real fondle.

He's going to make me wait this time, I'm sure.

It's clear before he's even produced the handcuffs, though especially so once I feel them clicking around my wrists. I've got my eyes closed and hardly know what he's doing – until that cold steel connects.

Then I understand. Yeah, I understand all the way through me, at that point. I just hear the sound like a gunshot going off, and that whimpering I've been doing becomes a series of frantic gasps. I'm suddenly panting like a well-run racehorse, mind full of all the possible reasons for a move like this. Does he want me flummoxed and flushed, already raw before he's done anything? It seems likely, but other ideas occur.

Like … maybe he doesn't want me to resist. He wants me tied and restrained and unable to do a thing, and oh, I wish that thought wasn't quite so electric. It sizzles and pops in a hundred weird places, like inside my gums and behind my knees, and the second I start to feel it I almost fall face down into his enormous bed.

But he saves me. He catches me, and keeps me upright. And he says soothing things, designed to calm my nerves and steady my resolve – or at least I think that's the intention. It's hard to tell when the soothing things are being said in a voice so choked with lust I'm surprised he manages to get out a single word.

He's as far gone as I am.

Which doesn't bode well for me, I have to say. He's probably going to do something crazy to me – something he doesn't have any control over.

And then he suddenly does the crazy thing, and it's *still* somehow a shock. I lurch forward again the second he does it, but this time he's prepared for it. He curls a hand around my hip, to keep me in place – and it works. However, I've no idea if it does so because his touch is so firm and sure and solid, or because the sensation is so strange I just have to experience some more of it.

I've never had anyone lick me there before.

Oh, sure, a couple of past boyfriends might have got a little lost on their way to other destinations. And once some guy passed out {uy wev drunk in that general area. I think I felt him drool a little over that one far too sensitive spot.

But this is different. This is *intentional*. He's intentionally licking over my tightly clenched asshole, and I know he is for certain because he isn't just working his way in there, in tiny tentative strokes. He's using his free hand to spread me open, and is actively working over that place in long, wet laps.

As though he likes it, I think, and then my mind tries to fly away. It visits calmer shores, where everything is reasonable and rational – because surely no one *enjoys* doing something like this. It can't possibly be enjoyable.

To anyone but me.

Oh, Jesus, it's so enjoyable to me. In all honesty, I don't see how it could be anything but. It just turns the dial inside me – the one that apparently loves things that seem filthy and naughty and forbidden. He shouldn't be touching me there, I think, and suddenly everything is so much more exciting. He isn't just touching me, after all. He's licking me, with his eager and oh so slippery tongue. He slides it over my entrance, setting off landmines of sensation that knock me sideways.

I had no idea there were so many nerve-endings – that being licked there could narrow your entire focus down to just that and nothing else. It's all I can do to keep breathing. I'm sure my heart's about to stop, to make way for this one unbelievable sensation. Then just when I'm about to pass out from it, he pulls away.

And replaces his tongue with something else – something slicker and more slippery but, oddly, so much cooler. It's almost soothing against my overheated skin as he slowly rubs and works it over me ... until I realise what it is.

After that, it's not soothing at all. It makes my fists clench and my back arch, that urge to both stay and get away reaching some kind of crescendo. Any more of this and I'm going to tear in two, but still he continues. Still he keeps on making a slick mess of me with the lube I know he's using. It's not thin enough to be saliva, so, really, what else could it be?

And more importantly, what else could it mean?

He's going to fuck my ass, I know. It's obvious before that maddening finger starts to exert some pressure, then impossible to deny once it has. I can feel that slow, insinuating push, feel it all the way up to the roots of my hair, almost painful but oh, so sweet at the same time. The slipperiness just adds this tingling, silky sensation that's pretty much driving me wild – and ultimately, that's what lets him in.

I flood with pleasure and everything just relaxes. Everything gives, in this rush I'm not quite ready for, and then suddenly I'm being spread open. His thick finger slides in, far bigger than it had ever seemed before. When he's busy doing ordinary things it looks almost normal, but now that it's inside me, slowly working back and forth ...

It's enormous. It's all I can focus on – that smooth slide, that sense of something intruding. Or at least it's all I can focus on until he speaks.

And then there's nothing but the sound of his voice.

'Yeah, you like that, don't you,' he says, but he doesn't really need me to answer. It's obvious how much I like it. I'm moaning and rocking back against his hand, and when he asks me if I'd like his cock there I don't tell him no.

I tell him:

'Oh, God, yes, yes, do my ass.'

'You want me to fuck it?'

'Ahhh {tife. The slh, yes, yes, go on.'

'You want my cock easing into that tight little hole?' he asks, and this time I think he really wants to know. There's a building note of incredulity in his voice, like he can hardly believe I want this. Or else he can hardly believe he's going to do it.

Either way, the answer is the same.

'I want it, oh, I want it,' I say, because I do – though I'm not sure if the reasoning is the same as it was a moment ago. Before, it was all about getting more of this strange pleasure, but now there's another layer. There's the thought of him doing something that makes his voice all shaky like that, and his hand so unsteady on my hip. It's almost as though he's never done this before.

And oh, that idea is thrilling. It makes me clench hard around his still working finger – much to his delight and possible consternation. He lets out a little gasp, followed by a stream of Hungarian words that make absolutely no sense to me.

Yet they make all the sense in the world. They spell out his feelings, as clear as day: *this is more than I can handle.*

However, he doesn't stop. He barely pauses. I hear his zipper go and the snap of rubber, and then a terrible absence. That slick finger leaves me, in a way that makes me whine and beg – but I don't have to do it for long. He mutters something more in that glorious, guttural language – half prayer and half praise – and then I feel the most incredible pressure. I feel the blunt head of his cock, rubbing and pushing against my entrance.

And just when I'm thinking he can't possibly fit ... just when I'm sure I can't take him ... everything gives again, and he glides in as though it's nothing, absolutely nothing. He's not fucking my ass. I'm not taking his big cock in my most private place.

This is all completely easy and ordinary, even if I know to the marrow of my bones that it's not. The way he's cursing and gasping tells me it's not. His hands are coated in perspiration, and when I glance over my shoulder at him he looks like someone who's lost his way. I can almost feel him reaching out for me with his eyes, and though that seems like a complete impossibility the urge to help takes over anyway.

It's a blind instinct, like feeling for someone's hand in the dark. I don't know if he needs it and am kind of sure he doesn't, but the words are there and I want to offer them.

'You can say the safe word, if you want,' I tell him, and for a second there's such a stripe of vulnerability on his handsome face. It breaks him in two, right down the middle, in a way that makes me think he can never be put back together again. He'll never be the same now, and I know he won't, because after a second he just reaches down and gathers me up. He pulls me close to him, my back to his front. My face in his hands.

And then he kisses me, he kisses me, he kisses me. He puts his mouth on my mouth as though that is the transgressive thing, while his cock eases back and forth in that forbidden place. My hands are chained and my ass is getting the fucking of a lifetime, but this one act of intimacy is so much more searing.

And not just for him. Oh, God, it's not just for him at all. It burns through me, too, completely unexpected and totally unprepared for. I'm not ready, I think, I'm not ready, but it's too late for that now. The fire is already raging, whether I want it to or not. In fact, I'm pretty sure he's stoking the flames higher as I flounder in the middle of the inferno.

He doesn't just kiss me – he covers my throat with one hand, in a way that's s {ay wheno tender and adoring I can hardly stand it. Suddenly it's me who wants to say the safe word, though it's not for any reason I ever thought I'd need it for. It's for messy feelings and gushing emotion, as brutal and shocking as any kinky sex.

I love him, I realise. And as we stumble towards our pleasure – heaving and hauling and grasping at each other desperately – I realise something even more subversive:

He loves me too.

Chapter Fifteen

I jerk awake in the middle of the night, half-panicked and completely unsure of where I am. Everything smells so unfamiliar – like his cologne and whatever his cadre of servants wash his sheets in – and, when I reach out for something to reassure me, there isn't anything there. All I can feel is the vast and empty acres of his immense bed, coated in sheets that make me think of skating rinks.

It's too cold and too smooth, and no matter how hard I search I can't find him. He must have got up, I think, but I'm not sure if that's really the discomfiting part. In fact, I know it's not the discomfiting part, because when I finally find him after seventeen years spent wandering in this bed desert, I don't feel relieved.

I feel unsettled. Somehow, somehow … I've slept with him. We're sleeping in the same bed, like a real couple who do real things together. And though I've done this before with other people, the idea of doing it with him is jarring. Did he even ask me to stay? I don't think he did, and yet here I am anyway – like some interloper in his world of cold liaisons and crisp sheets. In a moment he'll probably wake up and realise I'm still here, then point at the door like some silent harbinger of doom.

And the fact that he doesn't is disturbing in itself. I creep closer and he doesn't even stir. Apparently, my presence hardly troubles him at all. He's quite content to remain asleep, no matter how close I get. I actually manage to lift the sheets off his shockingly naked body, and I'm poised for a reaction that never comes.

I think I expect his hand to lash out and grab my wrist, though I'm not sure why. Because this is the first time I've really seen him naked? Up to this point I suppose it had seemed like something secret ... something he had to hide beneath his Prada suit of armour and his numerous rules.

But now I guess all of that is gone. He doesn't need it any more. He can just lie here bare and exposed, while I gingerly peel back the covers like *I'm* the panicked one.

Even though I'm not. I'm absolutely not. I'm just thrilled and startled by the sight of him, so fleshy and solid and real. When he's wearing his jacket and his shirt and his tie, you could almost believe that there's nothing but steel underneath. He's not made out of flesh and bone. He's made out of moveable mechanical parts.

Only he's not, he's not at all.

He's covered in rough hair, and much broader across the chest than his suit ever implies. Of course, he's always looked big in it. I've known right from the start that he isn't a small man. But to see it now up close and so naked … to see the jut of his collarbone like something found in a dinosaur's graveyard … to see his thick but firm pectoral muscles and shoulders like an enormous yoke …

It's unnerving. I feel like I'm sanding away the topsoil to get at the bones of some mythical creature beneath. Every new revelation makes me wonder what I'm going to find next, as though he doesn't actually have ordinary legs below th ~back ign="juste waist. He has great furred things that bend the wrong way and possibly end in heavy hooves.

Like that story I read as a child, about a woman who takes some charming guy home with her for some casual sex, then realises too late who he really is: the Devil, Satan, Beelzebub. He's just lurking there inside his man-skin, and when she least expects it he springs the trap and eats her heart whole while she's still breathing.

Or at least I think that's the way the story ends. I could be misremembering. It could be *her* who eats *his* heart while he still sleeps, and takes his power for her own.

In fact, I'm pretty sure that was the real finale.

So why am I thinking of another one? Why can I see her behind my eyes, with some great gaping wound in her chest? It's a ridiculous image, really, when you think about it, and a stupid story that has no bearing on anything here.

Which doesn't explain why I drop the sheets.

I mean, it's not as if I'm actually going to find anything. He's just a man, if 'just' is the kind of word you can apply to someone like Janos. And he's definitely not going to leave me with a sucking wound in my chest, either literally … or otherwise.

I'm safe, I think.

It's just that I don't feel it. I'm all restless and agitated, and completely unable to lie back down. I have to get up just to keep this buzzing, brittle sensation at bay, but when I do it doesn't get any better. I pad out of his plush bedroom and into a hallway that stretches on forever, and I'm immediately unsettled by the silence and the darkness and the sense that I'll never find my way out.

I have to grope along the walls for a light switch that probably isn't there – it's voice-activated, I bet, or maybe connected to him telepathically – until finally I discover a door.

Sadly, however, it doesn't lead to the relative sanctuary of a bathroom. It takes me to that enormous airy living space that spans the entire length of his apartment. I glimpsed it on the way in, but let it drift below the sex haze I was operating under.

And now it's back in all of its opulent insanity, both better and worse than I ever imagined it. There isn't much furniture, so I can't get too nervous about some platinum-plated this, or some antique that. In fact, there's so little in here you'd be justified in thinking the place was uninhabited. It looks rather like a showroom, with that smart and sharp-edged couch and the unobtrusive prints on the walls. Of course, they're probably originals. Hell, for all I know they're original Picassos.

But that's not the problem.

No, the problem is the wall of glass that dominates the place – no curtains, no blinds, no fancy coverings that I'm too plebeian to have heard of. Just a great glossy expanse, with a view so glorious it's almost intimidating. The entire city is beyond that wall, spread out in a mosaic of tiny lights and dancing shadows, near blue-tinged in the darkness.

And it's beautiful. I never knew the city could be so beautiful, not even after watching a thousand movies that start off with this very thing – the aerial view of some vast metropolis, steely and cold and just waiting for something terrible to happen. But then in the movies there's always a patina of lifelessness, as though London is just an unfeeling backdrop.

Whereas here it seethes with life.

It makes me want to cry, though I'm not entirely sure why. Because I've never really seen anything like this before?

Or is it because I've never been allowed to? I've gone through the motions for so long, I never realised my way was barred. I didn't know I was so small in a world that has things like this in it – this view, this life, this everything – and it's all so vibrant that emotion simply wells up inside me.

Yet I don't even think he notices. What stuns and scares me is, to Janos, this is just a backdrop, always expected but never admired. He doesn't have to admire it. He paid for it with money that means nothing to him, despite how much it could mean to so many people. It means something to *me* and I don't even need it. I'm not hungry, or cold, or poor.

But I'm still five hundred levels below whatever this is – and I always will be. I'll always worry that I'm sitting wrong on seats too expensive for my terrible clothes. And there'll for ever be that moment when I wonder if I've made a gaffe, or stood in awe of something when I should have been blasé.

I can't be blasé about this stuff. It makes me do funny things, like stand here in the middle of the night half-mesmerised by a view of the city. I even put my hand up to the glass, as though I might be able to reach through and touch it.

And then I hear his voice from the bedroom, and I react in an even stranger manner. I jerk around too fast, the way people do when they've been caught doing something bad. I had my hand in the cookie jar and he's just seen me, and now I have to explain. But how to explain this? How to explain this feeling going through me?

'I feel so small' sounds like a ridiculous thing to say, even to me. And 'the sight of the city moved me' is even worse. His eyes will go bright with amusement, the way they do, and that smile will hook the corner of his mouth.

While I quietly die inside.

In fact, I think I'm dying already. I lumber back to the bedroom like there are weights in my feet, still thinking of views and gaffes and the way he lives his life. I just can't shake that image of him walking past that window without so much as a second glance, even if I know that may not be entirely true. Perhaps he looks all the time, and I'm just being unfair. Maybe he takes none of this for granted at all.

Though even if he doesn't, his effortlessness is still real. I know it is. I've seen it first hand, in the way he walks and talks and moves inside his own skin. He belongs in this world of wealth and power, no matter what I tell myself.

And I do not.

I can't even walk back into the bedroom. I just stand in the doorway, gazing in at him like some urchin with her face against the glass – though, granted, his utter nakedness might have something to do with this paralysis. He hasn't even got the covers over him any more. He's just lying there with everything out on show, to the point where it seems deliberate. Apparently he's grown tired of hiding behind his suits, and wants me to see all of him.

But now I'm the one who isn't ready. I've grown used to him one way and don't know how to process this other him, with his flagrant nudity and his willingness to let me sleep over and his soft words, spoken just as I'm about to stumble over to him. 'Come back to bed, love,' he says, and I'm stopped in my tracks all over again.

'Love', he said. And he didn't do it in Hungarian, either. He said it in English, so I can't possibly pretend it's anything else, like with *szeretett*. I've come close to looking that one up a number of times, and always turned away at the last second. If I turn away, I don't have to find out that fin" ait means adored or amazing. I can just imagine it means sweet piece of ass, and keep everything on an even keel.

Instead of it being like this.

This is like being on the bow of a boat as it tries to negotiate a tidal wave.

'What's the matter?' he asks, but it's impossible to explain. Most women don't mind when their incredibly wealthy sex buddy decides that he'd like to be something more. In fact, isn't that the goal, according to *Cosmo*? To get him to love you?

I'm sure it is, though I wish they'd at least offer advice on the other stuff. The surrounding stuff, such as *he's massively wealthy and you're not. Six easy steps to negotiating class- and money-based landmines.* Or how about: *confronting your feelings of unworthiness ... or* even *being someone's perfect amazing magical blow-job-giving girlfriend is not the be all and end all of existence.*

Yeah, I'd appreciate that last one. Of course it would be a bit of a steep change in direction for them, considering all the money they make from persuading women to feel bad about themselves. But I'm sure they could do it.

They could do it if they were in my shoes right now.

'Should I ask again, or would you rather stay standing there in a state of what looks like abject terror?'

'I'm fine, really.'

'People who say they're fine, really, usually mean the absolute opposite. And especially when their actions confirm this theory.'

He's not just talking about the refusal to come to the bed, quite obviously. There's also the way I'm picking at the door frame, as if there's actually something there to be picked at. And every now and then I'll pluck at the hem of this shirt I'm wearing – his shirt, to be exact. It's seventeen sizes too big and smells so divine I could curl up inside its depths and never come out again, and yet I keep worrying at it anyway.

If there was a loose thread I'd pull on it until everything unravelled.

'I was just ... wondering ...'

Oh, I know that's not a good place to start. It leaves me too many options, and all of them so dangerous. If I go with the wealth thing, he might be offended. Or maybe I'll be offended. Or worse: we'll work things out and live happily ever after.

Lord, I just don't know how to live happily ever after. I can see that now. It should have been clear before but it wasn't, and so here we are in hell.

'And what was it you were wondering about?'

'I don't know. I don't know. Give me a second to come up with something, OK?'

'All right,' he says, just like that. No amusement, no ruefulness. Just an acceptance of my foibles, and a deep patience with my needs. He doesn't want to rush me or push me, and is quite content to stay quiet and wait for whatever it is I want to say.

In fact he's been that way all along.

He just *is* that way, and I love him for it. I love him so much that I can feel tears sparking behind my eyes. And it's silly, it is, but I understand why it's happening. It's like when I was a kid, and won a prize for the best-written essay out of thousands of entries. And rather than accept it and be happy with it, I wrote a letter to the board to make sure they had it right. I couldn't believe that it was me.

I was so sure it couldn't be.

I'm *always* so surys< bee that it couldn't be.

'Come here, love,' he says again, and this time I go. I stumble to him and curl around his legs – mainly so he can't see my face, but also because it feels good. It feels so damned good to be with him, no matter what my

235

insecurities tell me. I *hate* my insecurities for telling me these things. I hate them for multiplying like bacteria, growing dark spots I don't want to know about and illnesses I'd rather not face.

'What is it?' he asks, and as he does so he strokes my hair back over and over, and runs a hand down over my side, and generally makes me want to say more than anything in the world. He'll understand, I think.

But I still can't quite do it.

'I don't know.'

'You do know.'

'You're right, I do. I just don't know how to say.'

'Start with the words. They're these things you use to express yourself.'

'Couldn't I just make a series of complicated hand gestures?'

'I think you've already done that. I couldn't quite get a read.'

'You – supreme overlord of my every thought – couldn't get a read?'

'It's easier to guess when it's something as simple as sex,' he says, then pauses just long enough for me to notice. 'It's harder when emotions are involved.'

Now it's my turn to pause, but probably for different reasons. He just wanted a moment to catch his breath or organise his thoughts, most likely, whereas I need the extra seconds to gather my courage.

'And are they involved, with us?'

'What do you think?'

'I think I'm much more nervous about being involved than I thought I would be.'

'That's not such a strange thing.'

'It isn't?'

'Of course not. How could it be? You began all of this with the expectation that it would just be sex, and nothing more.'

'Well … maybe,' I say, but I really mean yes. Yes, that's exactly what I thought would happen. I even went so far as to imagine him having some kind of emotional melt-down, before backing off just as things got too heated.

Only somehow that seems to be me.

I'm the one having the emotional meltdown.

I'm the one who's backing off.

'And you believed that I would only ever require that from you, and this belief kept you safe,' he continues, so casual and yet so sharp at the same time. The sentiment practically stings as it sinks in.

'I suppose that could be true.'

'And now suddenly things are different, and you're no longer sure how to behave.'

'You don't know that. How can you know that?' I ask, half-laughing – though even as I'm making this little non-sound I understand what's going to happen. I can feel it in the falsity of my own amusement, and in his slight hesitation.

With Janos, the silences say as much as the words.

However, the words make a particularly good show, on this occasion.

'Because I feel many of those same things myself,' he says, and this strange prickling sensation runs up the back of my neck. We're not different at all, my mind whispers, and in this sudden quiet I could almostI cwidth="1 believe it. It steals over me like a comforting blanket, soft and warm – and all the while he's stroking and stroking my hair.

It would be so easy not to tell him anything else.

Too easy, in fact.

'So do you feel like you're not good enough, too?'

'Good enough for what?

'For swanky soirées and magnificent views and fancy restaurants,' I say, and brace myself for his amusement. I'm facing away from him, but I know I'll still hear it in his voice. It curdles the tone, like a throat full of clotted cream – unmistakeable and unavoidable.

And also completely absent.

'Ah, so that's what has you so worried, my lovely one,' he tells me, and there's nothing sardonic about it, no wry amusement. He doesn't even say that last part in a sarcastic manner, which means something rather disturbing:

I have to accept it at face value.

He really means that I'm lovely and his, and that I

have a number above any of the others. I'm not four or seven or twenty thousand and nine.

I'm number one.

'Perhaps a little.'

'And by "little" you mean so much that it's making you dig your nails into your palms – not to mention the night-time wandering.'

'Maybe the latter was just about needing the bathroom.'

'So that's why you got up.'

'It could be.'

'Oh, I'm sure it could,' he says, in this faux-solemn way that's becoming very familiar. He's about to spring a trap, I think, and sure enough here it is: 'Care to tell me where the bathroom is?'

'Sure,' I tell him, brightly, but in my head I'm frantically counting doors and identifying likely culprits. It wasn't the one on the left, which means it absolutely must be –

'The first room on the right.'

'So you pissed in my study.'

I don't know what's more jarring: that he nails me so effectively, or that he used the word 'pissed'. It sounds absolutely profane in his glassy, accented voice, like seeing a nun spit or watching the Queen run naked around a playing field.

'What? No, I –'

'Such a strange choice when the nearest bathroom is right there,' he says, and points a finger in the direction of the door at the end of the room – while I inwardly face-palm. Of course, I should have known. All places like this have en suites, after all.

But the fact that I had no idea only serves to illustrate my point. I'm still living in a world where people have to fumble around in hallways when they need the toilet in the middle of the night. In fact, I'm not so far removed from a time when most people like me had to go outside for things like that.

I'm not ready for this.

I'm not *right* for it.

'I don't belong here.'

'Because you don't know where the bathroom is? That seems like something of a leap.'

'You know that's not why.'

'I do, but I'm still waiting for you to say.'

'I don't fit in, Jan. I don't wear the right clothes or do the right things. You know what drink I wanted to have with my meal? Diet Coke. I desperately wantederat a Diet Coke, because I hate the taste of water and despise the taste of wine. And you know what? Next time I'll just ask. I'll just ask, and you'll have to sit there with a woman who drinks fizzy soft drinks, in a room full of people who probably don't even know what a fizzy soft drink is.'

I pause then, but only because I have to. I've run out of breath to say words with, and my cheeks are all hot with embarrassment. What a thing to admit, my mind barks at me, only once I've recovered there's some more.

Oh, there's so much more.

'Is that really who you can imagine yourself with? A girl who drinks pop, and probably burps after she's done it?'

'I like it that you burp,' he says, and I'm sure he means it to be comforting. I'm sure he does. But I'm still covering my face with one hand, anyway. I'm still moaning in horror.

'Oh, God, you *heard* me.'

'Well, I've seen the strange series of convulsions you do when you're trying to hide that it's happening. Does that count?'

'I don't ... I don't *convulse.*'

'Of course you do – though that's not really the point.'

'Then what is?'

'The fact that I don't *care*, and have no idea why you do. Have I ever made you feel as though your natural self is disgusting?'

'Well ... no, but –'

'Do I shame you for who you are?'

'Never.'

'And do you know why?'

'No.'

'It's because I adore who you are – don't you know by now that I adore you?'

The answer is yes, of course. It's yes in the morning

241

and yes in the evening, yes when I'm unsure and yes when I'm certain. And it's especially yes when he says:

'Do you know what that word I call you means?'

Because I do know. I didn't dare look it up, but I understand it anyway. I feel it right down to my bones before he even offers a definition.

And then he does, and I'm undone.

'It means "beloved". It means that there is and only has been you. I did not lie when I said I had not kissed any of the other women I met through the assignations, or taken any of them out. In truth, I have not been to dinner with a woman for the better part of ten years.'

I try to contain my shock, here, but I already know I'm failing. I started breathing hard around the time he used the word 'adore', and when he gets to the ten years I'm practically hyperventilating. I feel like I'm in some tense race I didn't sign up for, but I can't deny it's exhilarating, now that I'm here.

He just keeps upping the ante. He keeps peeling back more layers, as though he's never had a problem with talking like this.

And all I can do is listen, agog.

'You are the only one. The only one who spoke in such a way that I had to hear it again; the only one who did things that meant I wanted only to return to you. And most importantly: you are the only one I've ever felt compelled to touch. I spent every other assignation in that seat by the window, without the urge to rise and do a single thing.'

I'm no longer hyperventilating when he finishes, though that's hardly a good thing. It just means I've suddenly forgotten what breathen ne.

ing is. My body is starting to need oxygen, but I don't care. Did he just say he hasn't been with a woman for ten years? That he just sits there and ... and what? What does he do?

I have to know. It means using up my only remaining air, but I don't have any choice. I just need to blurt things out, immediately.

'Are you seriously saying that you only ever watch?'

He seems to take a moment – I think to muse over this concept a little.

But to me it's just an endless agony, waiting for him to finally speak.

'Well, occasionally I comment.'

'You comment? You *comment*? All this time I've been imagining you doing God knows what to God knows who – to the point where I've actually scared myself, thinking about limbs tangled like pretzels and women with hair like ice palaces. And the most you do is offer a few words, like some TV pundit?'

'Being incredulous won't make it any less true.'

'But you ... you went for me the first time we met.'

'Indeed I did. I wonder why that might be ...'

'Because you're crazy?'

243

'I'm fairly sure that isn't it.'

'You're going to have to give me more than "fairly sure".'

'Very well then: because I have never wanted anyone the way that I want you. With the others it was always easy to maintain my calm, and remain aloof – perhaps because they were all so similar. But with you ...' He trails off in this wistful way that gets me by the throat. I'm choking up before he's even finished, which isn't a good thing. Because, oh, his finish is spectacular. 'I've spent years building up my walls, and one look at you and your awkward little striptease was enough to tear them down. Everything you do is enough to tear them down. Even now, here, when you tell me you can't quite believe that you're worthy of something as meagre and miserly as my love ... as though my love is precious to you ... as though *I* am precious to you –'

I have to cut him off, here. I don't mean to, but there's really nothing else I can do.

He needs to hear. He has to know.

'You *are* precious to me,' I blurt out, in a rush of emotion so thick it almost trips me up. There are tears in my eyes and they're spreading to my voice, and in a second I know my words will stumble over them. I know it, and don't care in the slightest.

'You're my ... you're my ... that word you said,' I say, reduced to some gushy inarticulate fool. And he reacts as though I am, too. He laughs in that bemused way of his.

But it's OK, because he also tells me this:

'It's really so much easier in Hungarian.'

'Is that why you always say it that way?'

'Of course.'

'All right. All right then,' I say, but I'm just stalling. It's a struggle to get the next part out, and I need to buy time. Just a few a seconds, I think. Just a few and then I take a breath, and go for it: 'You're my ... *szeretett*.'

Only to have him laugh. He *laughs* at my efforts. I'm ridiculous, I'm awful; I shouldn't have said it – that's not the word he meant at all. He was trying to suggest I say something else entirely, and now I've completely given the game away.

And then he speaks, and I realise wnd ugghat an idiot I am.

'Ah, God, your accent is terrible,' he tells me, and just to sweeten it further he adds some more words on the end: 'And yet I've never heard anything quite so lovely.'

I turn to him then. Not because I no longer care if he sees my watery eyes and my probably runny nose – I still do. It's embarrassing to face him looking like this.

But my need to see him overrides all other considerations. I have to know if he's sincere, and the sound of his voice just isn't enough. I don't know if anything would ever be enough, but his expression is a start. His eyes are so warm I could sunbathe beneath them, and for a second I do.

I bask in that dark light. I let it wash over me, without a care in the world. He said those things and feels those things and nothing else should matter.

I wish nothing else mattered.

'But why?' I find myself asking – almost against my will. I know I need to stop with the questions. I know they're more about me than him. And yet they keep coming all the same. 'Why do you find my awkwardness lovely? Why is it my conversation and my way of doing things?'

He strokes a thumb over my forehead before he answers, like maybe he wants to soothe me first. He wants to rub out the worried wrinkles there, and he almost succeeds.

Then he speaks, and succeeds completely.

'You already know why – you just refuse to hear it. I could say "because you're different" a thousand times and in a thousand different ways, and I doubt you'd listen. To you, difference from some elegant ideal is wrong, and unappetising. But to me … to me your differences are a delight. They fill my life with the unexpected.'

'In what way?'

'In every way. You think of me as a mind-reader, but the truth is … I find you endlessly fascinating because I so often *can't* read your mind. I rarely know for sure what you're thinking, and cannot predict your every move – though I do enjoy trying.'

'Maybe I'm just novelty, then.'

'Is that what you really believe?'

'No.'

'But you still worry, though.'

'Maybe.'

'I don't think the answer is maybe.'

'Well, why not?'

'Because you're still making that little dent between your brows,' he says, and then he presses his thumb there, just to emphasise. And it's a good emphasis, too. It feels like I've got a great canyon of concern just above my nose, when he touches me like that.

'OK, so I'm worried a little.'

'About what?'

'I don't know,' I say, but only because it's a struggle to get the words out. In the end I have to frame my sentences as questions, just so I can say them aloud. 'That I'm not enough? That I'll never fit into your world?'

'Ah, I see.'

'I mean, is that so crazy to wonder? We don't exactly move in the same circles.'

'No, I suppose we don't.'

'But you don't see it as a problem?'

'Now who is the mind-reader?'

'Well, it wasn't that hard to guess. I can hear the laughter in your voice.'

'Forgive me, love. It's one of my many fe oorgive melaws.'

'What is?'

'The inability to hide my amusement when someone says something ridiculous.'

'So I'm just being ridiculous.'

'Not exactly. I understand why you might wonder, of course. But ... you see ... to me you fit in perfectly. Therefore, how can I find the idea anything other than absurd?'

I fall silent then. I have to. He's just presented me with the Chinese puzzle box of human interactions, and I need all my resources to work my way around it.

'You make a good point.'

'And yet you still don't believe me.'

'Afraid not.'

'Very well, then. What if I prove it to you? What if I prove that you can fit in wherever you choose to? Will you accept it?'

I go to answer automatically. 'Yes', I want to say, 'yes'.

But then I remember all the times he's spun a web and caught me right in its centre. He could do something really awful – so awful that I can't seem to imagine it. He could do a thing with some other thing that ends up really thinging me, and for a moment this insane notion is so strong I almost give in to it. I almost tell him: there's nothing you can do.

Before it occurs to me, in a hot rush:

What if it's just that I *need* there to be nothing he can

do? He might be good at designing traps for me, but apparently so am I. I make them for myself, intricately constructed and almost impossible to see – until it's too late. Next thing I know I'm bored and alone, sure that it was he who pushed when really it was I who ran.

My God, I think I always run.

'Do your best,' I say.

And he does. Oh, he does. He takes my face in his hands the moment I've given him permission, thumbs stroking somewhere inexplicably sweet – like my temples, and the tips of my ears. Then just as I'm about to say something more – 'I take it back,' maybe, because, Lord, this is too intense for me – he lifts my mouth to his.

Like he needs a long, long drink. The sips he had earlier weren't enough. He's already thirsty again, and if I'm honest so am I. I've gone all strange and shivery from what felt like an hour of emotional overload, and now I just need something to take the edge off.

His lips do the job admirably. They're hungry like mine, and hot like mine, but most of all they move against me in a slow, syrupy rhythm that reminds me of his promise. He's going to prove it by working this kiss into me, so deeply I'll never be able to get back out.

I don't *want* to get back out. It's better this way. It's better just to give in, and I have no trouble doing that. I relax back into his arms, and for once in my life I simply let myself be held. No questions. No doubts. No wondering if it would be better if I were standing alone over there, the way I usually seem to.

Just this kiss. Just his mouth on mine and the flicker of his hot, wet tongue, and oh, now his hand is moving down ...

He slides it over the line of buttons that currently lie between my breasts – promising so much but giving so little. A slight move either way would have meant he was cupping my already sensitive breasts, and if he had kept going when he got to the last button he'd be touching me between my legs.

But of course he doesn't keep going. He stops just shy, before easing back up again. Then down again. T dotwehen up again – and on and on until it crosses the line between soothing and maddening.

Lord, he's good at crossing that line. He always lets me think he might sway one way or the other, teetering on the edge of the chasm that lies in the middle, before pulling back. And then just when I'm close to begging or bursting, he starts on the first button.

Slowly, so slowly, but hey – at least it's something. And it's followed by the second and the third button, too, as though he's not going to tease me at all. Tonight is about something else entirely, I think, and I'm right.

It only takes him a few short moments to unfasten everything, and then he simply spreads the whole thing open. No fussing, no games, no tease. He wants me bare and I can't say I mind. It feels amazing to be laid like this over his legs – back almost arched, everything exposed. There's something so lewd about it, in amongst the tenderness, and it makes me want to really strain up towards him.

So I do. I stretch like a satisfied cat, stiff nipples poking up, ass almost off the bed. And in response he does the best thing possible. He runs and rubs his hand all over my bare breasts and taut nipples – not quite softly enough to be a caress, but not roughly enough to count as anything else. His touch lands somewhere in-between, and oh, it's making me moan. It's making me roll my hips, and doubly so when he starts plucking at my nipples.

First one, then the other, shifting back and forth until both are tight, stiff peaks.

Before moving on.

Though perhaps moving on isn't quite the right term. It implies something restless and maybe a little perfunctory, when this is anything but. It's a smooth, purposeful glide down the centre of my body, and it ends with him cupping my sex in this possessive grip.

However, I don't know if it's the sense of being so ready for him – so spread open and eager, legs almost flat against the bed in an effort to encourage him there – or his willingness to do a thing like this that gets me. Either way, arousal just gushes through my body in this great hot wave, so strong I have to turn my face away from his. I have to bury myself in the side of his throat, and let out an agonised sound.

But doing so provides no relief. Now his lips are close to my ear, and he's whispering and whispering. 'Yes, yes, you want a hand between your legs, don't you?' *he asks, as though there's any question at all. I'm practically humping his palm, and I know he can feel my wetness. He hasn't yet slid a finger into that plump seam, but he doesn't have to. I'm so slippery it's coating the sparse hair there – and it's obvious he's discovered it. After a moment of that holding and cupping, he starts to tease the slipperiness over my sensitive lips.*

Which is exciting enough on its own. But he couples it with constant murmuring, and that's more than I can take. He doesn't limit himself to pointed questions, either – now he's progressed to hoarse, aroused-sounding stuff like 'Ahhh yes, so wet, so eager.'

And he doesn't stop there.

'Did I tell you how much I adore your eagerness?' he says. 'Because I do, I do. I have fantasies about you being like this – spread out for me, straining for my hand, your sex all slippery like this … oh. Look how easily you take my fingers …'

By the time he's done I'm surprised I'm conscious. His tone is just so rough with lust, like he barely has control over it any more – and, even sweeter, I suspect he doesn't want to. He opened a door earlier and now everything is spilliningyet slig through, including stuff about his desires and his fantasies.

Apparently the latter feature me and my wet pussy – who knew?

Not me. But then, right now I know very little. I'm having to focus all my attention on him and his hand, and the thing he seems to be doing. The one he mentioned a moment ago, which seems to be burning a hole through my lower body. My stomach feels weird and tight and my thigh muscles are tensing like crazy, and all because he's slowly sinking two thick fingers into my wet and wanting hole.

They just slide right in, as easily as he claimed.

Though that's not the best part. No, no. I mean, it's good, sure. And I love how it feels to be filled and slowly fucked like that. But fucking me is clearly not his intended purpose – and it's this that makes it hot.

It's the way he rubs until he's gathered up my slickness – making sure his fingers are good and glossy – before gliding them back up through my slit, to stroke my stiff little bud. Oh, yeah, that's the thing that makes my body sing.

The pads of his fingers are just so slick when he finally rubs them over my clit. And it's such a rude thing to do. It's so loose and lewd and not like him, and for a moment I can't quite get over it. My head falls back on the bed, eyes rolling in disbelief or desire or both mashed together.

Followed by a sound that shouldn't ever come out of any human being. I think it's a groan crossed with something rattling inside a cement mixer – but I just can't help it. I skirt close to an orgasm the second he does it, and it's important I vocalise this. If I don't I might burst. In fact, I think I'm going to burst either way. I'm straining against his hand and nearly biting at his neck, and still he keeps on.

Of course he keeps on. He's got a particular goal in mind – one that he tells me about a second later. 'No no no,' he says. 'Not yet, not yet.' And just when I'm ripe with confusion, twisting and turning and wanting that yet to be right now, he lays out the rest of his diabolical plan:

'I want you to come all over my cock,' he says, and oh, the surge of sensation that follows,... It's like before in the elevator – this heavy, hot pulse just thuds through me, so similar to an orgasm you could almost call it one.

Only this time he stops it before it can fully develop into bliss. He takes his hand away and moves back on the bed, while I mewl and complain and do things I wouldn't have before. I reach for his cock – only not with my hands. I do it with my mouth, licking him wetly until he's close to giving in. I feel his hand hover around the back of my head, and I know he just wants to pull me towards him.

But there's something else he wants more than that, and after he's rolled on a condom he does it. He gets me on my back, and puts himself between my legs – so ordinary, I think, and yet it's completely not. All this position does is make me realise that we've never had sex like this before. We've only fucked with him behind me ... never face to face.

And oh, God, it's so ... I don't know. He's absolutely massive between my thighs – to the point where my muscles feel a little strained in their efforts to accommodate him. And the hair on his chest is all rough against my stiff nipples, which only adds to the agony.

Though it's his face I notice the most. Of course it is. He's staring down at me and I'm staring up at him, and suddenly everything is just so insanely intimate. I can feel the tears sparking behind my eyes again. I can feel my body trembling udy g thatnder the pressure.

And that's before he cups my face in his hands – just like he did earlier, with his thumbs rubbing and rubbing over my temples and his fingers in my hair. As though he knew how soothing I found that, and wants to replicate the feeling. He wants this sex to be soothing, which sounds strange until I realise there's another name for such a thing. It starts with an M and ends with an E, and I think there are the letters AKING and LOV somewhere in-between.

Or at least that's what my racing heart is telling me. I try to ignore it, naturally, but when you're staring up into eyes like his it's so hard. They're filled with so much feeling that I have to look away. If I keep going with this eye contact I'm liable to blurt out some really stupid things, and I'm afraid this will end if I do.

I can't let that happen. There's just too much to enjoy and thrill over – like the feel of his cock pressing between my legs, steel-hard and so heavy against my spread sex. When he rocks his hips just a little, that thick, swollen head parts everything easily, sending sweet waves of pleasure rolling through me.

And just as I'm revelling in that, he glides his solid length right over my clit and I'm completely gone. I don't care if this is sex with a capital M and a capital L, or that he's looking and looking at me while holding my face in his two hands.

I only care about the feelings, physical and otherwise. I give myself over to them, rocking with him in a way that starts off small but ends with me clinging to him desperately – one hand sprawled over his broad back, the other in his hair.

Then we simply move like that, as though we're fused together all the way down the length of our bodies. He pushes and I lean into it, and it's so good, oh, it's so good. I don't even need him to do the rest, in all honesty.

But I'm glad when he gives it to me. I feel him shift and that solid, swollen head is suddenly against my entrance, lingering just long enough to give me shivers. There's a hint of pressure and a sense of my own slipperiness sliding gloriously against the sensitive skin there, and then he starts to ease his way in.

He doesn't have to ease, though. I take him without a hint of trouble, everything just opening to him in this deliciously slow and slick way. And then once he's in to the hilt he stops, as though he wants to savour it.

Or wants me to savour it.

And, dear God, I do. I'm so swollen I can feel his length against every inch of those soft, slippery walls, pressing in places other men usually don't reach. And when I clench around him – even just a little bit – it sends pleasure radiating outwards through me. It makes me gasp, and I think the feel of me has the same effect on him.

He's just resting there in a way that seems designed to tease, until I give him that little squeeze. After which, his response tells me all I need to know. He's not teasing at all. He's trying to wrestle back some self-control. For some reason, he finds this so exciting he's close to triggering like some horny teenager.

However, he shouldn't feel bad about that. I think I'm about to trigger too. All I have to do is consider him suddenly spurting inside me, and those little waves of sensation become swells. It's still so startling to see him like this – quivering with tension, still full of feeling, and so deep into whatever this is that he may never find his way out. He's stuck seven miles down, I'm certain of it – but only because I'm in there with him.

I'm so flushed I'm sure my cheeks are glowing, and so bringgh to geathless I've been reduced to a kind of desperate panting. I breathe out in a long slow gasp when he rolls his hips towards me, and greedily devour the air when he pulls away, and I only just avoid a sob.

But the moment he starts up a more definite rhythm I stop bothering. I don't hold anything in, or hide an inch of my feelings from him.

What's the point?

He already knows. Of course he does. He's feeling the same way. His cheeks are as red as mine feel, and he isn't just shaking. He's shuddering all over, and clutching at me – yet still he doesn't speed up. He just carries on like this, working me over in these slow, steady rolls until I'm mindless and boneless.

And God, so close. Excruciatingly close. I feel like I'm hovering on the brink, and have been since the dawn of time. My sex aches and I'm making a sound like someone dying – so much more than a sob now. So much more in every way. There are actual tears rolling down my cheeks, and I don't even know why. It's not because it feels so good – though that's part of it. And it's not because this is love that we're making. It's something else, and as my orgasm surges up and up, breaking in a way I can hardly take, I realise what it is.

This is the proof, I think,

And yet I still don't believe.

Chapter Sixteen

My home looks different to me when I first walk in the front door – as though I've been away for a thousand years. It's like there's a layer of dust over my possessions, and it makes the colours dull. It makes the furniture shabby. I've been looking too long at the sun, and now everything is gloomy by comparison.

But I guess that's just part of the problem. It's a symptom of spending time with him, even though I so desperately don't want to be dazzled by his world. I don't want it to seduce me into forgetting what's important, and yet I think that is what's happening anyway.

My first reaction to the gift he's sent me is not offence or squeamishness. A little surge of excitement goes through me instead, and it lingers inside for far too long. It's there when I tear off the glossy paper, and there when I finally get to the box beneath.

It doesn't even go once I've drawn out the prize itself: a cashmere dress, cut at odd angles around the neck and even odder ones at the hem. It's all asymmetric and so soft you could probably blow on it and send it off on a breeze, and for a while I actually marvel. All of my worries drift away in the face of this luxury, and it's only this slowly dawning realisation that draws me back.

That love-making – it was never intended as the proof. *This* is the proof. This dress, the shoes that go with it, an appointment he's apparently made for me at some salon with a name I can't pronounce. He can't tell me I fit in yet, because I don't.

But he can *make* me.

He can take the round peg I seem to be, and slot me into a square hole. All he has to do is give me corners where none were before – and boy, are these some pretty ones.

The shoes are even more glamorous than the dress, perfectly matched and in possession of all the things my own footwear doesn't have. They've been fancily stitched – probably by hand – and they have real leather soles and heels with little metal tips, whereas mine ... well, mine are like these, without the extra finesse. All of this stuff is like mine, without the extra finesse. Once I've gone over everything it comes tofy">Bt to me: this outfit is practically the same as the one I wore to dinner with him.

Only *better*.

I can't deny that it's better, even if I want to. Without the denial I'm just left with a rather pointed comment, and I don't know how to process that. I flump down onto one of my dining room chairs and just stare and stare at this rich rubble all over the table, from the curls of fancy tissue paper to the puddle of that little black dress.

Is that what he wants? I have to change to be with him? I suppose that was roughly what I was asking for, but it's uncomfortable to suddenly face my own request. It makes me wish I had someone to talk to about it – someone who would say that I should only ever be myself and fuck everything else.

But of course Lucy is still on the other side of the world. There's a postcard from her amidst the mail I've been letting pile up, telling me what a fabulous time she's having – no secret mystery, no tortured love affair.

That was all me. I see that now. I just *wanted* there to be secret mysteries, and tortured love affairs, and in a way I guess I got it. I got so much. What's a little bit more, really? I can put on this dress and attend these appointments, and pretend to be cool for an evening in a dress worth more than I am.

I can. I can.

* * *

I go to the salon first, pulling up in a taxi on a street that probably doesn't even know what taxis are. This little tucked-away strip of London is used to limousines and chauffeur-driven BMWs, and it shows. I can already feel people looking as I step out of the car – though I suspect it has more to do with me than it does with the cab.

I shouldn't have worn jeans. I should have worn the dress, to an appointment that's intended to get me *into* the dress. Crazy logic, I know, but it's how I feel as I creep into a place that's just as glossy as everything else in his life. The floors are glossy, the seats are glossy, the sinks are glossy – even the faces of the people who greet me are glossy. Emotions skate over the surface of their features, eyes almost blank in an effort to be as perfect and precise as humanly possible.

Though I'll admit: they're nice enough to me. In fact, they're more than nice. They greet me like a long-lost friend – or as much of one as they're likely to have – fussing and plucking at the air around my face and hair as if they can't quite bring themselves to fully touch it yet. They have to remove the imaginary flies of poverty that are probably buzzing around me, before they can do anything like that.

'We'll do this,' they say. 'We'll do that. You're going to feel like a million pounds.'

And I suppose they're right in terms of money. But maybe not so right in terms of my emotional state. Whatever his intentions were in doing this, my insides still cringe away when they find little flaws and imperfections. It doesn't matter that they then buff and pluck and polish them away. They're still there, under my skin.

I'm still the same person – only now I'm smooth and glossy like them. They thread my eyebrows into elegant arches and wax every inch of hair off my body, until I'm down to a little landing strip above my completely denuded sex. And then once they've whisked me through these processes – once they've stripped me back to the bare essentials – they start building me back up again.

My hair is sculpted into a series of coils that I'm sure won't work on my out-of-control mess – but they do. bhe floor Everything stays perfectly in place once they've pulled and brushed and oiled it. It's a true feat of engineering, though I don't know what to make of it once I've seen myself in the mirror. They've given me all this height at the front, and when I make the mistake of standing I seem to be around seven feet tall. I'll be even taller in those killer heels, I think.

And it's then that I start to feel nervous.

Maybe I won't be the same person any more. Maybe you actually become someone else the moment you start down this path – though I can't halt proceedings now that I'm in the middle of walking down it. I couldn't halt them even if I wanted to. They're like an oiled machine, passing me down the assembly line until I get to the last stop:

Make-up.

God, make-up is the worst. It's like someone is affixing a mask over my features, to complete the disguise. And the girl doing it has to get so close. She has to get so intimate with me – colouring with her little pencil and sweeping with her little brushes, her face so near to mine I can see the flecks of gold in her pretty blue eyes.

At least with the waxing I didn't have to meet someone's gaze. I could look away at nothing while my mind went to a far-off place, but here it's impossible. She's actually breathing on me, despite it being the height of bad manners to breathe on a person. And after a while this silence is so stifling that I can't help speaking. I don't want to do it, because really, what could I ever say to someone like her?

But the pressure gets to me, and suddenly I'm jolting out a question.

An asinine, ridiculous question, that I wish I hadn't asked.

'Do you do this often?'

I mean of *course* she does this often. This is her job. She's probably plucked and peeled and attached masks to half the ladies in London, and judging by her expression I'm not wrong. Her forehead wrinkles just a fraction, before she catches it and smoothes it back into place.

'Indeed I do,' she says, and it's only then that I understand what I really wanted to ask. Not does *she* do this often, but does *Janos*? Does he send many women to this place, to be made over in one particular image? He could have been lying about me being the only one, after all. Maybe this is a hobby for him, tempering trash into gold.

But I can't restate the question.

I can't.

I have to.

'I meant … do you often style women who've been sent here by a rich man?'

I don't say his name. It seems better not to, and especially as I'm already being far more direct than elegant people are probably used to. I'm supposed to be silent and smooth, I think – like a fancy car that muffles the roar of its engine – and that theory is reflected in the flicker of her eyelids, and the hint of a downturn at the corners of her mouth.

I wasn't meant to do that, I know, but she's classy enough not to make me feel it too much. She doesn't comment on my mistake or roll her pretty eyes – she only answers, in her best and most noncommittal voice.

'No, not often,' she says, and then she hesitates for just a fraction of a second. Long enough to hear, but not long enough to mean anything – unless you want it to. Unless you're like me, and always think it does. 'And never for the man we're talking about.'

It's funny – she's answered the way I hoped she would. Apparently, Janos didn't lie about met lthe m being the only one. And yet I leave the conversation with this queasy feeling, and, once I'm outside, it occurs to me why.

She didn't mean that I was special, I think, as I stand on this posh street with my new hair and my new body and my new face. She meant that other women probably didn't need the work that she had to put into me.

But I did.

I needed an overhaul, in order to deserve a man like him.

* * *

The place he takes me to is even grander than the restaurant, and one hundred times more intimidating. Here there are no booths for us to hide in, no secluded spots where he can keep me a secret. It's a charity ball for a cause I've never heard of, and everyone is standing. Everyone is milling around.

There's no escaping.

I have to mill too, even if I really don't want to. The well-oiled machine is turned on again, and it simply eases me on through – like I've got my dress caught in it and can't quite get free. I have to move when it moves, or I'll get chomped up.

And, judging by the people here, that chomping will be painful.

There are women with peacocks on their heads, carrying bags that look like they've recently emerged from a diamond mine. Even the men are dressed in tuxedos that seem to shimmer and shine, depending on which way they turn.

Apart from Janos, of course.

He's in something subtler and darker – something that feels to the touch like the softest wool. I can't stop rubbing my fingertips over it as I clutch his elbow, trying to place the sensation. And then it comes to me … the material is very close to the stuff my dress is made out of. Not quite cashmere, but close.

Which is probably what he intended, now that I'm thinking about it. He wanted us to match. To go together, like bacon and eggs.

And we do, in truth. I can pretend and pretend, but I know we do. I can see us reflected a thousand times in the mirrored walls – Janos all darkly handsome, suit so sharply cut it could have been done with a razor, not a hair out of place and everything so poised.

And then this gleaming stranger on his arm.

Because she *is* a stranger. She doesn't even behave like me, which is undoubtedly the most frightening thing of all. The salon and the clothes haven't just made me appear different. They've also removed things they couldn't possibly have – like my awkwardness, and my unerring ability to trip in heels, and my tendency to say whatever is on my mind without thinking.

He introduces me to someone who must be a dignitary – he has an actual sash over his shoulder with various adornments all over it, and if he has a chin I can't see it. It's swaddled in seven thousand years of privilege, and all of these things should be enough to make me laugh nervously. They should be enough to force some stupid words out of me, like 'Is that a toupee or your real hair?'

Only nothing happens. I shake his hand as though I've been doing it all my life, and the most that comes out of my mouth is 'So nice to meet you.' I've been body-snatched, I think, but naturally no one else can see it. How I behaved at the restaurant – that was the jarring me. That was the me who caused offence.

This is how I'm supposed to be.

Though somehow I think Janos will disagree. I imagine turning to him to see horror all over his handsome face. He'll be unsettled by uning thingthis strange new person, and whisk me away somewhere to change everything back. All I have to do is glance at him to set everything in motion – but I know why I don't.

It's because he's not unsettled at all.

He's barely even paying attention. He simply glides me around the party like some new toy he just bought, showing me off to this person and introducing me to that. No secretive looks, like the ones he offered before. No admiring eyes aimed in my direction.

He doesn't need to aim them now.

I'm the finished product. There are no dents to be pondered, no flaws to fascinate him. Now he can just be as he always is – the way I imagined he was when I saw that view. He simply glides across the surface of his life, unseeing, and seems so content to do so it's almost excruciating. I watch him have conversations with people without registering a single word, and smile in a manner that they seem to like.

But I don't think I could – ever. His real smile – the one he tries to hide, and fights whenever it steals across his face: that's the one I love. I love it when he does things against his will and says things he doesn't mean to, all of it splurging out from some secret core of him that only I know.

But if he doesn't prefer the real me, than what hope do I have of ever being with the real him? He's turned me into this person now, and she is not the type to ask for proper smiles. She doesn't question why he's smooching with these insincere people, or wonder if he secretly hates it all.

And even if she does wonder, she never tells him. What could she possibly say?

What can *I* possibly say?

If this is the life he wants to lead, there's nothing I can do about it. I either go along with it, or end it forever – and I can't end it forever, I can't, I just can't. I'm not ready to go; I don't know if I ever could be. He still smells the same and looks the same and most of all:

He still feels the same, when he suddenly swings me into his arms for a dance.

How often have I wished to dance with someone? Oh, too often to count. I've had dreams of moments like this, where the handsome hero sweeps me up and spins me around, in a room made of mirrors. It's every woman's fantasy, I'm sure – or at least it's the fantasy of every woman who's ever seen the movie *Labyrinth*.

All I need to do now is eat the poisoned peach, and I can pretend that everything is perfect for ever. He's smooth and charming and still attentive. He even asks me after a moment:

'Are you having a nice time?'

And the truth is, I don't want to say no. I lean back a little so I can look into his eyes, searching for whatever was there before and must be still there now. He didn't just change into a different person, any more than I have. All I have to do is shake him back to himself.

'Does it seem like I am?' I ask, because he always knows. If he's the same as he was, he'll know. He'll see it in my eyes or feel it in my body language, and that will be the moment when he whisks me away.

But the moment never comes.

'It does,' he says.

And that's the end of that.

* * *

I know it's a foolish and rather melodramatic thing to do. But the truth is … I don't even really mean to do it. I just tell him that I'm going to the ladies' roe lsame, whom, fully intending that to be the case. I'm in desperate need of the bathroom, if only to unstrap myself from the iron maiden that is my underwear. I need some relief, I think.

Only, once I'm out of the ballroom, I turn left instead of right.

And then I just sort of … keep going. The hallway is too narrow and plush, to the point where it's almost stifling. I simply want to get past it, and out into a room that has more air. But once I'm in the entranceway there doesn't seem to be any more oxygen than there was in the place I've just come from – most likely because of the concierge, who seems to be sucking the life out of everything with his disdainful glare.

It's really no wonder I end up outside.

But it's more of a wonder when I find myself hailing a cab. I have to walk five blocks to do it, and my shoes are starting to feel like fire. Everything is starting to feel like fire, and yet somehow I'm doing this. I'm getting into the back of a taxi, and when he turns to me and asks where I want to go, I don't even hesitate.

So I guess I do know what I'm doing, after all.

I'm fleeing the scene of the crime, and that seems to fit. This certainly feels criminal, though I'm not entirely sure why. Because I didn't tell him where I was really going? If he truly is the person I saw back there, he probably won't even care. He'll just get himself a new doll to dress up, and cart her around instead.

While I do my best not to cry in the back of a cab.

For the record: I don't succeed. The radio is playing Adele, so I don't even stand a chance. She just starts singing about wishing the best for someone, and suddenly I'm pressing my lips together too tightly. I'm clenching my fists and gritting my teeth, as though all of these things could turn me to stone.

I *wish* they could turn me to stone.

I wish my face wasn't wet. I don't know why it is, to be honest, because nothing really happened. He didn't dump me in some spectacular fashion, complete with parting shots about my ass in this dress or the hair that doesn't quite suit me. And I didn't dump him for a terrible thing he didn't actually do.

It's just better this way, I think. He needs a woman who really *is* all of those things – not one who could probably force herself to pretend on weekends. And I need a man whom I can do all of those ordinary things with, like cuddling on the couch in front of programmes he probably doesn't watch, and walking through the park on Sundays and … and …

Oh, God, why am I torturing myself with these thoughts? I see that perfect picture of a happy relationship, and suddenly that ache behind my eyes is a sharp sting. There isn't a trickle that I'm just about restraining. There's a torrent that I can't hold back. I have to pass money to the driver with my mascara running down my face.

And of course he makes it worse.

'You all right, love?' he asks, but I don't answer. I can't answer. The floodgates are open, and it's all I can do to stumble out of the car. As it is I almost miss the kerb and fall flat on my face, and getting to the door is hellish. Getting upstairs is hellish. I keep missing steps and tripping over things that aren't there, and once I'm finally inside it's not any better.

I have to look at myself in the mirror in order to get this awful make-up off. I know I do, but I don't want to. I'm well aware of what I look like, and it's not a pleasing prospect – how could it possibly be? I feel like the biggest drama queenst ha in the world, and I'm sure that will be reflected on my pathetic face.

I bet I have mascara tracks a mile long, and lipstick smeared halfway around my face. My perfect hair is probably coming undone, and I'm sure I no longer smell like a gossamer haze of perfectly pitched perfume.

But at least it will be me.

That's one good thing amongst all of this – I am myself again. Battered and bruised and halfway indecent, but the skin fits again. And it fits comfortably, too, once I've removed every trace of this ill-advised makeover. I groan with delight once my feet are free of these stiletto shackles, and peel off the dress like I'm removing a suit of armour. I just did ten rounds on the charity ball battlefield, and now need to tend my wounds.

As silly as my wounds may be.

Because they are, and I know it. I understand it, before Janos even calls to tell me so. By the time I'm out of the shower he's left three messages on the machine, and all of them are a variation on that one theme: *why did you leave?*

Of course the first is sympathetic ... even conciliatory. He asks me where I am and if I'm OK, in so soothing a tone that I get a little pang. I picture him in that opulent entranceway, with a deeply troubled look on his usually so trouble-free face. There are suddenly lines where there weren't before, and he's picking at a thousand things that don't exist.

It's an unsettling image, and it almost makes me pick up the phone. I could just say I didn't feel well, I think, as my hand hovers over the receiver.

But then the second message comes.

'Are you running away?' he asks, in a manner that forces me to remember why I did. Or at least it pushes me into a mental argument with him, in my head. 'I had reasons,' I tell him, and try to ignore the part where my reasons seem flimsy.

They're only flimsy to him.

And even if they're not, he'll make them seem so. He'll handle me until I suddenly find myself being a completely different person at a million balls and banquets, in clothes that aren't me and hair that isn't mine. Or maybe I won't find myself at all. Maybe I won't even notice the change. It'll be so gradual, each alteration so small and seemingly insignificant, that by the time the transformation is complete I won't see it. This glamorous girl will be the person I've always been, and this hollow life of parties and pretentious people will seem like reality.

Instead of some nightmare I once had, about being trapped in a velvet-lined coffin made mostly of solid gold.

And I know – I do know – that this is probably an overreaction. I'm aware that everything could turn out fine. It's just that his messages don't make me feel like it *is* fine. They build the pressure until I get to the last one, and then they explode all over me. 'We need to talk,' he says, like some awful hammer coming down.

That phrase never means something good. It means what I thought –that I'm about to be handled – and even if it doesn't there are plenty of other horrible connotations. Most typically people say it when they want to end things, and somehow that's just as bad as my first interpretation.

I don't think I could stand here and listen to him dismissing me, like an employee. I'm not even sure if I could stand him doing it the other way, either. Heartfelt apologies are just as bad – in fact, everything is bad about this. I can't stop pacing and staring wildly at the phone, as though it's a bomb that's about to go off.

And when it doesn't I slowly turn my attention to the door. How long before he comes here? How long before he realises that I'm not going to answer his calls, and that maybe he should go for something face to face?

I can't have that. I'm already spiralling relentlessly out of control, and all I've had to endure so far are some phone messages. I'll crumble if I see him again and he looks at me with those warm, dark eyes. I'll give in without so much as a fight, and the thought is making me itch in my own skin. It's making me want to fly away.

And that's when I see it:

Lucy's postcard on my computer desk, propped up against the screen. It's an image of some distant ocean, sapphire-blue and oh, so calm-looking – a slice of heaven in the middle of the Mediterranean.

'Come and see me anytime', she'd written on the bottom, in that casual way of hers.

But now it doesn't seem so casual. It seems like a get-out clause, or an escape route. I don't have to sit here and wait for a conversation I don't want to have. I can leave and never return, just like she did. Someone will find my message stuck on the fridge. They'll rummage through my stuff in a frantic bid to figure me out.

But, by the time they do, I'll be long gone.

Chapter Seventeen

I'm not sure what I expected when I got on the plane. Some party island where everyone is naked all the time and constantly living it large? I guess that's partly the image I have of Lucy, but then again it's been so long since I last saw her that she's starting to fade. In my mind her face is blurry.

And this place brings her right back into focus. I remember how much she loved to lie in a hammock at the bottom of her mother's garden on lazy summer days. She liked peace and quiet as much as she liked parties, and her favourite thing in the world was the ocean.

So of course she's come here, to this quiet island. Of course she has. This is who she really is – secretive, like the town where they've piled one building atop another, full of hidden spaces and dark shadows, only blazing bright on the outside. And so beautiful, oh, she's just as beautiful as she ever was.

More beautiful, in fact. She looks so relaxed in her own skin I'm almost envious, and that's before I get to the caramel hue of her newly toasted skin, and the tangle of her red hair, and her pretty little bare feet.

'Lissa!' she says, like it's me who's the best person in the whole world.

Even though it's her. I'm the person who shut down our friendship just because she needed a long vacation. She's the person who welcomed me with open arms, the moment I bothered to pick up the phone. And she's also the person who did this – who went away to find herself – without any help at all.

She didn't need me to tell her to go.

But I needed her to ask me to come.

And I need her hugs even more. She embraces me warmly, smelling of coconut and sunshine and so many good things. Too many good things, in truth. I rest my head on her shoulder and breathe her in, and that's pretty much all it takes to upset me. My jaw clenches and I shut my eyes, trying to hold it back.

But that doesn't work on her. It never worked on her. She always knew when I was crying, even if I pretended not to. I've tried to fake her out, before today, with claims of sinus problems and head colds, but>'Ap wi she's never so easily fooled.

And she isn't fooled now. She doesn't even mistake it for happy tears, or a little emotion over our reunion.

She pulls away and I barely have enough time to glance at something else before she asks the dreaded question.

It's the one I'd hoped to avoid, somehow – as though we could just party-hearty-marty and forget everything. Hell, maybe that's why I convinced myself she was *that* person, instead of *this* person.

The one who asks:

'What happened?'

* * *

I don't think I'm having a nervous breakdown or anything. But she does all the things I imagine people do when their friends are having a nervous breakdown. She makes me tea, even though I don't drink tea, and runs me a bath, even though I don't take baths. And when I insist that I don't want to talk about it yet, she persuades me to have a rest until I feel ready.

I don't think I'm into that, either, but it turns out I'm wrong. I am into that. I'm so into it I pass out the moment I climb onto her shawl-covered bed, despite my refusal to lie down. I just prop myself up against the pillows while she gets my tea, and the next thing I know it's almost morning.

I'm still in my clothes, and everything is completely silent and dark – apart from the hush-shush of the ocean, somewhere off in the distance, and the first fingers of dawn creeping in under the makeshift curtains she's put up.

It's just a multi-coloured blanket, really. A shawl, like the ones she's using on her bed and over the back of her couch. They're everywhere, these rough little squares of material, and they give the place a wonderful feel. They turn the light from the window into a kaleidoscope of colour – but it's more than that.

It's more than the prettiness and the earthiness of her place. It's how *lived in* it seems. She's been here for a thousand years. She grew up from the ground and claimed it for her own, and I love it for that reason.

I love it for many reasons. There's something intoxicating about walking out into the living room to find the balcony doors open – no hermetically sealed wall of glass here. I step out into the dawn light and the ocean is right there, separated from me by nothing more than scrubland and a doable jump down. Its smell, its taste … I don't have to imagine it.

And no one could ignore it. The whole thing has my attention so firmly I don't even notice Lucy sitting there, until she speaks.

'Had enough not resting?' she asks, and I jerk and turn too violently. I'm on edge, I think – to the point where she's suddenly the villain waiting for the heroine in a place she doesn't expect. I'm actually imagining her stroking an evil cat.

But I don't know why.

Because I don't want her to ask?

Maybe, maybe.

Because I don't want to say?

Almost definitely. Saying is sticky and difficult, and there's that feeling creeping through my body again – the one that says I was a fool to let such a little thing bother me. The moment I explain she'll laugh, and tell me to knock it off, and I'll have to face the fact that I've blown the best thing that ever happened to me because of a little concern about my sense of self.

'Earth to Alissa.'

'Oh ... yeah. Yeah, I feel much better now, thanks.
ali, tdoable

'You sure, babe?'

'Definitely.'

'So you just travelled hundreds of miles, with holiday time I know you don't have, because you fancied getting a tan.'

'I *had* holiday time,' I say, and am actually quite proud of myself for taking the conversation in another direction. Now she's busy asking me about that, instead of anything dangerous. 'You did?' she says, and then I tell her yes and she's all 'Well, I guess Henderson must have softened.'

At which point I realise I haven't deflected her at all.

I've just brought her around to something even worse.

281

'Come on. What really happened?' she asks, followed quickly by the *something even worse*. She slaps the arm of her recliner and jerks towards me as she delivers *this* little doozy: 'If you tell me you're having an affair with him I will *kill* you, I will just *kill* you. He scratches his balls and then sniffs his fingers, Lissa.'

'He … what? Wait … what?'

'Are you sleeping with him?' she asks again, only this time she speaks each word in this robotic tone so as to be extra, extra clear.

Not that I need her extra clearness in regard to this particular concept. No, I'm all set on that. I'm not as set on *this*, however:

'I was hoping you'd explain the ball-sniffing, more than anything.'

She waves a hand in response. As though ball-sniffing is so commonplace it barely needs commenting on. Apparently I'm surrounded by men who are secretly doing this gross thing, and she's just let me go on in ignorance. Oh, the amount of times I've shaken his hand! And that guy at the charity thing with no chin – I shook his hand too. He almost definitely scratches his balls and sniffs his fingers, if not something way worse. Maybe he really rummages around down there, underneath the underwear.

Either way, I don't think she's right to say:

'It's not a big deal.'

'It *isn't*?'

'Absolutely not. Unless you *are* sleeping with him, in which case it's such a big deal it's kind of blowing my mind.'

'I'm not sleeping with Mr Henderson,' I say, as I take the recliner next to hers. It's cold and vaguely damp from the misty morning air, but I barely register it. I'm all in with this conversation now, and nothing else matters.

Not even a moist backside.

'In fact, I'm kind of offended that you could think so.'

'Well, you're leaving me very few guessing options. You suddenly want to come out here, you're being all mysterious, you're barely even trying to hide your tears behind that strain-face you do ... none of that is like you.'

I glance away at the ocean, searching for something that isn't there.

Myself, maybe.

'Then what *is* me?'

'Movie Friday nights and failed relationships.'

'That sounds *terrible*.'

'It's not so bad. The former is fun and you're usually much more excited about the latter.'

'Excited?' I ask, and though I try to stop my voice squeaking with incredulity, I definitely fail. I sound like Mickey Mouse on helium.

'Sure. You hate being in relationships. You can't wait to escape and once you have you feign sadness for five minutes before rolling right back into your safe little life.'

'That's … that's quite an assessment.'

'A cruel assessment?'

'Maybe a little,' I say, but what I really mean is *a lot*. I can't tell her that, however. If I do I'll have to explain how close it is to the bone. I'll have to talk about Janos and running away, when just thinking about it is making me hyperventilate.

Do I really have such an obvious pattern? I try to think back, but all I can make out as far as the eye can see is an endless stream of assholes and idiots, most of whom deserved relief after being discarded. There was Mick who stole from me and Derek with his penchant for prostitutes and Paul with constant passive-aggressive gaslighting. I remember him saying, once: 'No, I didn't say you were fat, babe. I said, wouldn't it be great if you could fit into a size eight?'

I can't be blamed for running away from these men.

But it's possible I can be blamed for running away from Janos. He didn't steal, or make me feel bad about my body shape. I'm not even sure if I can describe what he *did* do.

So, instead, more deflection.

'And anyway, you've got room to talk. What exactly are you doing here, in the middle of some Mediterranean nowhere? You know, I thought you'd gotten involved with some underworld criminal,' I say, and I swear I do it in all seriousness. For a while those were my real and honest thoughts, but in response to them she just cackles.

'Criminal *underworld*?' she asks, then again on an increasing scale of incredulity. 'I just wanted to relax in the sun, Lissa. Nothing bad happened.'

'Well, I can probably see that now,' I say, but my tone is too sullen and too whiny. I have to haul it all the way back before I can deliver my trump card: 'But come on – I find out you're going to these secret rendezvous, and the next thing I know you're gone. What was I supposed to think?'

She gives me a look I recognise only too well – her sly *I've got you now* look. Her little pink mouth purses and her eyes gleam in a way that reminds me too much of Janos, before she sing-songs her point.

'So you unearthed my diary.'

I flush red and fumble around for a second.

'It's not like I had to unearth it,' I say, and her smile broadens.

'No, I guess that's fair enough. I didn't exactly hide it.'

'You wanted me to find it, didn't you?'

'I might have done.'

'And now you're torturing me.'

'A tiny bit.'

'It wasn't Mr Henderson, you know.'

'That's starting to occur to me.'

'It was someone I met ... someone I met ...' I start, but I can't finish the job. There's this big chunk of oxygen caught in the back of my throat, and the more she leans forward – partly disbelieving, partly enthralled by something stupid old me is about to say – the harder it gets to say it.

So it's lucky, really, that she says it for me.

'Oh, my God. It's someone you met through an assignation.'

'It's ... possible that's the case.'

This time she doesn't just slap the arm of her chair. She yells aloud the words 'Shut' and 'up', and almost gets to her feet. I have the overwhelming impression that she's going to applaud – or wants to. I don't know why, but she definitely wants to.

'You mean you actually *went on one*, and shagged some guy, and then things *got serious*? Is that honestly what you're saying to me right now?'

'I want it to be, but I'm kind of frightened by your shock.'

She throws back her head and laughs, but it doesn't sting as much as it should. Mainly because she mitigates it with the sweetest gesture ever – a kind of squeezing of my upper arm, and a little shake, and these soft words that almost make me tear up.

'You have no idea how cool you can be, my good friend,' she says, and suddenly there's all this pricking going on behind my eyes. I guess I just didn't realise how much I'd missed her. And I especially didn't realise that she might have missed me. That I am important to her, or interesting to her, or cool – even though I'm always sure I can't possibly be.

'It wasn't really all that amazing.'

'No?'

'I hid the first time I went,' I say, and she laughs again. God, she's so sunny when she laughs. It's like the dawn breaking over my dark little melodrama.

'That's so you.'

'I thought I was searching for you – and I kind of was. But then later I realised ...'

'You actually wanted to see what happened,' she finishes for me, nodding in this knowing way. 'That's so you, too.'

'It is?'

'Oh, sure. You pretend to yourself that you don't really want something all the time. In fact, I think you once said to me that it's better not to hope for stuff, because then you can't be crushingly disappointed when it doesn't happen.'

I blanch, but I can't deny it.

'That does sound like me.'

'Is that what you did here? Blew something off before you could start hoping?'

I think her words turn me to stone. There's really no other explanation for the way I freeze in position, mouth pinched and eyes just ever so slightly wide. I'd say it was some sort of reaction to the truth, but it can't be, it isn't, that's not why I did this.

Even if it probably *is* why I did this.

'It wasn't ... really like that.'

287

'So what was it like?'

'I don't know. I thought it would just be some exciting sex. And it was, but then ...'

For once, it's her on the edge of her seat and me telling the gripping tale. She's really leaning forward now, but of course the problem is – I just want her to lean back. There's a reason why it's usually the other way around, and it's mostly because I don't know how to do this. I'm not good at the details, like her. I'm not good at framing the whole thing and getting right to the heart of it.

Though I suspect part of this is that I don't *want* to get to the heart of it. I'm not even sure how to describe the exciting sex part, if I'm honest. She gets this look on her face when I say those words – half-intrigued, half-disbelieving – and it's rather intimidating.

Maybe it won't sound real, I think.

Ben="coucause it doesn't sound real to me.

'We started ... meeting regularly, I guess.'

'You met one of the assignations regularly?'

'Yeah.'

'Like, more than once.'

'Uh-huh.'

'And you know how rare that is, right?'

'I've been told.'

'But it happened anyway,' she says, and now I'm sweating.

'I swear I'm not making this up,' I fumble out, but she doesn't narrow her eyes or anything. She just pats my hand, and says more soothing things.

'Hon, I know you're not. It's obvious you're not. This is just me, marvelling. I went to three of those things, and each time it was a different guy, and uniformly they were all as cold as ice. If I'd suggested meeting for a second time I'm pretty sure they would have asked why I was speaking in another language. It's just not that kind of deal.'

'So ... what made you go?'

She laughs.

'For the same reasons they did. I wanted to have fun. I wanted to be involved in something sexy and exciting – so did you! Everyone wants that, sometimes.'

'Then what made you stop?'

'I wanted a different kind of sexy and exciting. Which I guess is true of you too.' She leans back in her chair and gives me this long, considering look before continuing. 'Now you're in this deep, huh?'

'I guess you could say that.'

'What's up? He push for too much?'

I know it's possible that she means the right kind of pushing – the one I actually felt from him. But instinct tells me she means another kind of pushing altogether. She's still thinking in terms of the assignations, and all the kinky things he could have possibly asked me to do.

In her head she's got him dressed up a gimp suit, and me running around naked at some sex party.

I can tell.

Her expression is all curls and half-horror.

'Janos isn't like that. He didn't –' I start, but she cuts in.

She really, really cuts in. She even holds her hands up, as though she's a lollipop lady and I'm at some junction I'm not supposed to be crossing.

'Wait. Wait. Did you say *Janos*?'

I come close to just answering in the affirmative, and probably would have done if I hadn't heard that note in her voice. It's low and deadly, and it says, *Beware, Alissa. Tread lightly.*

'Erm ... no. I said –'

'Don't even try to turn Janos into John.'

'I wasn't going to.'

'You *so* were. Oh, my God, oh, my God, you're talking about Janos Kovacs. This whole cryptic conversation is about Janos Kovacs. Please tell me it isn't about Janos Kovacs.'

I wring my hands and little and sweat a whole lot, but ultimately answer.

'I don't know how to do that, now.'

'He doesn't even touch the women he hooks up with. Did you know that? Does he touch you?' she asks, but she's too breathless for me to formulate a response.

Suddenly I'm seeing the whole thing through new eyes, and it's making my heart beat too fast. It's making her heart beat too fast. 'No, waast align="juit, don't tell me. If he doesn't, I just want to live vicariously through you for a second and pretend he does.'

'Well, I –'

'Stop. Stop. I'm still pretending.'

She really is. She's got her eyes closed, and seems to be fondling the air with her fingers. And whenever I try to interrupt her she shushes me, until I'm fairly sure I'm just sitting here watching someone having imaginary sex with my boyfriend.

Despite the fact that he isn't my boyfriend. I don't know why I just thought of him that way, because he definitely isn't. And even if he was, he absolutely can't be now. He probably hates me. Or whatever he does that passes for hatred – mild condescension, perhaps?

'Do you think you could maybe describe his naked body a bit so I can imagine this better?'

'What? *No.* No! Stop … doing whatever this is,' I say, and then I flap my hands a bit in a manner that could be mistaken for jealousy. If I was a crazy person who is totally in love with him. Which I am not.

'Ohhhh, I bet that means it's really great, right? He's all burly underneath, isn't he? He has to be. And hairy, I bet he's hairy.'

'It's … possible that he's hairy.'

'And God, he's so handsome. Is he that handsome close up?'

I have to swallow thickly around a lump that isn't there, but I get some words out.

'He's very handsome.'

'Plus ... he's got to be charming.'

'I'd say so, yeah.'

'And dashing.'

'Oh, well. You could probably call him that.'

'And you love him.'

I'm looking at my hands when she slips those words in there, but I can't keep doing it once they're out. I have to hurl a sharp stare in her direction, to show my complete and utter disavowal of what she's saying. And I have words planned, too. Harsh words that imply she knows nothing.

It's just a shame they don't make it out of me. And the stare? It's not half as sharp as I'd like it to be. Actually, it's soft in the middle, and if I was really going to put a label on it I'd say it makes me think of two hands reaching out.

Thank God she takes them.

'It's going to be OK, you know.'

'You really think so?' I ask, but I do it in far too cheery a way.

It makes her crashing practicality that much more disheartening.

'Mostly? No. You're in love with Janos Kovacs – things could not be more terrifying. But the main thing is: I'm going to do my level best to help you through this trying time.'

'That's good of you. It really is. But I don't think there's anything you could do to make this feeling go away, to be honest.'

'That bad, huh?'

'It's like someone shot me, and I just don't know it yet,' I say, intending something light-hearted. I'm perpetually intending light-heartedness here. It's just that my words aren't coming out that way. They're coming out so red in tooth and claw, and, once they're in front of us all bloody and raw, her eyes do this awful thing.

I think a shadow actually passes across them.

'He's not worth it, Liss. A man like that … he's never going t nefy"o be more than what he is. He's never going to fall in love and sweep you off your feet. That's a fairytale.'

She's right, of course. I've heard the same story a thousand times before, in a thousand different ways. The rich prince somehow magically becomes a great guy with a big heart, despite how ludicrous that is when you boil it down. Nobody gets to be where Janos is by being good, and kind, and decent. Reality doesn't work that way.

Reality is the thing you have to face once you've finished convincing yourself that romance exists. I know it is. She knows it is.

And yet …

'So what happens if he really did fall in love and swept me off my feet?'

She falls silent then, for a long, long time.

Too long a time, if I'm being honest. I have to fill it with something, quickly.

'But I didn't feel like I fitted into his world, so I ran away without saying anything.'

I think I expect her expression to change here. Only no change comes. She just keeps on looking at me with that liquid darkness in her eyes, completely devoid of any disapproval.

It makes it easier to keep talking.

And maybe harder, at the same time. Partway through she puts her hand over mine, and the next thing I know I'm leaking. I'm leaking slow, sad tears like some pathetic cartoon puppy, while spewing words at a thousand miles an hour.

'I fucked it all up, Luce. He did all of this stuff for me – all of this *Pretty Woman* sort of stuff that every girl in the world probably likes, apart from me. I hated it. I hated it. I hated dressing up in the clothes he bought for me and going to the salon appointments he made for me. It made me think he wanted this glitzy and glamorous woman to fit into his precious perfect world and I … I just couldn't. I started to feel like a different person, and the next thing I know I'm on a plane. I'm on a plane, flying away from Janos Kovacs.'

Christ, it sounds so bad when I put it like that in black and white: I flew away from the man she just shit a brick over. I flew away from him, and no amount of her telling me *hey hey hey it's OK, it's OK* is going to change what I've done.

I'm a bad, stupid person, and need to express as much.

'But that's a terrible reason to just run away from someone, right?' I ask, then rush on before she can interrupt with the verdict. It's one I already know, anyway. 'Wait ... wait. You don't have to say. I know it is. I can feel that it is.'

'Calm down, babe. Calm down – stop clutching at yourself,' she says, before I even realise I'm doing it. She says the words and I glance down, and there's my hand making twisting shapes in the airplane clothes I'm still wearing. 'It's not that terrible a reason, OK? Or at least it doesn't seem like too terrible a reason based on what I can discern from all that frantic babbling. Most women like the idea of *Pretty Woman*, but don't actually want to live it, for God's sake. Who wants to be controlled by an eccentric billionaire? I'll tell you who: no one. No one in the known universe.'

'Some people might.'

'Such as?'

'Such as ... people ... who ... like billions of dollars.'

'Well, there is that contingency.'

'And ... women who fancy ... Richard Gere.'

'I'm sure he has fans,' she says, in a way that suggesty t="js she doesn't think so at all. She likes hot young studs more than anything else, of the sort I saw milling around on our way up here. She's never been a fan of older rich men, and to be honest neither have I.

That word – rich – keeps tripping me up, no matter how hard I try to avoid it.

'You don't really think he is, though, do you?'

'Think who is what?'

'Janos. You don't think Janos is a billionaire.'

She rolls her eyes at me.

'Of course he's not! Have you *seen* billionaires? Most of them look like something you'd find under a bridge. At the very least, none of them look like Janos Kovacs.'

'Excellent point, well made. But come on … you can hardly blame me for wondering.'

'Haven't you even Googled him?'

'I didn't dare. I was afraid of what I would find.'

'Like all his mounds and mounds of money.'

'I kept imagining a swimming pool, like Scrooge McDuck.'

'And maybe a lair in Antarctica, where he keeps his mutated menagerie.'

'I bet they can all shoot lasers out of their eyes.'

'And soon he'll use them to strongarm the UN into giving him the moon,' she says, and I'm laughing with her, I am. It's funny to reduce all of this mess to a silly story about super-villainy.

Even if I still have to face it, in the end.

'You realise all of this is just making it way worse.'

She nods, as she wipes away tears of laughter. And once they're gone she's suddenly serious again. She erased the humour with those little droplets, and now we're back to the awful, terrible matter at hand.

'Yeah, I do. And you know why? Because you don't want to be some rich guy's pet. That's what it boils down to, in the end. You don't want to think about his money and you don't want to be dressed up to play some part in his rich life – and that's OK. It's OK to want to be yourself. It's better to want to be yourself. I couldn't have this weird conversation about laser-eyed animals with anyone else. You shouldn't have to change.'

I'm breathless by the time she's done – too breathless to say what I want to. I've got all of these thank-yous to give her and lots of garbled words of probable agreement, but in the end I'm glad I keep them inside. They're too silly, and they don't go with the measured proviso she adds about a second later.

'That being said ... it might have helped if you actually spoke to him a little bit about these concerns. Did you speak to him about these concerns?'

There's really nothing I can say to that.

I think my silence says it for me, anyway.

'Even a little bit? A word or two? A note?'

'There might have been a note.'

'*Alissa.*'

'What? *You* only left a note!'

'Yeah, but I'm not your one true love.'

'I didn't say he was my one true love.'

'You didn't say he wasn't.'

She has me there. It makes my guts twist and my eyes bleed, but I can't deny her point, or the love thing, or any of this really. All I've got are silly ext ahascuses.

'I just didn't know what to tell him. I didn't know *how* to tell him.'

'You never know how to go about things when someone's hurt you. Like now – just now. That's the first time you've mentioned the note I left you in a way that suggests you maybe weren't so happy about that.'

'Well … maybe I am happy about it. I think it's cool that you did this.'

'But?' she asks, and I know then that she's right. I hate confrontation. I hate it so much that this paltry version of an argument is akin to being inside an iron maiden. Every time I speak or she speaks the screws get tighter. Any second now I'm going to be riddled with holes and screaming for mercy.

'But I … I felt like … you maybe … possibly abandoned me.'

'And you feel better for getting that off your chest.'

'Possibly,' I say, but only because the iron maiden is now five per cent looser.

'Good. So go call him. Go tell him. Don't pretend it doesn't matter, so you no longer have to hope and believe that it does. Hope isn't poison, Lissa. Hope is the thing that keeps you going when everything is awful and dark and you don't know which way to turn. It made you pick up the phone with me because you believed I was still your friend – and I *am*. I didn't abandon you. That's just what you tell yourself in your little reverse-hope world. You think the worst to protect yourself, baby, but it's not protecting you. Not really.'

She pauses just long enough to give her words weight, but she doesn't need to.

They sink to the bottom of me before she's even finished.

'If it was,' she says. 'Then why on earth are you so sad, huh?

'Why are you so sad?'

Chapter Eighteen

I try for the first time a few hours later, once I've eaten and had a shower and then eaten again. I'm eating when I dial, in fact, and bouncing on the spot. From across the room Lucy makes a *calm down* gesture, but if anything that makes it worse. I try to restrain my bouncing and end up in a spasm, and instead of compulsively eating I'm tapping and squeezing my fingers into fists and oh, God, why isn't he answering? Why? Why?

I shouldn't expect him to answer, and yet still.

Why isn't he answering? The persistent prrrrriiiinng of the phone is starting to drill into my head. It's becoming a taunt: *it's as bad as you think it's as bad as you think it's as bad as you think*. And it ends on the most horrible thing possible.

You shouldn't have hoped.

Though I suppose that last part is mostly Lucy's fault. I wish to God she hadn't told me that about myself. I mean, I knew. I did know. But even so: it's hard to take when it's shoved right in your face.

And it's definitely turning this into the phone call from hell. The damned thing just keeps ringing and ringing like there's suddenly no such thing as voicemail. Either that or he's turned off his voicemail service in anticipation of this moment. He's torturing me with technology, and no amount of fist pumps from Lucy are going to help me with that.

I deflate the moment I hang up. I deflate so much that it takes me a whole day to try again. I need twenty-four hours to forget the torturous agony of waiting to see if he will pick up, so I can come to ihatt fresh. I can pretend I'm blasé, this way, and hardly concerned at all.

Not that this pretending thing works. I've now progressed to biting my nails, even though I've never bitten them before in my life. And I wait, too, until Lucy's down at the market, so she can't give me moral support that only serves to remind me how much I need moral support.

A lot.

I'm staring at the ceiling and clenching my jaw by the time it gets to the third ring, and by the seventh I'm close to certain. I more or less was yesterday, but this is confirmation. He's already moved on. He's just not the sort of guy to wait around while someone he's dallying with decides what she wants, and even if he was ...

haven't I been cruel enough? If *he* cut out on *me* without a word I'd be devastated. I'd never forgive him.

It's not right to expect him to forgive me – though somehow I'm still doing it. I'm still doing the thing I never do. I'm *hoping*. Or at least I'm trying on hope for size. Lucy said I was sad anyway, so why not? Why not just let it take root inside me, and see where it leads?

Even if it leads to me lying awake at five in the morning, waiting for a call that will never come. Somehow I've turned into the kind of woman I never wanted to be, hanging everything on a man who simply isn't interested. He's no longer bothered, and it makes me want to be the same way. I don't want to toss and turn, wondering how things will turn out between us.

I want to get rid of him.

I want to not feel like this.

Which is probably how I end up on the beach in dawn's early light, still in my nightie and stumbling bleary-eyed like some fool. But if I am a fool then at least I'll be the strong kind. The independent kind. The kind who takes a snow globe to the ocean, with every intention of tossing it in. It'll be fitting, I think, for an idealised island to disappear into the waters around a real one. It's nice and symbolic. It's perfect and circular.

But when I get down there I can't do it. It's just too much. It feels like I'm giving up more than a stupid gift, or a chance of a passionate relationship. It feels like I'm giving up any chance of ever hoping about anything ever again.

This is it, I know. Once I've done this I won't believe any more. I'll go back to the way I was, eking out an existence in tiny cautious portions, never going for something more because something more is this. Something more is daring to go to an illicit meeting with a strange man; it's calling him and talking to him and doing all the things you thought you never could. I never thought I could be with someone like him.

I never thought I could be with anyone.

And if I throw it, then I'll know I can't. I'll just be this melodramatic idiot who refuses feelings, the way other people refuse meals at terrible restaurants. Lucy will look at me with pity and I'll spend the rest of my days knitting afghans, and all because I couldn't make a phone call or hold onto a snow globe.

I have to hold onto it, I think, but that just sends me into a spiral of options that make no sense. I'll put it in a sock drawer, I tell myself. A really deep sock drawer that probably doesn't contain socks. It'll have thorns in it instead, so I'll never be tempted to put my hand in and take it out.

Only that doesn't seem any better than tossing it away, to be honest. The end result is still the same, when you really think about it. I'm just locking my feelings away instead of hurling them into an ocean, and mn om>.y mind doesn't take kindly to that. Just get rid of the thing, it shouts, but I think my mind may well be an idiot. Because the moment I raise my hand up to throw – that's when I see him.

I see him coming down the beach towards me, like some insane mirage.

Oh, Lord, please don't let this be a mirage. It could be, because he's wearing something other than a suit and I'm sure that's never allowed. His suit is his secondary layer of skin, as essential to him as teeth are to a shark. It's just not him. And his feet are bare, which is even *less* like him. It's actually much closer to some romance hero on the cover of a book, and that definitely makes me think I've gone temporarily insane. I'm losing my mind, one piece at a time.

But if I am, that's OK.

I'll gladly trade my sanity for the sight of Janos striding towards me over the sands like something out of the Sheik's Runaway Mistress, dressed in white cotton and with his hair hardly brushed at all. You can see the slight curl to it and there's almost no parting, and after a moment of intense study I realise what that means:

His hair is *tousled*.

He's all *rumpled*.

I may well be swooning. Is this what swooning feels like? My head is suddenly too heavy for my body and my body has turned to jelly, and there's this incredible urge going through me – one that doesn't quite fit with fainting on a chaise longue. It's more like … it's more like I really need to break into a run. And I know it is, because the sensation is so unfamiliar it stands out a mile. I never run. I hate running. I don't know why I want to run here – I only know that I do.

For once I hoped, and it turned out OK.

It's OK, I think, and then I barrel down the beach to him at something just past the speed of light. If my feet had wings I'd fly. I fly anyway. I don't even feel the sand as I run, and I hardly care how I look – probably crazy, I know. And definitely crazy when I get to him and just fling myself at his body.

You don't fling anything anywhere near Janos. He likes measured handshakes, arm's-length greetings, polite hellos. He's probably going to pat me now and laugh and tell me to calm down – though I swear I won't mind. He can do anything he likes as long as the end result is me and him together.

I actually want to be together with someone. Even if it's hard and there are conversations about hurt feelings and confrontations I don't like. Even if he hates me. Even if he's the kind of man to stop and offer a handshake. I'll take handshakes, I think.

But I don't have to.

After a second of my desperate hugging, I realise he's hugging me back. In fact, he's not just hugging me back.

He's squeezing me hard enough to deprive me of oxygen. One hand is going to leave an imprint on my back, and the other is definitely doing something to my head. He's got hold of the back of it like he doesn't want to let go.

I don't want him to let go. We could just stay like this for ever, and I would be fine with that. And even better:

I suspect he would be fine with that, too.

'Don't leave me again,' he tells me, only he doesn't just do it once. He says it over and over, until I'm melting. He's going to have to let go, because hands traditionally can't hold onto liquidised people.

But I'm glad when he doesn't. He keeps holding me and holding me and saying all these awesome things, like 'Never leave' and 'I n'alieed you' and 'I want you'. So it's unfortunate that all I can think to say back is 'I'm sorry'. I mean, it's good to get it out there. And he seems to appreciate it. However, it's not quite as committed as:

'What would I be without you?'

Because he also says that, while cupping my face in his hands and staring deep into my eyes and oh, I must have broken the no-hoping machine. It's somehow operating backwards. I dared to hope and I got all of this, instead of absolutely nothing.

Despite the fact that I probably deserve nothing. I've just offered him the weakest apology in the world, and after five minutes of his unconditional love and his unrestrained hugging, the best I can do is this:

'I didn't mean to run away.'

Which is pretty poor, even by my standards. It has the word 'mean' in there, as weak and wishy-washy as a wet sheet on a windy day. And no matter how hard I search through it, there's no hint of an explanation. If I was on trial for freaking out on him, I'd be on death row right now. The judge and jury have heard it all before – I'm guilty as sin, and everyone knows it.

Apart from him.

'I know,' he says, then just for good measure: 'It's OK. It's always OK.'

I never realised how lovely that word is, before. *OK.* Though I know why I feel that way. It's because I've never heard a man say it to me like that – until now. None of them have ever told me it's OK to be this way, and that this state may continue for an indefinite amount of time. Not a tiny amount of time, or the amount that elapses before I blunder in some way.

Just this:

Always.

'Even though I messed up?'

'You didn't mess up.'

'I did. I did. I thought –'

'You thought I wanted someone else,' he interrupts, but I'm glad he does. The words I wanted to say were high and tight, whereas the one I actually end up offering is as soft and sighing as the falling wind.

'Yes.'

'And that I could only love you as that new person, that perfect person, that glamorous Gucci-wearing doyenne of the social scene.'

'Yes,' I tell him again, only the word is not the wind any more. It's the sound of something breaking, after being too long held in. He isn't just willing to overlook. He *understands*. He understands me, completely.

'But you're sure you can never be that. You need to be yourself.'

'I do.'

'And you didn't know how to tell me.'

'I didn't. I didn't. Oh, God, you really do have psychic powers. I should have just waited a while for them to kick in,' I say, and now he laughs. It isn't cruel, however. It's warm and good and so easy to sink into. I'm crying like a massive imbecile, but I find myself joining in.

And especially when he says:

'I don't have psychic powers, Alissa – your *friend* told me all of this. I called her the moment I couldn't get in touch with you, and she told me everything,' he says, like it's just so simple. He must have searched her out and tracked her down and God knows what else, but it's simple. And so is this, apparently: 'Then I took the first flight out here.'

'You took the first flight?'

'Of course.'

'You just … dropped everything?'

'I couldn't do anything else. She said you were hurting and I didn't – I *couldn't* – think of anything else. I couldn't think of anything else anyway. But if that's too much …'

'Too much?'

'If you need more space, more time, if you're afraid of something serious –'

'*Ohhhh*, she told you that too. She told you that I'm an emotional moron,' I moan, and for the first time since I ran to him and glued my body to his, I want to step away. I need to step away so I can put my face in my hands. I can't let him see me like this – hiding is the only option.

But thankfully he doesn't let me.

'She may have done,' he says, and as he does he strokes the hair away from my face so he can see everything, all of me, right down to the roots. He studies every inch of me for signs of pain, and oh, *oh*. I've never felt so safe. I've never felt so loved.

'I don't need more space. I need less space. I need the minimum amount of space possible. This right here –' I say, then gesture to the place where our bodies are glued together '– is too much space.'

'How about this?'

'That's better.'

'And this?'

'Oh, yes, I can definitely deal with that.'

309

'I love you, Alissa.'

'Also very good,' I tell him, only now my words are up and down and inside out. They're clotted with tears, and all the better for it. Otherwise, how could he possibly know how I really feel? I can't say it back – not even after he's said:

'I love you the way you are.'

Instead, I go with the only thing I can.

'You do?'

'How could you ever think anything else?'

'Because of the dress. Because ... because of the place and the makeover,' I say, as he strokes my tears away. 'You just seemed to like it so much.'

'I didn't like it, love. I was asking you a question.'

'What sort of question?' I ask, and in answer he puts his lips to my ear.

'If it's so easy – if it only takes a day, a moment, a new dress and some shoes and a hairstyle that didn't quite suit you – to transform someone into something that fits into my world, why on earth would it matter to me at all?'

My eyes drift closed the second he says it, as though I'm sinking into something soft and comforting and, most of all, obvious. Oh, it's so obvious I could kick myself, but instead I do what I should have all along. I should have done it the moment I met him, or at the very least five seconds ago.

He flew hundreds of miles to make me feel better. He's holding me and loving me and, more importantly, he wants me to be myself. He's OK with me.

I am OK with me.

'I love you, Janos. I love you for everything you are, and everything you've done. In all my life I've never met anyone like you. I didn't think I *deserved* anyone like you. But you make me believe I do, every day.'

'And do you know why?'

'I think I can guess.'

'Because it's true, love. You deserve to be happy. And if I can, I will spend, Idth="1em every second I have making sure you are.'

'Even if I'm not fancy?'

'Especially if you're not fancy.'

'And if I'm a fool, what then?'

'I'll make you believe again.'

'I might be difficult.'

'You always are.'

'I could fight you, and run from you, and tell you I don't really love you at all.'

'And if so I'll say what I always do, whenever you try to hide from me,' he murmurs, against the side of my face. His lips are almost on mine and my lips are almost on his, and all I need is to hear it, before we finally kiss.

'Say it for me now, then,' I tell him, and he does, oh, he does.

He speaks the word as though it's the sweetest sentiment in the world.

And here, now, it is.

'Liar,' he says.